※ ※ ※
THE STRINGER

THE STRINGER

TERRY CUBBINS

Copyright © 2016 Terry Cubbins
All rights reserved.

ISBN: 1532764545
ISBN 13: 9781532764547

Chapter 1

* * *

It was late June, and the National Basketball Association's season had finally ended. Unfortunately, so had the life of one of its promising young players, Larry Lavorini. The headline in the *San Francisco Chronicle* blared: "NBA Star Found Dead." Next to a photo of the player, the accompanying story detailed that "Larry Lavorini's fully clothed body was found by fishermen early Wednesday morning along the Truckee River, approximately thirty miles north of Lake Tahoe. A car registered to Lavorini was found nearby. An autopsy is pending although early reports indicate Lavorini may have accidentally fell into the river and drowned. Alcohol may have been a contributing factor."

Alcohol a contributing factor? Really? Now, there's a surprise.

Sitting alone at his kitchen table, totally engrossed in the story, along with about two hundred thousand other *Chronicle* subscribers, was twenty-five-year-old Michael Fletcher, freelance sportswriter. Like the rest of the sports fans in the area, he was stunned and saddened by the news. But unlike most of the rest of the fans, he had actually known Lavorini. They had grown up in the same South San Francisco neighborhood and played sandlot sports together.

Michael finished reading the front page and flipped over to page two, where the story continued. "Lavorini was known as the 'Italian Stallion' and had just completed his second year as a power forward with the Sacramento Kings. He struggled in the recent playoffs and was suspended in game five for punching John Skelton of the New York Knicks, breaking Skelton's jaw in several places."

Michael put the paper down and poured himself another cup of coffee. He thought back to when he was a kid playing hoops in the alley by his home. Lavorini was bigger and stronger than most of the other kids in the neighborhood and could have thumped any of them at any time if he'd wanted to. There were occasions during games when a scuffle would break out, but it was usually Lavorini who acted as the peacemaker. He may have had a hot button like a lot of other athletes, or most humans, for that matter, but Michael thought of him as more of a gentle giant than an Italian Stallion.

He remembered the last time he'd seen Lavorini. They'd literally bumped into each other on a sidewalk on Fremont Street in the city. At the time, Lavorini was attending the University of San Francisco on a basketball scholarship while Michael was studying sports journalism at St. Mary's in Moraga. They were both underage at the time, but Michael convinced Lavorini that they could bluff their way into a bar. Once inside, the Italian Stallion had ordered an iced tea.

And what's this about drowning? Lavorini had been a lifeguard at their local Boy's Club. He had been an excellent swimmer, very strong.

Michael read the story again and collected his thoughts. He knew what he was going to do. He'd been doing basically the same thing over and over for the past five years.

He opened his laptop and began a letter to the sports editor at the *Chronicle*. *Will this be the e-mail that finally gets me noticed? Will this lead to the break I've been hoping for?* Probably not, but this time, he didn't care. This time he wasn't writing for notoriety; he was writing for a lost friend.

Twenty minutes later, he hit "Send" and stared at the computer screen. *Now what?* It was only eight in the morning, and a mostly empty day lay ahead of him. Work on his blog? Pound the pavement, figuratively speaking, via the Internet and social media? At least, literally speaking, his pounding had produced a job delivering an underground flier once a week. It wasn't the newspaper job he had in mind, but it was something.

Since he had entered his chosen job market, the *San Jose Mercury News*, the *Associated Press*, and a few other wire services had picked up some of his articles. Unfortunately, they were usually small-ticket items, and few and far between. In the past year, Michael had covered a minor league baseball playoff series, a couple of local rugby matches, a high school basketball championship, two sailing regattas, and a fishing derby, none of which lead to anything steady. He would have covered a marbles tournament if someone was willing to pay him for it. All in all, the work that he was finding was barely enough to pay the rent.

His thoughts gradually shifted from his childhood chum to the calendar on the wall. His wife, daughter, and dog had been away for over a month now. If he wanted his family back, all he had to do was find a real job. Soon.

Chapter 2

✳ ✳ ✳

"Where's a good serial killer when you need one, huh?" Len Wrighton, venerable sixty-seven-year-old reporter for the *San Francisco Chronicle*, was just wrapping up a conversation in the office of his friend and fellow employee, sports editor Bo Kimble.

Kimble was a generation younger than Wrighton, and the physical differences between the two were like those between Laurel and Hardy. Wrighton was tall, slender, and sported a full head of silver hair worn just long enough to suggest distinction and independence. Kimble was built closer to the ground, more like a Rocky Marciano, his black, wavy hair showing only minor signs of receding and graying at the temples. He had a slight paunch but moved with an athlete's grace. There were hints of crow's-feet around his eyes, indicating that the man did a lot of squinting, grinning, or maybe yelling.

Fifteen minutes earlier, the dialogue between the two had started out in its usual fashion with Wrighton's butt perched on the corner of Kimble's desk. Wrighton was questioning his mentee's career choice. "You coulda had class! You coulda been a condenda! You coulda *been* somebody."

"Yeah, and maybe you coulda been an actor." Kimble folded his hands behind his head and leaned back in his chair. Kimble liked to spar with his reputable elder but did so carefully. After all, the senior reporter was a legend at the *Chronicle*.

Len Wrighton had cut his journalist's teeth changing typewriter ribbons when the likes of Herb Caen and Paul Avery roamed the halls of the *Chronicle*. He had a dry wit, and his sense of humor could be cutting, but he was a dedicated newspaperman and loved his job. Rumor had it that he suffered a paper cut once…and bled black ink.

Besides the good-natured jabbering, the two men had been talking about the paper's circulation numbers, which, like most other newspapers', had been trending down for years.

"Yeah, and maybe I should just retire before they close us down, you know, like Candlestick Park?" Wrighton said. "That was supposed to be a state-of-the art stadium, you know. Or maybe they'll turn this building into a museum, like the old mint building across the street. Christ, the only thing that hasn't faded away around here is Tony Bennett."

"You raise a good point," Kimble chuckled, "not just about Mr. Bennett, but about where they used to print our dinero. Just because the Treasury Department moved out next door doesn't mean the feds quit printing money. They just don't do it from that location anymore."

"So?"

"So…you don't retire. You keep working. You keep writing."

"Yeah, for who? AOL? Or those Yahoos downstairs?"

Bo Kimble shook his head. He'd been down this road with his friend before. He knew Wrighton had started working for the newspaper when it had occupied all three floors of the *Chronicle* building. Before the paper began downsizing. Before the newspaper rented out the bottom two floors to global web services.

"Newspapers will still be around long after we're gone," Kimble said. "You can have all the social media you want. All the television and radio, too. I don't give a shit. If a story's interesting enough, people will still want to read about it in print, even if it's just to confirm what they've already seen or heard."

Wrighton raised his eyebrows mockingly. "Even sports stories?"

"*Especially* sports stories."

"Like the NBA kid that drowned…what was his name? Lava-something. Lava…tory?"

"Lava-*rini*, asshole."

"Hmmm. Lavorini Asshole. Now there's an interesting name. Too bad he wasn't murdered. Woulda sold more copies."

"Still looking for another Zodiac Killer, huh?"

Wrighton shrugged. "Well, no. But it sure was an interesting time around here then."

Kimble knew that Wrighton was kidding about Lavorini having been murdered, but he was also aware that the man knew a thing or two about sensational headlines.

Wrighton was just a twenty-two year old swamper for the *Chronicle* when the so-called "Zodiac Killer" randomly murdered at least five people in Northern California. While the murder spree was going on, the newspaper began receiving letters from a person claiming to be the killer. These letters contained cryptograms, suggesting clues as to the killer's identity. One letter was sent to Paul Avery with a Halloween card that read "Peek-a-boo, You are doomed."

"You'll never see another newspaper commandeered like that again," Wrighton said. "A killer demanding front-page coverage? And the paper bowing to his demands?"

"Maybe they just wanted to sell more papers, kinda like what you're suggesting now?"

Wrighton took a deep breath and shook his head. "I remember how tense it was around here then. Police detectives hovering everywhere, waiting for the next communication from the killer. Editors constantly in meetings with lawyers and top city brass, figuring out what they should do. Everyone in this building was on edge.

"In the end, I think the paper decided they couldn't take the chance of not complying with the demands. That they might somehow be seen as responsible for someone else being murdered. Of course, it also bought time for the police to try to catch the guy. They're still not absolutely sure who he was, you know?"

Kimble raised his hands in mock surrender. "Yeah, yeah, yeah. I *know* the story, Lennie. You've told me about it enough times. Plus, I've seen the movie."

"All right." Wrighton stood up and stretched his back. "I can tell when I'm not wanted. I better let you get back to work, or whatever it is that you do around here." He shuffled over to the doorway, stopped, and looked back. "By the way, which NFL team is leading this year?"

"Leading?"

"Yeah, you know. In felony arrests."

Chapter 3

✳ ✳ ✳

(SIX YEARS EARLIER)

Spilling beer down a girl's blouse is probably not the best way to go about meeting women, even for a college student. But that was how Michael Fletcher met Annie Ireland.

It happened one night at Duke's, a pizzeria-pub near the campus of St. Mary's College in Moraga, twenty miles east of San Francisco. Duke's was a popular hangout with students and was only three blocks from Michael's tiny studio apartment. With finals coming up, Michael was getting ready for some serious studying, and he thought a pizza would be the perfect belly-wadden to get him through the night. After calling in an order to go, he hustled over to Duke's.

As usual, the place was jammed. Waitresses with trays of beer held high over their heads swivel-hipped around tables and chairs. Music from an ancient red and gold Wurlitzer cranked out some bluesy honky-tonk.

Michael had snaked his way through half of the crowd when suddenly, someone scooted a chair away from a table, bumping him into one of the waitresses. The gal did an admirable job of stopping a pitcher of beer from falling completely off her tray, but not before most of its contents splashed down onto one of the four coeds seated at an adjacent table.

"Goddamn it" were the first words Michael heard from Annie's mouth. She jumped up and began furiously wiping beer from her clothes. Her white satin blouse had taken most of the hit, but there was a large wet spot in the crotch of her faded blue jeans as well. Annie was about five foot seven, with light brown hair pulled back into a loose ponytail. She had soft, tanned skin and dark walnut-colored eyes. Although her face was scrunched up in anguish at the moment, Michael could see that she was a very attractive girl. He stood transfixed, watching the lovely young woman frantically wiping her crotch. The faster she wiped her pants, the more her breasts jiggled beneath her wet blouse. It was now painfully obvious (for her, anyway) that she wasn't wearing a bra. When she looked up, she looked straight at the dumb son-of-a-bitch who had caused the trouble, her dark brown eyes blazing.

"Oh, hey. I'm really sorry," Michael said. In desperation, he picked up a napkin and said, "Here, let me help you."

She stopped wiping her crotch long enough to give him an incredulous look.

"Oh, well, ah…okay, maybe not," he stammered. As he stood there like an idiot, the waitress slapped the table twice with a wet rag, tossed Annie a dry one, and then hurried away.

One at a time, the other girls sat back down. Annie made a few more passes over her pants, threw the towel on the table, and shot Michael another frosty look. As she stood there with her arms folded over her breasts, a strand of wet hair fell down in front of her face. Without moving from her defiant stance, and still staring at him, she curled her lips and blew the hair away. There was an awkward silence for a beat or two, and then the wayward strand dropped down again. The other girls looked at Annie and started to giggle. Annie gave the hair another blow, but this time it didn't budge. The giggles turned to laughter. Annie remained stoic for a moment or so, but as the laughter around her grew, a dimple slowly evolved into a smile.

Michael stood there uncomfortably while the girls yukked it up, not knowing whether to laugh or leave. He looked around the crowd and tried to form his exit strategy, but when he looked back at Annie, he could see that the fire in her eyes had softened.

"You don't go out much, do you?" she said with a slight smirk.

Michael took a lame stab at humor. "You won't tell my parole officer about this, will you?"

Annie's eyebrows arched. "Oh, I'm sure she's used to it by now."

The girl didn't miss a beat. Michael's next move was the only thing he could do at that point—he raised his hands and surrendered. "Look, I'm really sorry about this. My name is Michael, and I will gladly pay for any cleaning bills."

"Well, we'll just see about that bill, Mikey, but, for now, if you'll excuse me, I need to go powder my nose along with the rest of my body."

As Annie Ireland marched off to the ladies' room, the girls at the table smiled up at Michael and shrugged their shoulders. Michael was just short of six feet tall, a trim one hundred seventy-five pounds, and had almost wavy, sand-colored hair and dark-brown eyes. And despite his crooked nose (previously broken while playing street hockey) and a crooked scar on his chin (a remnant from catching a football and a street sign at the same time), most women found him cute, as if he could use some mothering or something. He apologized once more and said, "Well, excuse me, I think my pizza's ready."

Michael made his way over to the counter and picked up his order, but didn't leave. He waited there for fourteen minutes before Annie came out of the ladies' room. Her hair was back in place, and she looked reasonably dried off: at least, her blouse was dry.

"Here's my number." Michael handed her a slip of paper. "Call me with the bill."

He practically speed-walked to the front door, carrying a less-than-warm pepperoni with everything on it under his arm.

As he was walking home, an image of Annie Ireland floated into his mind. She was in the ladies' room, topless, holding a wet blouse under a hand dryer.

Chapter 4

* * *

A week after the beer baptism, Annie called. Yes, there was a bill. Apparently blouses by Rachel Zoe didn't come beer proofed. She got right down to business and told Michael how much the dry-cleaning tab was. It was slightly more than what he'd paid for his best shirt. When they discussed how payment should be made, Michael threw caution to the wind and suggested that they rendezvous at the scene of the crime. He was surprised when she agreed.

* * *

When they met again at Duke's, Annie was there early and ready for him. She was sitting at a table by herself, dressed in light brown shorts and sandals and wearing a sweatshirt in St. Mary's colors. Over the sweatshirt, she wore a clear plastic raincoat.

"I see you dressed for the occasion." Michael said as he pulled out a chair and sat down.

"Yes. Protection. A girl can't be too careful these days, you know."

He looked at her with a smile. "It's not as busy here tonight. I think you're safe."

She was prettier than Michael remembered. She wore her hair down, and it framed her face in a way that softened her features and gave her a more sensual look. She removed the cleaning bill from her purse and placed it on the table in front of Michael.

After a quick glance at the tab, he frowned a little before saying, "Does this mean your pants survived? They weren't that expensive kind that are made to look old and gritty?"

"Oh no, they *were* old and gritty. Like these. No problem."

Before he could catch himself, Michael glanced at her crotch. "Oh, I didn't mean…"

"That's okay. The beer washed out."

Michael studied the bill and then pulled out his wallet. "You want to take another chance?"

"Whaddya mean?"

"How 'bout a beer?"

Annie removed her raincoat and hung it on a chair next to her. She pushed her hair back off her shoulders and smiled. "Sure, why not?"

A waitress clearing a table nearby acknowledged Michael's wave and hurried over to their table. She spent nearly twelve seconds scribbling their orders, said thank you, and then swished away.

"So, what—?"

"Are you—?"

When they finally got the pecking order straightened out, Annie methodically filled in a few of the blanks. "Well, let's see.

I'm an only child. Born in Walnut Creek. My parents had a small farm there where I tried to grow up."

"Tried to?"

"Yeah, well, I was a bit of a tomboy back then. Loved horses and stuff. Didn't mind getting dirty. That all changed when we had to sell the farm and move into the city. Pop got a job driving a bus for the Rapid Transit Authority until he couldn't stand it anymore. When I was about thirteen, we moved back to the country, up near Healdsburg. My folks bought another small farm and raised wine grapes. My dad's still there trying to make a go of it by himself. My mother died of cancer the same year I enrolled in St. Mary's."

"Oh, I'm sorry."

Annie's eyes clouded slightly, and she swallowed before continuing. "Thank you. My mom always used to say, 'Get all the education you can. Nobody can ever take it away from you.'"

"Good advice."

"Yes, it is. I went to junior college in the city before transferring to St. Mary's. I'm majoring in business accounting and hope to graduate this year."

Annie took a breath and smiled. "So, that's me. Now, who are you? If you tell me you play tuba in a marching band, I'm leaving."

"I've never played the tuba," Michael said with a grin, "but I used to play a lot of sports, some organized, some unorganized, like the kind you played in the streets."

"Stealing hubcaps, tagging, that sorta thing?"

"No." Michael laughed. "I grew up in San Francisco in a neighborhood where all the kids played stickball, whiffle ball, street hockey, hoops in the alley, that kinda stuff."

"And your parents? They let you run around like that?"

"Oh, sure. They were cool, as long as I kept my grades up, anyway. My dad always liked sports and encouraged me to play.

He'd toss a football around and play catch with me when he could. Mostly on weekends."

"Your folks still live in the same neighborhood?"

"No, they moved down to Carlsbad. North County, San Diego?"

Annie nodded. "Nice down there."

"Yeah, my dad needed to get to a warmer climate. He worked at the Pier 70 shipyard in the city until an overhead crane dropped a load of steel on his right leg. He uses a cane now, but he gets around pretty good. By the way, I'm a senior too, at St. Mary's."

"And your major?"

"Sports journalism."

"Sports journalism?" Annie looked doubtful.

"Yeah. I'm writing for the school paper. We usually have a pretty good basketball team, as you probably know."

Annie's countenance didn't change. If she knew anything about the basketball team, she wasn't saying.

Michael surged ahead. "Sometimes I write about what some of the alumni jocks are doing since they graduated. 'Where are they now?' kinda things. You know. Human interest stuff."

"Do you do any other kind of writing—other than sports, I mean?"

"No, not really."

"Why not?"

Michael shrugged. "I dunno. Probably suck at it, I guess. Besides, I like sports. When I was a kid, I dreamed of being the next Mickey Mantle. I wanted my Dad to be proud of me. I was gonna buy my folks a new house once I made it in the pros."

Annie smiled. "Okay, that's admirable."

"Yeah, well, when I figured out I wasn't gonna make it as professional athlete, I decided I'd settle for the next best thing: writing about them. My dad really encouraged me, too. He loved his sports pages and thought being a sportswriter would be an awesome way to make a living. He subscribed to the *L.A. Times* just so he could read Jim Murray's column in the sports section."

"Jim who?"

Michael rolled his eyes and feigned indignation. "Jim Murray. One of the, if not *the*, greatest sportswriters ever to stroke a typewriter."

"Stroke a *what*?"

"A typewriter. The ancients used them. They were writing devices."

They studied each other for a moment, brown eyes to brown eyes. Finally, Annie brushed back her hair, took a sip of beer, and said, "Sportswriter, huh? Sounds like a great hobby. What are you going to be when you grow up?"

"Grow up? Why grow up? Besides, you're the one who came dressed like a shower curtain tonight!"

"Yes, based on a mature decision."

"Well, anyway, you know what they say about doing something you enjoy?"

"Yeah, find something you like to do, and you'll never work a day in your life. Right?"

Michael shrugged. "Well, there you go."

"And here you go," the waitress said as she set their order on the table. "Let the games begin."

Chapter 5

✳ ✳ ✳

Soon, Michael and Annie were seeing each other two and three times a week. And for all her presumed disdain for sports journalism, Annie wasn't a bad athlete herself. She could handle her own on a tennis court, and one afternoon, when Michael suggested a little one-on-one basketball, she didn't hesitate. "I love it when you talk dirty to me," she said. "You're on!"

As their relationship developed, their desire for each other escalated. It seemed as if they tore their clothes off every time they saw each other. They made love in the back seat of his car, in every room and on every floor of her apartment, and even once in the ladies' room of a fancy restaurant. They would have done the big naughty in a phone booth if they could have found one. It was soon evident that they were crazy about each other, and they started making plans.

Although Annie wasn't thrilled with the idea of Michael making a living as a sportswriter, she loved him and wanted him to be happy. She was sure love would trump everything. Besides, she would have her own career to keep her busy. They were confident that they would find jobs that fit their degrees. He would be offered a salaried position at one of the newspapers and write a story that would earn him a Pulitzer in a week or two. She would parlay her diploma into a position at one of the high-powered firms in San Francisco's financial district, or FiDi, as the locals called it. She would wear smart business suits and clickety-clack around in high heels. They would join a country club and raise a dog and two perfect kids.

Despite all the time they spent touching each other, Annie and Michael kept up with their studies and stayed on track for commencement. The graduation invitation to their parents also included their wedding announcement.

* * *

After a wonderful honeymoon in Hawaii, the newlyweds moved into a modest, one-story, two-bedroom house in a residential area in South San Francisco. The house was fronted by an attached two-car garage, with the home's main entry door on the left of the garage. Or at least the rental arrangement *said* it was a two car garage. The building was actually constructed in the 1940s, when cars were much smaller. Annie knew they'd be lucky to squeeze Michael's Jeep and maybe a bicycle in the garage. If they did get a couple of bikes, her Volvo would have to stay outside. At least the garage door had been updated with a remote control opener.

The Fletchers' bunker was squished between hundreds of identically shaped houses that were each painted a different color. The neighborhood was the inspiration for a folk song that was popular in the '60s called "Little Boxes."

"Little boxes on the hillside
Little boxes made of ticky-tacky

The Stringer

Little boxes on the hillside
Little boxes, all the same.

"There's a pink one and a green one
And a blue one and a yellow one
And they're all made out of ticky-tacky
And they all look just the same."

The neighborhood denizens were friendly enough, though. And typical of San Francisco, they came in all shapes, sizes, and shades. A Korean family ran a small general store called Kim's on the corner just up the street. Kim's grocery sold everything from Band-Aids to boxer briefs. The aisles of the store were so narrow that if you met another soul while shopping, you had to stand sideways to allow him or her to go by. Some inventory high on the wall behind the cash register had been there since Elvis's last bowel movement.

Michael and Annie's new abode fit the song lyrics, with one exception: their home had a tiny backyard enclosed by a cyclone fence and gate. The lawn wasn't in the best of shape—a few bare spots here and there indicated the previous tenant had a dog, or maybe practiced his short golf game there. Access to the backyard came via a cracked cement walk that ran along the left side of the house or from a back door that opened off of the kitchen.

A week after moving in, Michael and Annie started their family by rescuing a ten-week-old female golden retriever/Lab mix they named Scooter. Scooter took to the backyard like a dog who knew where the bones were buried.

* * *

Like many young couples starting off, money was tight. But Annie and Michael were in it together, and together they would figure out the road ahead. They sat down and wrote out individual goals that they hoped to reach within five years. They agreed if they didn't reach their goals in that time frame, they would re-evaluate their career choices and make changes if necessary. These things were easy to say at the time.

Michael did his best to find work as a sportswriter and applied to every newspaper and publication business in the area. He made sure to send his resume to Bo Kimble at the *San Francisco Chronicle*. He knew Kimble was a graduate of St. Mary's and, like Michael, had written for the school paper. Michael had high hopes that Mr. Kimble would favor his resume in some way, if for no other reason than the commonality they had with St. Mary's.

In the meantime, Michael scanned the want ads in weeklies and trade magazines. He stayed in touch with professors and fellow journalism students, looking for leads. He read everything regarding sports, always taking note of the article's author. He would then send a complementary note to the author about how much he enjoyed the piece, and, "Oh, by the way, do you know anybody who's hiring?"

Annie tried to keep her end of the bargain and went to several interviews in the canyons of Wall Street West. With each meeting, she came away feeling she had nailed the interviews. But as time went by and nothing came from the prospective employers, she began to look elsewhere for work. When she finally did find a job, it was with the San Francisco Port Authority as an assistant web designer in the public relations department. What web designing had to do with business accounting was anybody's guess. But it helped pay the bills. For a while.

And then, less than a year into their marriage and without meaning to, Annie became pregnant.

"What are we going to do?" Annie asked Michael after giving him the news.

Michael was rocked for a moment. Then he looked deep into Annie's eyes and said, "*We* are going to have a baby, that's what *we're* gonna do!" He took Annie's hand in his. "Of course, you'll have to do most of the heavy lifting."

Chapter 6

※ ※ ※

Sadie was a beautiful little girl with large brown eyes and dimples like her mother's. She was smothered in love by both parents. They painted her room a light pale blue, sprinkled with yellow butterflies. They consulted the Consumer Product Safety Commission before buying her a crib or any toys. They shared diaper duties and doted on their baby constantly. They were a happy family, and for the first couple years together, the joy of having a child was enough to keep Michael and Annie happily distracted.

But by the time Sadie started kindergarten, the young Fletchers' five-year plan was nowhere near where they'd hoped it would be. Their address was still the same. Michael was still plodding along doing temp jobs and freelance stuff for anybody who might be interested.

Annie was still working for the Port Authority, but there was talk of impending layoffs. Her hours had already been cut, along with some of her benefits. The mandatory health care bill was still in its infancy, and nobody could tell yet whether the term

"Affordable Care Act" was an oxymoron or not. For the Fletchers, it was just another burden to throw onto the pile.

And, like rust on steel, the monetary pressures slowly strained the harmony of the young family. Annie and Michael began snapping at each other over trivial things: turning the thermostat up too high. Leaving a light on in the hall. Wasting hot water. The cost of Scooter's premium dog food versus cheaper brands. And Michael's career choice. It was becoming increasingly hard for Annie to watch her husband pursue a job that seemed to be leading nowhere.

Then one evening, Michael and Sadie sat at the dinner table discussing different cartoon characters and waiting for Annie to serve supper. Annie had been strangely quiet since coming home from work, but finally brought the food to the table. She shooed Scooter away and sat down.

They ate in silence until Michael cleared his throat and said quietly, "Well, I got a little good news today. I've got a good chance at getting hired as the P.A. for the Coyotes. Their regular guy is having a problem staying off the juice."

When Annie didn't say anything, Michael continued. "And the Web Dot Com golf tour is at the Olympic next week; somebody will probably call me for that. Plus, I think…"

Suddenly, Annie dropped her silverware, buried her head in her hands and began sobbing.

"My God, honey, what's wrong?" Michael asked.

Sadie immediately started crying too. Scooter whined and retraced her steps back to the table.

Annie immediately straightened up and wiped at her face. "I'm sorry…I didn't mean to…"

Michael reached for her hand. "Please, honey, tell me. Are you okay?"

"I'm fine, but...I...ah...I lost my job today." She burst into tears again as she said it.

Michael quickly scooted his chair over to her and let her cry against his chest. A few seconds passed before Michael took a deep breath and laughed. "Jesus, honey. You had me worried there for a second."

Annie stopped sniffling long enough to look up and punch him in the chest.

* * *

A few weeks later, as the two were sitting at the kitchen table having their morning coffee, their conversation segued into unofficial come-to-Jesus talk about their future.

"You remember the pact we made?" Annie said. "About digging ditches if we have to to make things work?"

Michael nodded, sensing where the conversation was going.

"Well, I think we should really take a time-out from our career choices and accept what we can."

"You mean me, right? You want me to find another job?"

Annie looked thoughtfully at her coffee cup. She didn't answer right away, but when she did, it was in a low, slow voice he hadn't heard before. "Job, Michael?

She looked out the window and continued in a wistful tone. "You write about *games*, Michael. *Games* people *play*. But life isn't a game. Our life isn't a game. I just think you should consider changing course to help make this work."

Michael was stunned. "Make this work? I suppose you'd like me to take your father's offer to work at his farm? Whadda you think he could pay me? Ten bucks an hour? Eleven? To be his foreman? My Spanish isn't that good, you know. I'd—"

"Whatever it is, it would be better than what you're doing now."

* * *

Two weeks later, Michael was sitting on the couch in the living room, tapping away on his laptop, when Annie and Sadie returned from visiting Annie's father. After Annie hung up her coat, she took Sadie to her room for a nap, and then joined Michael on the couch.

"How's your dad?" Michael asked as he put the finishing touches on a story.

"He's good. He's fine." Annie said, her voice trailing off. Michael knew there was more coming.

"And?"

"Well, Pop is having some trouble with his books. You know, Mom used to do all that stuff—pay bills, handle taxes and payroll—but since she died, he's let things get away from him."

"*And?*"

"And, he wants me to help him straighten things out. He's offered to pay me."

"Good. We can use the money."

Annie studied her fingernails. "He wants us to stay with him for a while."

"Us?"

"Me and Sadie."

"Oh."

"Did I tell you Dad just hired another hand?"

"How long we talkin' about here?"

"I'm not sure. Maybe a month?"

"Then what?"

"Then we'll see, I guess."

They sat in silence and stared at nothing. Finally Michael took a deep breath and reached for her hand. "Alright, honey. I promise if I don't find a steady job writing by the end of the year, I'll go buy a shovel. Okay?"

Annie smiled and said, "I'll still love you whether you have a shovel in your hand or a pen. Just remember that."

* * *

A week later, outside his house, near the curb, Michael hugged his daughter, kissed his wife, and then watched them drive away. When they were gone, he went inside, sat on the floor, and cried onto Scooter's head.

Chapter 7

✳ ✳ ✳

Determined to provide for his family, Michael had doubled his efforts at finding steady work. He kept up his blog, Twitter, and Facebook networking. He continued pestering newspapers and magazines. He made a daily checklist of people to see or call. Usually, his phone calls to prospective employers and editors were intercepted by assistants who promised to pass along his message.

While making one of his calls, Michael listened to the buzzing on the other end and realized he had forgotten who he was calling. He started to panic, but then thought whoever was going to answer would just be a gatekeeper and would identify his or her office, or it would be a recording: "Hi, you've reached *The Gilroy Gazette*. For the job of your dreams, please press one..." Michael was stunned when a voice came on the line and simply said, "Kimble."

"Oh...hi. My name is Michael Fletcher. Ah...is this *Bo* Kimble?"

"One and the same."

"Oh, hi, Mr. Kimble. I'm Michael Fletcher, ah, I'm—"

"I know who you are."

"You do?"

"Yeah, you just told me."

"Oh, ha, yeah. I guess I did, huh?"

If there was such a thing as a time machine, Michael would have sold his soul to go back five seconds.

"Well, anyway, Mr. Kimble, I'm a graduate of St. Mary's, and I…"

"And you're looking for work, right?"

Michael hung his head in resignation. "Yeah, I'm looking for work."

"You and a thousand other guys," Kimble laughed. "Look, I'm sorry. I don't mean to sound so negative, but times are pretty tough right now. Have been for a while."

"Yes, sir. I understand." Michael picked up a pencil and drew a line through *"Chronicle."* There was silence from Kimble's end of the line, and Michael wasn't sure if the editor was still listening or not. Michael looked at his cell phone and was about to hit "End call" when he heard Kimble mumble, "St. Mary's, hmmm, let's see, have you sent us your resume?"

"Yes, sir. It was a while ago, though."

"But you've sent us stuff in the past, like e-mails?"

"Yes. Usually just—"

"I hope you understand why I can't acknowledge everything sent my way?"

"Oh, sure, I'm sure—"

"Did you, by chance, send us something recently about Larry Lavorini?"

"I did. I said—"

"You knew him, right?"

"Yes, sir. We grew up together."

"Am I right to assume he grew a little more than you? Physically speaking."

Michael laughed. "Yeah, I stopped at five-eleven; he kept going."

After a few more heartbeats of silence, Kimble said, "Well, listen, son. I suppose I could spare an alumnus a few minutes. Maybe point you in the right direction. Can you meet me for lunch, say, this Friday?"

"You bet. Ye-s-s, sir."

"Good. You know where Sal's is?"

"I do. Nice place."

"Okay, see you there at eleven forty-five. The bartender can tell you where I'm sitting."

"Yes, sir. Thank you. I'll be there."

Chapter 8

✳ ✳ ✳

He had only been in Sal's once in his life, but Michael knew the history of the place well. Except for the short time-out during Prohibition, Sal's Bar and Grill had been serving up food and drinks for almost as long as the *Chronicle* had been serving up newspapers. Patrons entered through a single door off of La Selva Street. A long mahogany bar ran to the left of the entry, lined with enough stools to accommodate thirty butts. On Friday nights, a standing space between bar stools was almost as valuable as the seats themselves.

Opposite the bar, there were a dozen or so small, round wooden tables and chairs where the lunch crowd could order the special of the day and get in and out in a hurry. Hardwood flooring ran parallel to the bar and lunch area before giving way to carpeting in the back room. A few tables were positioned in the middle of the room, while private booths, upholstered in red Naugahyde, circa the 1960s, horseshoed the area. And although the lumpy-looking seats and high back cushions of the booths looked uncomfortable, they actually provided some massage action if you moved your back and butt muscles just right.

* * *

Michael walked in to Sal's at 11:45 a.m. on the dot. A chalkboard sign mounted on an easel greeted him at the entry. The lunch specials were listed in yellow chalk, followed by instructions to seat yourself. An early lunch crowd was already jockeying for position. Most of the bar stools were taken, and only a few tables were left unoccupied. The sound of a blender from behind the bar whirred over happy Friday chatter. A lone bartender was busy setting up drinks and taking orders. The name tag on his vest identified him as Frank. He looked like a Frank. He was about fifty, medium height, almost bald, and almost pudgy. He had a stubby pencil behind his ear, and the plaid vest he wore over his white shirt probably wouldn't get buttoned in its lifetime. His sleeves were rolled up over hairy forearms that sported blurred black tattoos. A waitress scurried between the bar and the lunch tables, while another waitress worked the back room.

In Michael's eyes, not much had changed in the place. The walls of the establishment were covered with framed historic newspaper headlines from the past. A lot of tragedies, a lot of triumphs. Sal's was within easy walking distance from the *Chronicle*, and the ambiance fit perfectly. Michael remembered that it was the first place he'd ever seen a sports section from a newspaper tacked above a urinal in the men's room. He assumed that the *Chronicle's Sporting Green* section was current and in place today, the Niners probably getting most of the ink.

Michael positioned himself next to an empty stool and waited to catch the bartender's eye. It didn't take long. After ringing up a customer, Frank turned and looked over, raising his eyebrows as if to ask, *Yeah? Whaddya want?*

"Bo Kimble?"

"Far corner, by the window."

Michael looked in that direction and saw a man sitting at a table by himself. He was wearing a dark sports coat, pale blue shirt, gray slacks, and a red tie loosened at the collar. He wore bifocals and was holding a folded newspaper while sipping coffee.

As Michael approached his table, Kimble's eyes shifted, and he looked up over his cheaters.

"Mister Kimble?" Michael asked.

"Ah, you must be Michael." He rose and extended his hand. "Call me Bo."

"Yes, sir. Thanks for taking the time to see me."

"Well, I don't know if I can help you or not," Kimble said as he pointed to an empty seat. "But at least I can advise you on what's good to eat around here."

Michael promptly sat down, but as he pulled his chair forward, he bumped the table, causing some of Kimble's coffee to slosh and stain the white linen tablecloth.

"Ah, sorry about that," Michael said as his face turned crimson.

A waitress appeared out of nowhere with a cloth and began dabbing at the spill. When she finished, she squared herself up and looked at Michael. "May I bring you something to drink, sir?"

"I'll just have a water, thank you."

"Good choice," the waitress said. "It's easier to clean up."

She gave Michael a wink and walked away. Michael glanced at Kimble. The editor took a sip of coffee, smiled, and said, "Welcome to Sal's. The one thing they don't serve around here is slack."

Michael quickly decided the crinkles around the man's eyes didn't come from yelling. And then, by design or not, Kimble eased the situation further by asking about St. Mary's. "So, what're some of the programs they're using now at the school paper? Can't be the same antiquated crap they had when I was there."

Michael laughed and filled Kimble in on the latest systems. The newspaperman listened with genuine interest. He had a few questions, but for the most part, he let Michael roll. The coffee stain slowly faded.

When Kimble asked about Michael's experience since graduating, Michael filled him in as best he could, embellishing on some things but mostly sticking to the truth.

Kimble listened patiently for Michael to sum things up before he asked, "So, is it fair to say that you are still looking to write that one big story? The one that establishes you as a bona fide writer? And that your career hasn't exactly taken off like you thought it would?"

Michael nodded in agreement, but stopped short of saying what he was thinking: *Well, my career hasn't really taken off, but my wife and daughter have!*

Kimble seemed to be reading Michael's mind. "Are you married, son?"

"Yes."

"Then maybe you've already figured out that pursuing a career as a newspaperman automatically adds a challenge to any marriage."

* * *

When their lunch arrived, Kimble brought up Michael's letter regarding Lavorini. He speared a tiny tomato from his salad and pointed his fork at Michael.

"You know, that wasn't the first time an NBA player was suspended from the league for that type of action. Back in '77, in a game between the Lakers and the Houston Rockets, L.A.'s Kermit Washington punched Houston's Rudy Tomjanovich in the face so hard it damn near killed him. Had to have surgery to reconstruct his skull and eye socket."

Michael nodded and said, "I remember my father telling me about that game. He saw it on TV. He says he can still remember the sound of the punch. Sounded like a watermelon being dropped on concrete."

"Yeah, it was brutal," Kimble continued. "There was some pushing and shoving going on between the players earlier in the game, before Washington threw the punch, but the way it went down, everyone called it a sucker punch.

"The incident was called 'The Punch that Changed Basketball Forever.' Looking back on it, about the only thing it changed was Washington's status around town. He was branded a thug and was traded soon after. His wife was pregnant at the time, but suddenly her obstetrician didn't want anything to do with her. Told her to find another doctor to deliver her baby. In fact, in a lawsuit filed later, Tomjanovich was awarded three and a quarter million. Hell, his lawyers were only asking for *two* million! But all that was before Lavorini's time. Apparently Lavorini never got the memo."

* * *

After the lunch plates were taken away and the crowd started to thin out, Kimble got down to the business at hand.

"As you know, the newspaper business has been in a downturn for quite a while now. Many syndications are struggling. Social media has really taken off. And I have to tell you, I've probably got ten or twenty resumes sitting on my desk right now, and just about every one of them has something you don't, and that's experience. So, how do you get experience if nobody gives you a chance? It may sound kinda like a catch-22 situation, but I suggest you continue to do what you've been doing—you know, watch all the sports you can, keep sending your material out to the wire services and publications. Who knows, you could stumble on a story on your own. Break something big. Get lucky. Maybe you could do a little digging on your own, say, on concussions in the NFL. That's a pretty hot topic right now, as you know. Maybe find out why woodpeckers don't get concussions or something. Use your imagination. As far as your blogs and Twitter accounts, what I would suggest…"

Michael just nodded and kept his mouth shut. He had heard all of this before and was ready for the letdown. He even started thinking about the lunch bill. *Will Kimble pick up the tab?* Michael would offer to pay his share, of course, but maybe he could come out of this with a free lunch.

"However, I just had a thought," Kimble was saying. "I'm thinking of sending someone to cover the dedication of the new Sam Dornam Field next Saturday. You know, the one over at the Presidio?"

Suddenly, Michael's thought-train jumped the track. *Dornam?* Sam Dornam had been one of his heroes growing up. The former Forty-Niners fullback was earning even more fans now as a respected pediatrician. During his playing years, Dornam had been well liked by fans and players alike. He always gave one hundred percent on the field and credited his teammates for any success that he had. He went to college at Oregon State and later studied pediatrics at the University of Washington. When he retired from football, he finished his medical studies, then returned to

San Francisco as a licensed pediatrician. He opened an office in Broadmoor, and along with his wife Barbara, became active in many fundraisers for the Boys and Girls Clubs. He initiated a college scholarship program for underprivileged kids in the Bay Area. And as far as Michael knew, Dornam still held several rushing records for the Niners.

"Most likely there'll be some bigwigs there," Kimble said. "Including Dornam, of course. The mayor'll probably break a bottle of Gatorade over the goalpost or something like that. Then they'll play a Pop Warner football game on the field. We may run a feature on it, maybe use it in our society section, or we might not use it at all, *but*, if you wanted to cover it and send it to me, at least you'd be in our files. Would you be interested in doing that?"

Suddenly, Michael was interested in everything Kimble was saying. They worked out the details, and when the lunch bill arrived, Kimble picked up the tab and waved it at Michael. "This may be all you'll get for your story, you know that, don't you?"

Chapter 9

※ ※ ※

Michael woke up the next morning in a great mood. It was at times like these that he couldn't imagine living anywhere else in the world, especially in the fall. The skies were usually sunny, the average temperature around seventy degrees, and the Grateful Dead weren't all dead yet. It was even better considering the Giants were in a pennant race, the Forty-Niners were in first place in the NFC West, and the NHL's San Jose Sharks looked good to make another run at the Stanley Cup.

Michael felt that the Bay Area was nirvana for a sportswriter. Within a sixty-mile radius from his home, there were seven major league sports teams; two baseball, two football, one basketball, one soccer, and one hockey team. If he wanted to, he could get in his Jeep after breakfast, drive to every professional venue, and be home before dark.

Many people, including Michael, thought that for any professional team to be successful, it had to have at least two things: savvy upper management and owners with deep pockets. A few exceptions existed, such as the Oakland A's, who, at times, didn't pay well, but played well. Their way of doing business was known as "Billy Ball." Brad Pitt got it right in the movie.

The San Jose Sharks had gotten a lot of things right, too, since moving from the old Cow Palace in Daly City to San Jose. Since 1993, they'd only missed the playoffs a handful of times in spite of playing in a building known as The SAP Center (named after that lovable German tech giant Systeme, Anwendungen und Produkte in der Datenverarbeitung, who bought the naming rights for more than three million dollars, which called into question the part about savvy upper management…SAP?).

One of the big reason Sharks fans were optimistic that season was because of a young man named Troy Polanski. He was a local boy who had made his way to the NHL by playing like his team's nickname. He was fearless, aggressive, always moving, and didn't care what he ate.

Polanski was now in the third year of a five-million-dollar-a-year contract that included incentive bonuses. If he could stay healthy and out of the penalty box, he seemed a good bet to cash in on those bonuses and help the Sharks get back into the playoffs. The early odds out of Las Vegas made the Sharks a 6–1 favorite to win the Stanley Cup.

What Michael didn't know, however, was that not everybody agreed with the bonus clauses in Polanski's contract, although they thought his cashing-in part had a ring to it.

* * *

After breakfast, Michael loaded Scooter into his Jeep, pulled out of the driveway, and headed north to Healdsburg to see his family. Before he made it through the city, Michael encountered splashes of rain, splotches of sunshine, and a few areas of fog. The weather was still trying to make up its mind about what to do. It was behaving more like a spring day than one in November. Above the city's skyscrapers, small, confused clouds darted around the sky.

As they crossed the Golden Gate Bridge, Scooter stuck her head out the window, ready to give her occasional bark of disapproval at the slow-moving traffic.

Forty-five minutes later, traffic congestion had eased and the scenery had given up its cluttered, city look for a more relaxed one. Vineyards and farmland spread out over rolling hills dotted with black scrub oak and eucalyptus trees. Two miles south of Healdsburg, Michael exited the freeway and headed east on a frontage road. Soon he came to an intersection marked by an overhead, blinking yellow light. In the corner of one of the fields, the rusted hulk of an old red Farmall tractor sat tilted under a huge oak tree. Michael turned right and headed up a gravel road, passing three mailboxes and a small sign that read, "Ireland's Acres."

As he drove toward the farm, he recalled Annie's stories about her family when they had lived in the city, and how her father had shuttled grim-faced commuters back and forth from San Francisco to Oakland while her mother worked out of their modest home, electronically filing insurance forms for various medical companies. When the weekends came, Annie told him, her parents would pack up the Subaru and head for the rolling hills of the wine country north of San Francisco. They would critique farmhouses as they drove by. "Oh, honey, look at that one. Nice barn. Fence needs work." Or, "That one's beautiful. Too close to the road, though." They went on wine-tasting excursions and delighted in meeting like-minded people. It seemed like such an idyllic life.

According to Annie, the daily grind of Jesse's job began to wear him down. Every day, he would imagine how life would be back in the country instead of behind the wheel in traffic. But when Jesse broached the idea of moving out of the city and getting involved in the wine industry, Janice was sure her husband was having an early midlife crisis. "Not at this point in our lives, honey," she would say. "We don't have enough money saved. It's too risky."

But Jesse Ireland didn't give up on his dream. He researched the wine business from top to bottom. He took wine-making classes. He studied weather patterns. They continued their drives in the country, and he would stop and talk to as many farmers as he could. Then one day, on his way home from work, Jesse barely avoided a nine-car pileup east of the Golden Gate Bridge that left three people dead. Two of them were children. The next day, Jesse called a Realtor.

* * *

As Michael continued up the gravel road, he passed twenty acres of young grapes with dark-green leaves on the vine. One his right, there were thirty-five acres of mature grapes, their leaves an even darker hue. A quarter of a mile later, Michael pulled into a circular drive and parked in front of a large, two-story Tudor house. Michael knew that the house had been built in 1983, but it had all the features of a medieval structure: a steeply pitched roof, tall, narrow windows, exposed timbers, and a stone chimney. A wooden barn with a rounded shake roof stood directly across the drive, its two large doors opened wide.

Sadie appeared out of the shadows of the barn. A split second after the car door was opened, Scooter bolted across Michael's lap and flew toward the ground.

"Scooter!" Sadie let out a yell and ran across the drive to meet her dog, who was already running, hell-bent, toward her. After

Scooter had been kissed and petted thoroughly, Sadie smiled and looked up. "Hi, Daddy."

Michael scooped up his daughter in his arms. "Hi, sweetie. How ya doin'?" Looking over Sadie's shoulder, Michael saw Annie and her father stepping out of the barn. Jesse Ireland was in his late forties, but stood erect, with a solid frame. He had just a hint of gray in a full head of light-brown hair. His eyes were green and clear. His handshake was firm and calloused. "Hello, Mike."

"Hey, Jesse. Good to see you."

Annie waited until the men had exchanged their greetings before she offered hers. "Hey," she said with a slight smile.

"Hey to you, too."

They stood there without saying anything more until Jesse excused himself and headed for the house. When Sadie ran to find a stick to throw for Scooter, Annie and Michael turned to follow.

In better times, if Michael didn't have to work, the Fletcher family had enjoyed spending Sunday afternoons doing something fun together: maybe a trip to Fisherman's Wharf, where Sadie would run around with an ice cream cone and squeal in delight at the barking sea lions, or maybe a visit to McLaren Park to toss a Frisbee for Scooter.

Now, strolling behind Sadie and Scooter, Michael asked the same question that he'd asked every time he had come out to the farm. "Have you finished with your dad's books?"

Annie smiled, a pensive look on her face. "I'm not sure I'll ever be. He was really in a mess."

"Well, I'm in a mess, too. I want my wife and daughter to come home. You said you were only going to be gone—"

"How about you?" Annie asked. "You find anything yet?"

"Well, I had lunch with the sports editor for the *Chronicle* yesterday."

"And?"

Michael explained how he would now be on file at the newspaper, and added, "He picked up the tab for lunch."

Annie stopped walking and looked directly at Michael. "Michael, listen to me. Sadie loves it here. I think it's where she should be. Lots of animals and fresh air. No traffic or smog to speak of. Haven't heard a siren since we've been here."

Michael looked down and kicked a pebble. "What about you?" he asked. "What do you want? Where do you want to be?"

"I want to be with you, Michael. You and Sadie are the loves of my life, you know that. And I want us to be happy. I want us to be together."

"Yeah, and you know…if we were, like, together, we could copulate and everything!"

Annie's eyes drilled through his.

"Copulate. It means—"

"I know what it means, butthead. Can't you be serious?"

"I am serious." He looked over at the barn. "Is there any hay in there?"

She frowned and then poked him in the stomach. They took a couple of steps and stopped again. She tossed her hair back and looked out over the vineyards. "I just don't know right now. I see things differently out here."

Michael followed her gaze but remained silent. After a moment, Annie took his hand, and together they walked past the barn and out to a line of oak trees that fronted a stand of grapes, Scooter and Sadie zigzagging in front of them.

Then they saw Jesse waving from the veranda at the back of the house. "Hey, you guys! Lunchtime.

Come and get it!" Before they could answer, he disappeared through a slider door.

Annie and Michael changed course and followed Sadie and Scooter through a gate in the backyard. Jesse re-emerged from the house carrying a platter of sandwiches and walked across the flagstone deck to a round, glass table that was surrounded by wicker chairs. He set the platter down on the table and said, "You guys wash up if you want to. I'll bring some coffee out."

Annie sent Sadie to wash her hands, then went to help her dad. Michael shooed Scooter away and pulled out a chair. Five minutes later, everyone was back at the table, chowing down.

"So, Michael, you stayin' busy?" Jesse asked after they had all had a bite of lunch.

"Well, sort of. Tomorrow I'm covering the dedication of a new football field near the Presidio. That's kind of a big deal for—"

"Will we have lots of money then, Daddy?" Sadie asked excitedly.

Annie quickly stepped in. "Sadie! It's not polite to talk about money at the table."

"But you and Daddy do," Sadie whined. A second later, she laughed. "Daddy-doo, daddy-doo."

"That's enough, young lady," Annie said, hiding a smile.

"How 'bout that other stuff you're doin'?" Jesse asked. "The blogs and twitters, or whatever you call them?"

"Oh, yeah. I keep up with all that."

"What's a blog, daddy? Is it like a log? Or a frog?" Sadie giggled.

Michael frowned at his daughter. They'd had this discussion before, but he felt that for Jesse's sake, it wouldn't hurt to reiterate. "You know what it is, honey. It has to do with my work. I write stories about sports. Football, baseball, hockey, whatever's in season. I write my opinion on what I've seen or learned, and then I post the stories on—"

"Do you have a boss?"

"Well, no. Not really."

"How do you get paid?"

"Ah...that depends, honey. You see, I—."

"Are you more richer than Grandpa?"

Annie jumped in again, "Sad-*dee!* I told you—"

Jesse quickly saved the day. "You listen here, young lady. Nobody's as rich as I am!" He reached over and tickled her side. "Long's I got you around, anyway."

After Sadie's giggles died down and for the rest of the lunch, the conversation was steered away from what Michael was doing, or not doing, for a living.

An hour later, Michael headed home. Alone again. Naturally.

Chapter 10

✳   ✳   ✳

The mayor of San Francisco stood on a small platform that was positioned to one side of a yellow goalpost. Seated around him in gray folding chairs were two park officials, Sam Dornam, his wife, and an attractive, dark-haired woman whom Michael didn't recognize. From their position on the stage, the dignitaries could look out over an adjacent baseball diamond and soccer field. A red cinder running track encompassed the two fields.

A stalled high-pressure area just off the coast made for an unusually warm morning, with just a few high, puffy clouds and a light breeze. It was a perfect day to dedicate the new athletic facility. The people there to make speeches were dressed in coats and ties, but the audience in the crowd and around the park were mostly stripped down to tees and shorts.

At precisely 12:00 p.m., the mayor stepped up to the microphone, which squealed as soon as he touched it. An aide jumped up onto the small stage, made a quick adjustment, then hopped back down. The mayor tentatively touched the microphone again, then, assured his voice could be heard clearly, began: "As some of you may or may not know, Mark Twain visited our town years ago and took issue with our weather. He said, 'The coldest winter I ever spent was one summer in San Francisco.'"

The mayor, like the polished politician he was, paused just long enough to let the scattered chuckles quiet down, then added, "Well, apparently Mr. Twain was never here in the fall! Isn't *this* a gorgeous day?"

The crowd immediately responded with loud applause and whistles. The ceremony was off to a nice start.

Michael had met Sam Dornam on a couple of occasions. The first time, Michael was a kid asking for an autograph after a game at Candlestick Park. The second time, Dornam had been retired for a couple of years, but was one of the celebrities attending a benefit dinner for the local Boys Club. On both occasions, Sam Dornam was approachable and gracious. And on this day, as Dornam delivered his speech and thanked everyone in sight, Michael felt that nothing had changed about the man.

After his speech, Michael followed Dornam and a group of dignitaries to the south end of the field, where a red ribbon was strung across the goalpost. The man of the hour was handed a huge pair of scissors and then positioned alongside the mayor for a photo shoot. When all the smiles were in place, the mayor's aide gave a thumbs-up, and Dornam snipped the ribbon, saying, "This one's for the kids!' There were shouts and whistles, and the deed was done.

Minutes later, two Pop Warner teams took to the field for pregame warm-ups. One team wore dark blue jerseys with white numerals on their backs. Their pants and helmets sparkled white as well. Their opponents were decked out in bright-red jerseys with black numerals, black pants, and gray helmets. There was nary a grass stain on any of the uniforms.

When the number of people around Dornam dwindled to a handful, Michael walked up and introduced himself. "Hi, Mr. Dornam? I'm Mike Fletcher. I'm covering today's event for the…ah…local newspaper."

"Yes, how are you? Good to see you." Dornam said, as if he remembered Michael.

"Thank you, sir. Would you mind if I asked you a few questions? I pretty much know about your football career, I've been a fan for a long time. But I would like to ask you about your medical practice and some of the things you've done for the kids in this area."

"Sure, that'd be fine," he said. But then, in typical fashion, Dornam deflected credit to someone else. "But wait, let me find Dr. Scott. She's the one who's responsible for so much of what's going on here."

Doctor Laurie Scott was chatting with some women a few feet away when Dornam caught her eye and motioned her over.

Dornam had introduced Dr. Scott to the crowd earlier as his associate who had played a tremendous role in establishing some of his childcare charities and programs. When she addressed the audience, she captivated them, not only with an eloquent and uplifting speech, but with her physical beauty as well. She wore a dark business jacket and skirt and a white blouse, and even in low heels, she was taller than most of the men around her. She had long, silky black hair that touched her shoulders. Her olive-colored skin and dark-brown eyes hinted at Native American ancestry. When she smiled, dimples showcased dazzling white teeth.

When she walked over to the men, Michael couldn't help but notice her long, shapely legs.

"Laurie, this is Michael Fletcher. He's with the—I'm sorry, son, who are you writing for again?"

"Well, Bo Kimble asked me—"

"Yes, of course. I know Bo. He's a good man. Anyway, Laurie, Michael here is with the *Chronicle*, and he's interested in some of the programs we have for the kids in the area. Would you mind?"

Michael saw no need to correct Dornam about his position with the *Chronicle*, and although he wanted to talk with the man of the hour a little more, Michael wasn't too upset when Dornam excused himself and trotted out to midfield for the coin toss to start the football game.

"Nice to meet you, Michael," Scott said, offering her hand.

Michael had never seen eyes quite like hers. Her touch was a low-voltage tingle.

"Oh, ah, yes, I'm doing a story for, ah…well, the *Chronicle*, and…"

"That's great. How can I help you?"

"Well, ah…how was it that you and Mister, er, Doctor Dornam got together on these projects for the kids?"

"Well, that's a good question. I'm glad you asked it." Dr. Scott smiled and pushed her hair back. Michael noticed she wasn't wearing a wedding ring.

"When I first started my practice, I met the parents of a young boy named Jason, who had been diagnosed with a condition that affects the spinal column. He underwent surgery to correct it, and all went well until it was time to start his physical therapy. The boy was very reluctant to do the exercises and, on a couple of occasions, refused to do them at all. He seemed to be afraid of the equipment around him. And he didn't want me to touch him."

Michael forced himself to look down at his notes as she continued.

"Then I saw Sam on a newscast, working out with some kids at a local gym. The children looked like they were really having fun. I knew Sam was connecting with those kids. It was a connection I was missing with Jason."

Suddenly, whistles blew, summoning both teams onto the field for the kickoff. Michael and Dr. Scott turned and slowly made their way toward the field while continuing their conversation.

"Anyway, I decided to take a chance and call Sam to ask if he would come by and see Jason. Well, of course he said he would. And it worked. In no time, Jason was doing his exercises almost to a point of showing off. I knew then that I had to find a way to partner up with Sam."

Scott stopped, looked at Michael, and flashed her smile. "So, like a brazen slut, I propositioned the poor man."

"Well, ah, obviously, Dr. Dornam accepted your, er, proposition," Michael stammered. "And the rest, as they say, is history, huh?"

"Yes, well, we'd like to think we're making history. We try to keep up with the latest technology and medical research that's available, but like everything else, funding is sometimes an issue. But thanks to Sam, we've got the latest exercise equipment at our facility."

As if she were reading Michael's mind, she looked at his camera and said, "If you have time to come by, I'd be happy to show you around the place. It isn't too far from here."

"Today?"

"Sure, why not?" She reached into her purse and handed Michael a business card. "I was planning on watching the first half of this game, then going to the office. There's usually no one there on Saturday, which is nice because it gives me time to catch up on some things." She placed her hand on Michael's arm and leaned toward him confidentially. "Besides, I never turn down a chance for publicity. It helps when I ask the government for grants."

She smiled and walked away to rejoin some people on the sidelines, leaving Michael with a hint of her sweet fragrance.

Chapter 11

The kids' football game got underway with lots of proud parents urging them on. Some sat in the small sets of bleachers that were on both sides of the field; others lined the sidelines. It was an evenly matched game without a lot of scoring, but nobody seemed to care. Some people strolling in the park wandered over to see what was going on.

Mark Twain would have been impressed.

Michael was meandering around the sidelines, snapping photos, when he heard his name called out.

"Fletcher? Hey, Mike Fletcher!"

He turned and saw three men standing twenty yards away from him and the playing field. One of the men was smiling and looked vaguely familiar. He had red, curly hair, a stocky build, and was about Michael's age. He wore Levi's, running shoes, and a gray hooded sweatshirt with the sleeves pushed up to his elbows. The other two men were a little older and looked as if they could have come straight from Las Vegas: sports coats with open shirt collars, deep tans, dark glasses, and assorted bling on their chests, hands, and ears. Michael was too far away to smell if they were wearing cologne, but he could imagine it.

"Mikey, it's me. Dan Kelly!" He waved Michael over to the group.

In an instant, it all came back. Dan Kelly was one of the kids from the neighborhood where Michael grew up. He was a bit of a bully and had a temper that was always getting him in trouble. He was pigeon-toed and walked as if he was about to run. Michael hadn't seen him since the ninth grade, when he and his parents moved away.

"Hi, Dan." Michael walked toward the men and stuck out his hand to his former neighbor. "Been a long time. How you doin'?"

"Good, good. Hey, I thought that was you. I saw you writing stuff and taking pictures. You're a reporter or something, right?"

The two other men exchanged a glance.

"Well, my business card says sports journalist," Michael said.

"Yeah, cool. I've read some stuff by a Michael Fletcher. I wondered if that was you."

"Ah...'scuse me, Danny." It was the taller of the two other men. "We gotta go. But hey, listen, it was good seein' you, right?" The man didn't wait for an answer and had already turned away.

"Yeah. Yeah, you bet. See ya." Dan Kelly watched the two men walk toward the sidelines. He turned back to Michael and shrugged. "Assholes."

"Who are they?" Michael asked, mildly interested.

"Aw, the big guy's an agent. Carl Weinstein. Thinks he's hot shit."

"Sports agent?"

"Yeah. Fuck 'em."

Kelly dropped a shoulder and faked a left hook to Michael's stomach.

Michael jumped back a little, then quickly raised his hands in mock surrender. "No mas, no mas! Me give-oh."

"You pussy." Kelly tapped Michael's chest and laughed. "You always were a pussy."

Michael nodded. He really wanted to ask Kelly more about the sports agent, but tried to be polite. "Yeah, that's me. But what about you, Dan? Whaddya doin'? Last I heard, you were living in L.A."

"Yeah, I was there for about six years. I went through the police academy there. I live in San Bruno now. I'm a cop."

Michael raised his eyebrows at that. What he remembered about Dan Kelly certainly didn't fit the profile of a police officer.

"But, hey," Kelly said. "You being a sportswriter and all, I bet you get the inside shit on injury reports and who's gonna play each week, huh? You know, in the pros."

"I don't really…"

Their conversation was interrupted by a commotion on the field. A minor scuffle had broken out, and whistles were blowing and penalty flags flying. The referees quickly broke up the fight and sent two players to the sidelines. One of the players was limping.

"Aw, shit. I think that's my son," Kelly said as he strained to get a better look. Then he turned back to Michael. "Hey, Mikey, I better go. Listen, it was good to see you again. You in the phone book? I'd really like to talk more football. Fantasy league and shit. You know?"

There was concern in Kelly's voice, but Michael couldn't be sure if it was for his son or his football picks. As Michael watched, Kelly hustled over to the players who were huddled near the sidelines. He pushed his way through the group, grabbed one of the players, and started to shake him by the shoulders. One of the coaches quickly intervened and pointed Kelly back to the grandstands.

Some things never change, Michael thought.

* * *

Just before halftime, Michael noticed the two men who had been talking with Kelly. They were off by themselves on the far side of the field, near the end zone, watching the football action across from them. The offensive team was slowly grinding its way toward pay dirt. The two men were smiling and talking, and seemingly enjoying the game from a distance.

Michael thought it might be interesting to talk with the agent, find out who he represented, and maybe get a quote or two. It took him two minutes to walk around the end zone. As he approached the men, they stopped talking and looked his way.

"Scouting for future clients?" Michael said, smiling.

The two continued to stare at him, saying nothing. Michael began to feel as if maybe he had dog shit on his shoes. He considered walking past the two men.

Finally, the one that Kelly had said was an agent nodded slightly. The shorter man looked at his pal and shrugged, as if he was saying, *What the hell. Go ahead. Talk to him.* Michael took that as an opening.

"Hi, I'm Michael Fletcher. I'm doing a little piece on the ceremonies here today." He held his camera in his left hand and gestured with it toward the gridiron. He kept his right hand free, thinking there might be a handshake coming.

The bigger man finally spoke. "I'm Carl Weinstein. This here's Tony."

Tony just nodded. Weinstein offered his hand. Michael took it. It was clammy.

"I understand you're a sports agent?" Michael said as he shifted his camera back into his right hand. It kept him from wiping his hand off on his pants.

"Yes, I am. And you're with…who again? Who do you write for?"

"Well, right now I'm sorta doing this thing for the Chronicle, but usually I freelance…"

Suddenly, cheers erupted from the sidelines. One of the defensive players in a blue jersey had recovered a fumble and was returning it as fast as his little legs could carry him. Michael and company watched number nineteen race toward their side of the field. The boy's oversized helmet was bouncing and twisting on his head with each stride he took. For a moment, it looked like he was going to stumble and maybe lose the ball, but at the last moment, he caught himself and continued his run to glory. A few of the opposing players were giving chase, but their hearts weren't in it, especially the heavier kids. The boy finally made it to the end zone, where he tripped and fell down. He struggled to get up and tried to spike the football, but the ball flew backward out of his hands. He turned, picked up the ball, and was in mid-spike when his teammates trampled him, and he whiffed again.

"He's gotta work on his end-zone routine if he wants to make it in the NFL," Weinstein said out of the side of his mouth.

"No shit," Tony said.

Michael saw another opportunity to bond. "Well, at least somebody finally scored. You think they'll cover the spread?"

Bond? "Bomb" was a better word. The air temp around the three men suddenly dropped about twenty degrees. Tony glared at Michael.

"Look, Flauker, or whatever the hell your name is, you say you don't really work for anybody full time, huh? You're just a stringer, then?"

Michael's hackles stirred. "Yeah, I guess you could—"

"Let it go, Tony," Weinstein said as he put a hand on Tony's chest. But Tony wasn't through.

"Then why don't you take your camera out to the Golden Gate and wait for someone to take a dive? That's the kind of stories you guys like best, isn't it?"

Chapter 12

✳ ✳ ✳

"Seething." It's a great word.

There are no gray areas in "seething." No sorta, slightly, or kinda. If you're seething, you're on fire inside.

Michael watched the two slowly walk away. *You do the dive, dickwad, I'll be happy to do the story!*

Michael was seething.

A few deep breaths later, he decided to go home, take a shower, and cool off mentally and physically. Hopefully, he'd remember to write a story on the dedication of the new playing field.

He was still rattled and halfway home when he remembered Dr. Scott's invitation. He took a perfunctory sniff of each armpit, decided he was okay in that department, then spit out the window as if to expel any residue of his conversation with Weinstein and Ass-hole-ciates.

Fifteen minutes later, Michael turned west onto Geary Boulevard and found the address Dr. Scott had given him. He pulled up to the curb adjacent to a one-story, modest brick building with a flat roof. Lettering on the glass entry door read "Dr. Laurie Scott & Associates, Physical Therapy."

Michael grabbed his camera and notepad and headed for the front door. His mood temporarily dropped back a notch when he pushed on the door and found it locked. But as he shaded his eyes against the glass and peered in, Dr. Scott floated into view, smiling, and unlocked the door.

"Michael. I'm so glad you could drop by. Please come in. I just got here myself, through the back door." She was still wearing what she'd had on earlier, but as she led Michael inside, she stopped at a standing coat rack behind a reception desk and took off her jacket. "Excuse me, but I'm always so glad to get out of these clothes, especially on days like these."

She steadied herself with one hand against the wall and slipped off her shoes. She unbuttoned the top two buttons on her blouse and then tossed her hair back off her neck.

"There, much better," she said, smiling. She padded toward Michael in her bare feet. "Now, let me show you around."

She led him through a hallway that was adorned with autographed pictures and posters from the San Francisco Forty-Niners. One poster displayed Sam Dornam in his uniform and was signed, "Dr. Laurie, good luck with the kids!"

The hallway opened into one large room that was filled with shiny, black-and-chrome exercise equipment of every description, some of which Michael was sure he'd never seen before. Full-length mirrors adorned much of the surrounding wall space.

"This used to be a dance studio," Dr. Scott said as she surveyed the room. "It didn't require much remodeling when we moved in, which made it nice."

"I'm impressed with all the different equipment you've got here," Michael said, "although it might seem like a house of horrors to some folks. I could see how a couch potato might be intimidated by it all."

Scott laughed and leveled an eye at Michael. "You don't look much like a couch potato to me, Michael. You're not intimidated, are you?"

"No, no," Michael blustered. "But, ah…I'd need a trainer or someone to explain how to use half of this stuff." He held his camera up and took a couple of quick pictures.

"Well, most of its not as complicated as it looks. Come, let me show you."

They wandered around the room with Scott explaining what certain equipment was used for and how it worked. She glowingly shared success stories about some of her patients and how proud she was of them, and then added, "Of course, without Sam's help, none of this would have been possible."

As they were winding down the tour of the room, Michael stopped and pointed to a padded stool that had a flat, vertical paddle directly in front of it. "Okay, what's that for?"

"Well, I actually used that myself for rehab. It's used for Patellar disorders, meniscus tears, things like that."

"Oh, sure, right."

Scott smiled at Michael, went over to the stool, pulled her skirt up a few inches, and sat down. With the paddle between her knees, she twisted her hips, swiveling the stool.

"It strengthens the muscles around your knees, as well as the vastus medialis." She demonstrated by pulling her skirt up another inch and running her finger along the outside of her thigh, tracing what Michael guessed was her nicely defined vastus medialis. He also noticed a small, white scar above her right knee.

"You can adjust the resistance between the paddle and the stool. It really works quite well." Scott stood up and pulled her skirt back down. She looked directly at Michael without saying anything. A long moment passed before either of them spoke.

"Well, ah, thanks for the tour, Doctor," Michael said, finally. "I appreciate your time. I guess I better let you get to work, and I better do the same." He knew that there was a good chance that someone would edit most of the pictures he had just taken, if they used any of them at all. He was feeling a little guilty about taking up the woman's time.

"It's been my pleasure, Michael," Scott said, her eyes still locked on his. "And I know Sam recognizes what you're doing."

Michael let her lead him back to the front entrance. At the door, Scott extended her hand. "Thanks again for coming by. I appreciate your interest in our project here."

"You bet," Michael said as he held onto her hand. "Maybe our paths will cross again."

Chapter 13

※ ※ ※

The following Tuesday morning, Michael had every reason to be excited. Bo Kimble had called him the day before and told him that he was pretty sure that Michael's story about the dedication of the new playing field would be in Tuesday's edition. It had been edited down to four paragraphs and would appear in the society section, page five.

Now, dressed in a bathrobe and slippers, Michael hurried outside to get the paper. He had already put the coffee on and told himself not to get too excited. Bo had said *"pretty* sure," which didn't mean *"for* sure." Maybe they had to cancel the article for some reason, or they'd edited out the good stuff, or something.

He picked up the newspaper and headed back to the house, unrolling the blue rubber band off the paper as he went. He stepped back into the kitchen, tossed the paper onto the table, and reached for the coffee pot. He poured a cup, turned to sit down, and saw the front-page headline, "Pro Hockey Player Found Dead. Sports World Suffers Another Loss in Bay Area."

What?

Are you kiddin' me?

Michael sat down and read, "Troy Polanski, star forward for the San Jose Sharks, was found dead in a hotel bathtub by a cleaning lady late yesterday morning. An investigation is underway, and the cause of death has yet to be determined; however, early indications suggest a possible drug overdose. A source close to the investigation said police have reviewed hotel security footage, but aren't saying if anyone was seen entering or leaving Polanski's room after he checked in. An autopsy is pending."

As the day went on, Michael wasn't surprised to see that Polanski's death had birthed a media frenzy. It was the main on local sports radio and opened on the five o'clock news. Social media was all atwitter, too. Soon, everyone knew the rest of the story.

Polanski was born and raised in Morgan Hill, California. As a boy, he played all school sports, including junior hockey. After graduating high school, he briefly attended the University of Colorado, where he was an outstanding left wing on the Buffaloes hockey team. He left school early to pursue a career in professional hockey and was soon offered a tryout by the San Jose Sharks. He had scored a goal and been instrumental in the Sharks' victory on the night he died.

* * *

That night, Michael was compelled to write something about Polanski on his blog, but what could he add that somebody hadn't already said? Could he juxtapose the story with Lavorini's in a way that nobody else had?

Before he went to bed, he typed out a narrative that included words like "tragedy," "loss," "senseless," and "profound." He also added a hackneyed opinion about drug policies in professional sports. He thought he should mention something about the glaring coincidence of two local professional athletes dying accidentally in a relatively short time, but in the end decided against it.

Maybe happenstance really does just happen.

Chapter 14

✳ ✳ ✳

By Friday, the Earth was still spinning on its axis, still tracking in its solar orbit. The moon was still mooning, and the Polanski story began to fade like the comet it had been. There was a rumor that the Niners were posted as a two-and-a-half point underdog in Sunday's game.

Friday was also the day Michael got his first phone call from the *Chronicle*.

"Hey, Mike, it's Bo Kimble. You got a sec?"

"Su...sure. What's up?"

"Well, first, I thought your coverage of the Dornam deal was very good. Glad Jack could use it over in Society."

"Thank you. It was...ah...well...mostly..." Michael had to clear his throat before he finished the sentence, but he squeaked it out: "fun."

If Kimble noticed Michael's hesitation, he didn't let on. "Yeah, well, there was a little bit bigger story that day, as you know."

"Yeah, no kidding. I read your coverage on Polanski. Terrible stuff."

"What, the writing?"

"Oh, no, no. The writing was fine. I meant..."

"I know what you meant." Kimble chuckled.

Michael let out a breath and felt his face flush.

"But, hey, the reason I'm calling is this: Polanski's funeral is tomorrow in Morgan Hill, and we'd like someone there to cover it. I'm shorthanded again and wondering if you'd like the job?"

"Oh, well...sure. I'd be happy to help."

"Good. I wanna keep it low-key and not bother the family. I'd like you to take a few shots without sticking the camera in everyone's face. Polanski wasn't married and didn't have kids, but he had a sister. One of our guys knows her, says she's okay with us being there. I'm not sure Polanski's stepfather will be thrilled with the idea, but that's another story. As long as we observe from a distance, so to speak, I'm sure it'll be fine. You think you could handle it? We can pay you our contractor's rate."

"Sure. No problem."

"Atta boy. Use your own judgment about who you talk to there. I'm assuming that a lot of his teammates will be attending. Probably his agent too."

"His agent?"

"Yeah, Winesteed? Winestead? Something like that."

Chapter 15

※ ※ ※

Saturday morning came with a steady drizzle of rain. Perfect funeral weather.

Michael sat at his kitchen table and watched the raindrops wriggle down the bay window.

He wondered if it was raining in Healdsburg.

He wondered if the grapes were being affected by the rain. Wondered if his wife was sitting in their kitchen, drinking coffee and wondering about him. Michael had been excited the night before after the phone call from Kimble and had called Annie to tell her about it. When her voice message had come on, he'd tried to sound casual and upbeat at the same time, but twenty seconds in, he'd sort of trailed off.

She hadn't returned his call.

Are they still called answering machines if they're cell phones and nobody answers? Michael wondered again.

Cell phones can take pictures and videos, send e-mails and check the stock market, give you the weather forecast, show you a calendar, point north. They can keep you entertained in myriad ways, maybe even tell you how your hair looks, but as answering machines go, they suck. They still can't make the other person answer.

* * *

By the time Michael left the house and pointed his Jeep south, the rain had lightened to a mist. He jigged and jagged his way over surface streets until he hit the nearest onramp to the 101 south. He accelerated up onto the curved onramp and took a quick glance over his left shoulder. Traffic was moving at moderate speed, and there was room for him to enter the stream easily.

Cool.

Michael was sixty-two mph and one second away from engaging the cruise control when the wail of a siren suddenly grabbed his attention. A state patrol car, red and blue lights blazing, quickly filled the driver's-side mirror. Before Michael had a chance to slow down or pull over, the patrol car flew past him. It went by so fast, it was three seconds before Michael's adrenaline surged and caught up with his heart.

The patrol car seemed to vanish into traffic as quickly as it had appeared, its siren Dopperling away. Michael stayed in the slow lane and let his heart rate return to earth. *What was it Annie said? Oh, yeah. They haven't heard a siren since they've been out at the farm.*

Michael's thoughts turned to Sadie. His little girl did seem to be happy at the Ireland farm. There were plenty of things for a five-year-old to do, especially one who wasn't always engrossed in electronic games; especially one who loved animals and bugs, loved climbing apple trees and discovering frogs. *Will she grow out of that?* Michael wondered. *Maybe. Maybe not.*

Was she safer out there? Probably. As long as she stayed off the machinery. As long as she didn't climb too high in the apple tree. As long as she didn't...

Michael moved over another lane and kicked his speed up a notch. He glanced at the Jeep's odometer and noticed the blue, digital numbers read 99,998. He instantly thought back to when he was a kid, about the same age as Sadie, riding in his grandfather's restored 1953 Buick Roadmaster. They were driving up the coast from Monterey. "Look, Mike," Leo Fletcher had said, pointing to the odometer with its boxes of mechanical numbers, "the odometer's gonna turn over!" He said it as if some life-changing event was about to happen.

"The what's gonna do what?" Michael asked.

His grandfather slowed the big car, and the two of them watched the row of nines rise together in slow motion. Just as the numbers reached the top of the instrument, they seemed to hesitate for a last look around, and then, as if knowing they couldn't go back, rolled up and over, into oblivion. Then, a breath later, as if being pulled into a new world by the expiring numbers, a fresh set of zeroes slowly climbed into view.

"How 'bout that, Mikey? Pretty neat, huh?"

"Yeah, I guess. What happens now, Grandpa?"

"Ah, well, I dunno." His granddad shrugged as he stepped on the gas. "Let's see if we can get another hundred thousand outta the old goat."

Would Sadie be impressed by such an event?

Michael's reverie was cut short when a Volkswagen van in front of him suddenly slowed. He braked hard, regaining his focus. When he looked back at the odometer, the blue, digital numbers had already morphed away. *Blink, blink. Now you see me, now you don't!*

Life in the fast lane.

Chapter 16

✳ ✳ ✳

The First Methodist Church of Morgan Hill sat alone at the top of an imposing knoll. A long, winding drive, lined with neatly trimmed hedges and flowers, led upward to the building. As Michael swung onto it and started up the hill, he noticed a sign posted just off the road that read: "Dead End. No Exit" He laughed and continued up the asphalt lane. *What the hell, nobody gets out of this alive anyway.*

At the top of the hill, it became evident that the church's architects had taken advantage of its location. The structure was a circular design that afforded a 360-degree view of the town and the gently rolling hills that surrounded it. Tall eucalyptus trees ringed a parking area already jammed with cars.

Michael nosed the Jeep around the lot until he found a spot and squeezed in between a Lexus and Jag. The sky had brightened, and the sun was gallantly trying to prove the forecasters right by fighting through some lingering clouds.

Inside the cavernous church, it was standing room only. Mourners in dark clothes leaned toward each other and spoke in hushed voices. Some smiled, some sniffled. An occasional cough could be heard over solemn organ music that filtered around and through everything. Michael quietly took a standing position along a wall, near the last pew, and waited. He thought he spotted Weinstein in the front row but couldn't be sure.

After what seemed like an eternity to everyone but Troy Polanski, the organ music mercifully faded out, and everyone quieted down.

A tall, thin man dressed in a black robe, with a lime-green scarf draped over his shoulders, emerged from the black curtains behind the podium. He looked to be about sixty-five years old and was wearing glasses, and what little hair he had was combed east to west in dark, narrow wisps. He placed his notes on the podium, cleared his throat, and looked out over the crowd. When he finally spoke, his voice was soft and syrupy, with pauses between phrases.

"Thank you all...for coming *heeere* today. I'd like to begin... our service...with a prayer I know Troy...found faith in."

Michael's religious beliefs were about on the same level as the sports he'd played growing up: unorganized. His parents weren't exactly strong churchgoers, but they weren't on the atheist side of the spectrum, either. The Fletcher family bowed their heads before Christmas and Thanksgiving dinners, and sometimes on Easter. They did so mostly to remember family members who had shuffled on ahead. And they did so in silence, leaving it up to each individual to fill in the blanks however he or she saw fit.

You wouldn't find the Good Book in the Fletcher library, but you could find good books. One such book was a science publication titled *The Amazing Universe*, published by the National Geographic Society in 1975. It was about astronomy and the early, brainy guys who had studied night sky centuries ago, thinkers such as Copernicus, Herschel, Newton, and Galileo.

Michael had always been interested in science and the moon and stars and all of that, but as far as who or what started it all, he wasn't sure that the human mind was capable of understanding any of that. Why was way out of reach. He was curious, though.

The book was short, relatively speaking, just under two hundred pages. But the contents of each page kept Michael turning them. There were magnificent photos of planets, nebulas, and distant galaxies. There was even an artist's rendering of what the proposed space shuttle would look like. For Michael, this was the Bible.

At the end of the book, there was a chapter titled "The Cosmic Order," which dealt with different theories about how and when the universe was created. It suggested that philosophically, there can be just as many versions of how the universe began as there are philosophers. As Michael read furiously toward the final page, he was ready to put his chips on the Big Bang theory. But when he came to the last hypothesis, by Nobel laureate Bertrand Russell, he wasn't so sure. Russell tossed all the other theories aside by saying, essentially, "The universe could have been created five minutes ago, complete with its apparent history and all our memories."

Five minutes ago? Really?
Well, shit, then.

* * *

The pastor finally ended his prayer, and quiet amens murmured through the crowd. Then he began the eulogy. The tenor and inflection in his voice was such that he seemed to caress each word in an effort to pimp the next. He would speak softly, pause, and then power up when appropriate. Not that the man speaking wasn't eloquent and sincere sounding—he was—but two minutes into his extolling, Michael couldn't help but wonder if the preacher ever spoke in a normal voice. How did he sound when he answered the phone at home? Hell*ooo*, may I help *yoooou*? Or, if he was out bowling with the guys, "Hey, fell*oows*, would you like a bee*eer*?"

As the sermon progressed, the preacher mentioned how Troy Polanski had been blessed with a God-given talent to play hockey. Michael wondered why God would bless Troy with the ability to play hockey, but not bless him with the ability to think clearly enough to avoid overdosing on drugs.

Oh, that's right. He works in mysterious ways.

The tempo of the service picked up considerably as a few of Polanski's teammates took the podium and shared some anecdotes that produced a few polite chuckles. Michael discreetly wrote down their names and usable quotes. Then Carl Weinstein took the podium, decked out in a black Armani suit and a dangling gold necklace. His black hair was gelled and combed straight back. A diamond stud earring glinted in the sunlight that streaked in through the stained glass windows. In his best baritone, Weinstein gave a moving testimony about Polanski's character and how he felt he had lost a friend and a brother.

As Weinstein continued to speak, a man sitting in the pew directly in front of Michael looked to his left, then back to his right. Unaware that Michael was a few feet behind him, he leaned over to the guy next to him and whispered, "Yeah, Weinstein lost something, alright. Ten percent."

The other man tilted his head and said out of the side of his mouth, "Naw. He probably had Polanski insured to the hilt."

* * *

At the conclusion of the ceremony, Polanski's family gathered outside to accept condolences as people filed by. Michael skirted the family and went directly to the parking lot. From a distance, he snapped a couple of pictures of people coming out of the church, mostly just to show the size of the crowd. Ten minutes later, satisfied that he had what Kimble wanted, he climbed into his Jeep and drove away.

* * *

Ninety minutes later, he pulled into his driveway. Scooter greeted him at the cyclone fence gate with a slobbery green tennis ball in her mouth.

"Okay, Scoots, I'll give you a couple." Michael felt a little guilty for not playing with his dog more often and wished that Annie and Sadie were home to help with her exercise program.

After a few quick tosses, Michael went inside, zapped a cup of coffee in the microwave, and settled in with his laptop on the kitchen table. Within an hour, he had regurgitated the events of the funeral into a short but effective piece. He didn't mention Weinstein. After a final spell-check, Michael hit "Send"…and then he thought about the two men in the pew in front of him.

Chapter 17

※ ※ ※

On Sunday morning, Annie answered the phone on the first ring.

"Hello?"

"Hi, ho...ney." Michael choked a little on his coffee. He was somewhat surprised to hear his wife's voice so clear. He almost blurted, *"Are you okay? Is Sadie alright?"* But instead, what came out of his mouth was, "How ya doin'?"

What came out of Annie's mouth was, "Oh, hi, Michael."

Suddenly, the sparring began.

"*Oh?* Oh, hi? Is that all I get? You *do* remember me, right? I know you have caller ID."

"Jesus, Michael. Don't start. I was expecting a call from Dad."

"Okay, okay. I'm sorry. I'm just checking in." Michael took a breath. "I was thinking about coming up there this afternoon. I've been doing some—"

"Uh oh. I think there's a cop in front of us. Sorry. Sadie and I are in the car on the way to the farmers market. I better get off the phone."

"Yeah, sure. But call me back, okay?...Hello?"

* * *

While trying to decide whether to drive up to Healdsburg, Michael took his coffee and newspaper into the living room and flicked on the TV. He settled into his recliner and punched in one of the NFL pregame shows. The five analysts on the program sat on a curved dais and mostly yucked it up, argued, and predicted. They consisted of a former field-goal kicker, a defensive end, an ex-quarterback, one retired coach, and one fired-in-waiting coach.

The host of the show was a middle-aged man who, probably while in college years ago, had discovered that he didn't have the skills or the testosterone to play sports professionally, so he had studied telecommunications and found his niche in broadcasting as a color commentator/comedian. It was his job to keep the other talking heads from all talking at once. Sometimes he succeeded, other times not. Of all the people on the show, he was the least annoying.

There was a brief mention of the Polanksi tragedy and the obligatory, "Our thought and prayers go out to his family," and then it was business as usual. At the end of the show, the experts were asked for their predictions of all the games to be played that day. When it came time to pick between the Niners and the Cowboys, there were mixed views, with a final tally of three-two in favor of San Francisco. The one thing they did agree on, however, was that the Cowboys offense would do well to stay away from Marshal Decker.

"The Forty-Niners' defense is number one in the league and has been ever since they drafted Marshal Decker." This came from the ex-quarterback, who knew a thing or two about being run over by linebackers. "The man is ferocious and determined to be the highest-paid linebacker in the league. You know what they say about home field advantage being worth three points a game? Well, I would say there's a Decker advantage, and it's worth at least three points, too."

Michael remembered reading newspaper and magazine articles about Decker when the young phenom was still in high school. And even though they were about the same age, Michael's interest was not so much in Decker himself, but more in how the articles and stories were structured. Were all the whos, whats, whys, whens and wheres accounted for? How did the stories begin? How did they end? Was it new information? What was old? What made the stories interesting? What kind of questions were asked, and how were they poised? How much was cliche?

Most of the stories about Decker described him as "one to watch" or "a promising prospect," and said he "can't miss." Through these narratives, Michael learned that Decker was somewhat shy and reserved in interviews, but his father was always close by and never at a loss of words. Also, anybody who knew Marshal Decker knew that his determination came not from his love of God or a fiery coach, but from his father, Merle. Merle Decker was a strong and proud African-American who worked as a foreman for a road construction contractor. He raised his son alone after his Asian-American wife died of a brain aneurism when Marshal was only four years old. It was then that his father shoved a football in his stomach and said, "Here, son, play with this. Sleep with it."

In high school, Marshal played halfback on the football team and earned all-city honors. He struggled with his grades, but always seemed to get by, thanks in part to some creative, sports-minded teachers. When he wasn't busy with practices and games, his father kept him working out in their home gym. "You'll have your choice of women once you make it to the pros," Merle Decker was known to tell his son.

Sadly, Merle made the news one day on his own. The day after his son received a huge bonus for signing with San Francisco, Merle was wrapping up eight hours at work when he dropped dead of a heart attack.

* * *

His first year in the NFL, Marshal Decker's career took off, and the media circus around him grew accordingly. He set a team record for most tackles and ranked second in quarterback sacks. He had four interceptions, two of which he returned for touchdowns. In the forty-yard sprint, he was faster than most of the players on the team. His work ethic and competitive fire were such that his coaches asked him to tone it down during practice scrimmages. People started calling him "M.D.," not because they were his initials, but because the letters stood for "Mean Dude."

When Decker was voted Rookie of the Year, Michael thought that his agent was probably salivating at the thought of renegotiating Decker's contract.

As the sports media followed him in to his second year, reporting his every move, Decker started making up for lost time. He bought a condominium in the city, and a Hummer to go with his Mercedes. He changed his wardrobe completely, and spent lavishly on flashy jewelry, including diamond studs for both ears. And though he knew nothing about boats, he bought a fifty-four-foot Hatteras and kept it moored at the San Francisco Marina Yacht harbor. He even changed the boat's name to *Deck Mate*, scoffing at the notion it was bad luck to rename a vessel. He was soon making the rounds at all the hip and not-so-hip restaurants and nightspots. Tabloids tagged him "San Francisco's most eligible bachelor." Women were now much more available and easier to come by. Even though some wise sports scribe tagged him "all steam and no rudder," his star continued to rise with each game.

* * *

When the pregame show on television ended, Michael thumbed the remote's off button. He stared at the blank screen. *What to do, what to do?* Two minutes went by. He drained his coffee and absentmindedly clanked the cup down hard on the table next to him. Then it became clear. He would take Bo Kimble's advice. He would watch as much goddamn football as he could and write about it all. He would pay special attention to the Niners game and send it to Kimble. It was his job. He was a sportswriter, damn it.

As the early games started, Michael set the TV to record one of the games while he watched the other. But as far as drama went, there were hardly any surprises. The chalk bettors had their way as Atlanta covered a thirteen-point spread by crushing Jacksonville, forty-one-seven, and Philadelphia shut out the Jets, twenty-zero. The TV shots of empty seats in the stadiums confirmed the amount of interest.

After a lunch of canned chili poured over two boiled hot dogs, Michael settled in for the afternoon competitions and hoped for something more entertaining. He got his wish with the Niners home game.

The contest opened with a fast pace, and both teams scored touchdowns with their first possession. Tensions were high, bodies were flying everywhere, and the smack talk spewed from both sides. Although not many penalties were called, the referees were kept busy separating the two teams after nearly every play. At halftime, the two playoff contenders had battled to a fourteen-fourteen draw. There were no empty seats at the athletic field that was soon to be formerly known as Candlestick Park.

When play resumed in the second half, the tempo of the game remained fierce. Nobody blinked. When Dallas scored a field goal, San Francisco answered with one of its own. When one defense caused a three-and-out, the other team's D did the same. Nothing was easy. Every play was important. This one was going the distance.

They continued to slug it out well into the fourth quarter, tied at seventeen. With 6:05 left in the game, the Cowboys had worked their way across midfield and had the ball on the Niners' 46. According to the script, it was their turn to score. But the Forty-Niners' defense stiffened and put Dallas in a crucial third-down situation. Needing six yards for a first down, the Cowboys' quarterback dropped back and fired a bullet to his wide receiver, Wallace Jones, who was running a crossing pattern over the middle. A split second after Jones caught the football, the Forty-Niners' Marshal Decker came up from his outside linebacker's position and leveled Jones with a vicious blindside hit. As the pass fell incomplete and Jones crashed to the turf, Decker struck a bodybuilder's pose and screamed over the fallen receiver.

While most of the sixty thousand fans in the stands roared their approval, two people sat quietly watching the game on television, not far from the stadium. One of them picked up the TV remote and said, "They say that man is worth three points a game. I say we make that man go away."

And poof, the TV went black.

Chapter 18

* * *

Sunday night, Michael zapped his version of the Niners game to some satellite in space, which, he assumed, would rezap it back to some cyber address on Earth. On many occasions, Michael spent three or four seconds wondering if his message had been received, or how it was even possible to send his thoughts through space. He would then remind himself that he had probably just wasted three or four seconds. His wasn't to wonder why, his was to write or die. Some editor could be reading his message while climbing Mt. Everest, for all he knew.

At the thought of an editor, Michael remembered something else that Kimble had suggested he do: research the NFL's studies on concussions. Like most people, Michael was aware that there was a growing problem with head injuries in football, but to what extent, he wasn't sure. So, with nothing else to do, he decided to spend a few minutes researching the matter.

* * *

Three hours later, Michael finally closed his laptop and shook his head. Before he'd started his research, he had been cognizant of the lawsuit against the NFL by former players asking for compensation for head trauma during their careers, but he'd had no idea the sum they were asking for was almost a billion dollars.

He had also heard of the acronym CTE in relation to head injuries, but hadn't known that it stood for chronic traumatic encephalopathy. CTE was defined as a progressive, degenerative disease of the brain found in people with a history of repetitive brain trauma. The symptoms included memory loss, confusion, impaired judgment, aggression, depression, impulse control problems, anxiety, suicidality, Parkinsonism, and eventually, progressive dementia.

He read that since the 1920s, CTE had been used to describe a boxer's condition known as "punch drunk syndrome," or dementia pugilistica. The disease was later found in hockey players and football players.

Some other interesting things he found out were that Tony Dorsett, former running back with the Dallas Cowboys and Denver Broncos, was showing symptoms of CTE to the extent that his own children were afraid of him, and that when Junior Seau, linebacker with the Chargers, committed suicide, an autopsy showed he had suffered from CTE. Also, Dave Duerson, Chicago Bears defensive back, committed suicide by shooting himself in the chest. He left a note explaining that he had shot himself in the chest instead of his head so doctors could examine his brain. The autopsy showed he too suffered from CTE. Michael found it amazing that the man wasn't able to deal with his demons, yet he was lucid enough to spare his brain for the sake of science.

He was also surprised to learn that CTE could only be diagnosed accurately by an autopsy.

In a sidebar to his research, he learned that in 1905, after nineteen players died of injuries on the gridiron, an effort to abolish football had gotten underway. An editorial in the *Cincinnati Commercial Tribune* depicted the grim reaper sitting on a goalpost like a vulture, eyeballing a twisted mass of fallen players below him.

In an effort to save the game back then, President Theodore Roosevelt bullied up and lent his support by saying, "Manly sports builds character." Also, two new inventions were added for safety purposes: helmets and the forward pass.

Michael wasn't sure if all this was old news to Kimble, but he decided to write up a condensed version, put a little spin on it, and ship it off.

* * *

It wasn't until Wednesday morning that a least some validation came for Michael that he wasn't just writing in the wind. It came in the form of the *Chronicle's* sports pages with his story titled "Overflow Crowd Says Good-Bye to Hockey Great." It was pretty much the way he had written it, and he was pleased that Kimble hadn't changed it much.

After he finished reading his article, Michael turned the page to "Letters to the Editor." Polanski's life and death were still hot topics, with posts written in a mostly supportive narrative. Today was the exception, with one of the letters reading, "Why must we continue to idolize athletes who consider themselves above the rules, both in sport and civility? Polanksi is dead because as a society, we elevated his status to godlike, and he couldn't handle it. And now we're all shocked to find out he was just human after all. No wonder other countries and cultures take issue with capitalism.

We must stop glorifying overpaid athletes who eventually fail not only themselves, but our country as well." The letter was signed, "No symbols. No numbers. No Polanksi. Know justice."

Hmmm…very strange.

Michael had just read it for the second time when his cell phone rang.

"Hello?"

"Hey, Mikey. It's Dan. Dan Kelly. From the old days, 'member? I just saw you the other day."

"Yeah, yeah. Sure. What's up?" Michael couldn't remember giving Kelly his cell phone number.

"Oh, not much. Just thought I'd give you a call. I read your article this morning on Polanksi. I always knew you'd make it big someday."

"Yeah, right." Michael laughed. "Obituaries and dedications. Big time, for sure. How'd you get my cell phone number?"

It was Kelly's turn to laugh. "Hey, I'm a cop, remember?"

"Detective?"

"No, I'm not. I'm a…well, I'm just callin' you to tell you I enjoy reading your shit. How 'bout that game Sunday? Huh? You see that hit by Decker?"

"I did. It was a good game. Big hits on both sides."

"No shit. I love smash-mouth football."

"Sure, I do too. Just as long as they leave it on the field." Michael instantly regretted bringing up more fodder for Kelly to chew on.

"Whaddya mean? That domestic violence shit?"

"Sad, isn't it? But, you probably get your share of—"

"A lot of its bullshit. I'm not sayin' it's right or anything. I get it. Men are bigger than women. We're naturally stronger. But I think a lot of it's taken outta context. Don't quote me on this,

Mikey, or I'll have to kill you, heh, but hey, I think the media is blowing this thing way out of proportion. I mean, come on, pal, what guy hasn't wanted to throttle a chick at some time? Shit, what about the time you knocked Betsy Tyler on her ass. Remember?"

Michael was stunned. Betsy Tyler had been in his eighth-grade class. She was skinny, wore braces, and never talked to anyone. One day during lunch, she went berserk and attacked Michael for not paying attention to her.

"She dropped her tray and came screaming and scratchin' at you. She tried to kick you in the nuts, if I remember correctly, right?"

Michael didn't know if Kelly was screwing with him or not, but he had the story right. Except for the "tried to" on Betsy's part. Betsy had connected on her first attempt to kick him in the gonads. Michael's breath had blasted out of him, and he had immediately doubled over in pain. Ms. Tyler had drawn back her other leg and launched another shot, but Michael had seen it coming and instinctively thrown his arm up, somehow catching his attacker flush on the chin. She'd gone down like a sack of Joe Fraziers.

"That's a little different, Dan. Jesus, we were what, fourteen years old? She was mentally disturbed. Kids made fun of her all the time. She probably shouldn't have been in public school. I was just protecting my—"

"You were just protecting yourself, right?"

"Yes, I—"

"Well, there you go, my friend. Everyone's got a right to protect themselves, man or woman, that's all I'm sayin'."

Michael was at a loss as to how the conversation had gotten to this point, but he knew he'd had enough of it. "Okay, great. Look Dan, I've got a ton of stuff to do here. I better get back at it."

"Sure, sure. I just wanted to say hi. Hey, one more thing—who do you like tomorrow night in the Raiders game? I don't understand how Oakland is favored by four and a half. What's goin' on?"

Actually, Michael thought Cincinnati would run over Oakland by at least two touchdowns. The Raiders had lost their starting quarterback for the season and were on a two-game losing streak. They didn't look to improve anytime soon.

"Take Oakland and give the points, Dan. But don't tell anybody I told you…or I'll have to kill you."

"That's funny, Mikey. But hey, thanks."

Michael's thinking was that the Bengals would win easily, and then maybe Kelly wouldn't call him again. Of course, there was always the chance he would just have Michael killed, too.

Chapter 19

✳ ✳ ✳

Michael had just finished his conversation with Kelly when his home phone rang. Unlike his cell phone, the land line actually made a ringing sound. This time it was an incoming friendly from his father.

"Hi, son. I getcha at a bad time?"

"No. No, it's fine."

And it was fine. Michael loved his mom and pop. They were hardworking and honest and had always been there for him. They brought him up in a lower-middle class neighborhood instilled with high-class values.

Ray Fletcher was built a little closer to the ground than his son and had a bit of a beer belly from his bowling days. What was left of his gray hair ringed a shiny bald head. But what he lacked in leading-man looks, he more than made up for with his good nature and contagious chuckle. At Michael's commencement, he had tossed his son a set of keys, saying, "There's a new Jeep Wrangler that goes on the end of these. It's dark green. But don't go get all gushy on me or anything, we only gotcha one of em'."

Michael's mother, Bette Fletcher, was a sweet, gentle woman with twinkling eyes. These days, her short red hair was highlighted by streaks of silver. She complemented her husband perfectly. When Ray Fletcher would tell an off-color joke, Bette Fletcher would smile sheepishly, roll her eyes, and say, "Oh, Ray."

They were a tight family and knew each other well. And now that father had son on the phone, he thought he heard something in Michael's voice. "You sure things are fine? You sound a little tired."

Michael laughed. "Well, I just got off the phone with Dan Kelly, for one thing. You remember the Kellys? When we lived on Dalcamo Street?"

"Oh, hell yes. I remember the Kellys, all right. Had personalities like sandpaper. You walked by their house, you could hear 'em gratin' on each other all the time. Always had their windows open, for some reason. How come you're talkin' with Dan? I didn't know you two stayed in touch."

Michael explained the impromptu meeting with Kelly at the dedication ceremony.

"That little peckerhead's a cop?"

"Says he is. I'm not sure why he called me, though, to tell you the truth."

"Whadya talk about?"

"Football, mostly. Then we got into the domestic violence thing in the NFL. He's got some strange views on it." Michael repeated Kelly's rattle to his dad.

"I'm not surprised, Mike. Hell, he's a product of domestic violence his own self, for Christ's sake."

"Yeah, well…"

There was a silence on both ends of the phone connection, and then Ray Fletcher tried to lighten the mood. "Speaking of domestic situations, I'm sure yours is a lot better than most. How's little Sadie-Bug and Annie? Your mother and I miss 'em so much."

"Oh, they're—"

"I…I mean, well, you know, we miss you too, okay?"

Michael laughed. "Yeah, yeah, sure. I just don't remember you doting on me like you do Sadie."

"That's different. She's a girl. She's our 'grandgirl,' as your mother likes to call her."

Michael could hear his mother's voice in the background. Ray Fletcher said something to her and then came back on the line.

"Your mother wants to know if Annie would like to have our antique lamp that she likes so much. The one your mother and I got for a wedding present a hundred years ago. We've been downsizing, and…"

Michael spoke before he thought. "I'll ask her the next time I see her."

A few moments of dead air passed over the phone. Michael heard his mother in the distance again, something about a hundred years.

Ray Fletcher came back on the phone. "Ah…is Annie still up at her dad's place? With Sadie?"

"Yep."

"When they comin' home?"

"Good question, Dad. I dunno."

Ray Fletcher lowered his voice. "Is everything okay, son? Sounds like, maybe, you know, somethin's off a little?"

Michael took a deep breath and let it out. "Well, it's kinda hard right now. I think Annie wants to stay out in the country. She says it's safe and more affordable."

"Is that the only thing? Is that what's keeping you guys apart?" The man knew his son well. He knew there was more to the story.

"Oh, she thinks I'm being stubborn, I guess. Wonders why I'd wanna work with a dying breed like a newspaper, with most of them downsizing or going out of business."

"Hell, I've read newspapers all my life. Gotta have one every day, you know."

Michael smiled to himself, as if his father was personally keeping the industry alive with his habit. He remembered very well when his dad would come home from work, take his paper and a beer into the living room, and relax while Bette Fletcher fixed supper.

"I know, Dad. But...well, I promised Annie I'd look for another line of work if things don't work out soon."

"Newspapers ain't goin' away, son."

"Yeah, well, Jeff Bezos just bought the *Washington Post*. He must know something."

"A bozo bought what, son?"

"Never mind, Dad."

"You need some money? Your mother and I can loan—"

"No, no, thanks. We'll be all right."

"Well, if you need anything, let us know. In fact, if you want me to, I can give Ernie a call down at the shipyard. He owes me, you know."

"That's okay, Dad. I'll get it figured out."

"I know you will, son." Ray Fletcher lowered his voice. "You know, your mother and I went through some patchy times, too. Our marriage wasn't all creamy peaches, but we hung on."

"Don't worry, Dad. We'll be fine."

"Atta boy. I think you'll...uh oh. It looks like my cook is serving up. I better get off the phone."

Michael imagined his mother in her apron and pearls, setting the plates on the round oak dinner table, just like an old episode of *Leave It to Beaver*, or something like that. His visualization was complete when he heard his mother call, "It's ready! Come get it while it's hot!"

"Uh oh. I better go, son. I think your mother wants to have sex with me."

"Oh, Ray."

Chapter 20

※ ※ ※

Michael remembered how uncomfortable he'd been shopping for the negligee. It was displayed on a mannequin above the sales counter in an exclusive woman's clothing store in downtown San Francisco. It was very sheer and very red. He had stared at the mannequin and tried to imagine how Annie would look in it. The young salesgirl had wisely let Michael's imagination roam a moment before complimenting him on his choice and coyly guaranteeing his satisfaction.

Annie wore the lacy garment on their honeymoon, and she was wearing it again tonight. Michael lay on their bed and watched his wife move from the bathroom door slowly to him. Michael felt the bed sag slightly as Annie knelt down and then moved her hips to straddle him. She smiled down at him and slowly untied the front of the negligee, shaking her breasts free. She leaned forward and flicked the tip of her tongue against his lips. She moved to his ear and did the same thing. Michael groaned and reached for her...

"Annie!" Michael woke from his dream in a sweat, his heart pounding. Something wet and slippery was in his ear. Scooter's face came slowly into focus, just inches away. Her tongue was hanging out, and she was panting.

"Oh, Jesus." Michael closed his eyes and pulled the covers over his head. He tried to go back to sleep and catch up to his dream, but it was no good. He knew his dog was still inches away, staring at the lump under the blankets. Finally, he gave up and rolled out of bed. Scooter jumped down and led the way to the kitchen door that opened out to the backyard.

After Michael finished his own morning ablutions, he returned to the kitchen and hit the switch on the coffeemaker. He was just taking out some bread for the toaster when his cell phone sounded. It was a new ringtone, a blues piano riff. Bo Kimble was calling.

"Are you working, Mike?" he asked.

"Well, not at this moment. I just got up."

"I mean, you haven't committed to anything steady with anyone, have you?"

"No, well...yes, if you count my blog and Twitter accounts."

"Good. Can you work for me here at the *Chronicle*? For the next couple of weeks, anyway?"

Michael's grip on his phone turned his knuckles white. "Can I do *what*? I mean, sure...I think. What's goin' on?"

"Okay, Mike, here's the deal. Due to some unfortunate situations with two of my top people, you've just moved up the food chain. You know Charlie Duncan, the guy who's been with the paper forever? Well, he just gave his two weeks' notice. Poor guy's wife has MS, which I knew about, but I didn't know it had reached an advanced stage."

"That's too bad," Michael said. "I never met the man, but I read his stuff. He's good."

"Yeah, he is...or was. And so is, or was, Brenda Taylor."

"Brenda Taylor? Your beat writer for the Niners?"

"Yeah, she was involved in an accident last night on Turk Street. Some drunk asshole plowed right into the back of her little KIA while she was sitting at a red light. She's at St. Francis as we speak. Doctors haven't said much yet, but I'm guessing she won't be going anywhere soon."

Michael took a deep breath and waited for Bo to continue.

"Meantime, I'll need someone to keep a finger on the team's pulse while she recovers. Strictly a temp position. Having said that, I'm sure you're aware that the Niners have a good chance of making the playoffs. They're seven-two now and play Denver at home Sunday, and have a good chance at another W."

"Yeah, right," Michael confirmed. "They should win that game, I think they're favored by seven and a half, last time I looked."

"We have them at eight, but whatever it is, they could go deep into the playoffs. Anyway, this job is a temporary position, but I need someone to commit full time to the Niners run. There'll be some travel involved, interviews and player profiles, smelly locker room stuff. You're born and raised San Francisco. You've covered press conferences on a college level. You know anyone might be interested in this job?"

* * *

Immediately after the phone call from Bo, Michael took a deep breath, and then let it out. "Yeeesss!" he cried.

Scooter was outside the kitchen door with her nose planted against the glass, tail churning. Michael quickly pulled the door open, and his dog bounded into the house.

"This could be it, pal. This could be our chance!"

Michael grabbed Scooter's front paws and stood her up for an impromptu dance around the kitchen floor. Scooter could do a lot of good doggy things, but two-stepping wasn't one of them.

After a couple of cha-cha steps, Michael mercifully returned his dog to her full and downright position.

"Damn, this is good!" Michael picked up his phone again and punched in Annie's number. "Maybe we'll drive up and see Sadie this afternoon. Whaddya think, Scoots?"

Scooter wagged her approval.

"Maybe we'll even stay there tonight?"

"Woof! Woof!"

Michael's excitement faded slightly when he heard his wife's message on the phone, "Hi, this is Annie, I'm sorry I missed your call…blah, blah, blah, and I'll blah-blah you back."

Michael left a brief message, as instructed. "Hi, honey. Good news. Call me." Then he made three laps around the kitchen table, saying "Hot damn! Hot damn! Hot damn!" He stopped to pet Scooter each time around.

Finally, he slowed down long enough to pour himself a cup of coffee. He had just pushed the lever down on the toaster when his phone played his new ringtone again.

Michael grabbed the phone and answered before the first riff had ended. "Wow, that was quick!" he said.

"Oh, I'm sorry. What was quick?"

The voice on the phone was female, but it wasn't Annie.

"Oh, I'm sorry. I thought you were…ah…someone else."

"Is this Michael Fletcher?"

"Yes."

"Hi Michael, this is Laurie Scott. We met at the—"

"Oh, hey! Yeah, sure. How are you?"

"Fine, thanks. Did I get you at a bad time?"

"No, no. Not at all. I was just sitting home practicing clever ways to answer the phone."

Laurie laughed, and Michael visualized her smiling.

"Well, Michael, the reason I'm calling is to thank you for that wonderful piece you wrote about our facility and the dedication of the new park. It was really well written, and Sam and I are truly grateful."

Michael thought of her on the thigh master machine. "Well, thank you. That's nice of you to say that."

"Not at all, Michael. We really appreciate it. *I* really appreciate it. In fact, what I wanted to tell you is that I'm holding a check in my hand right now that was sent to me by a man who read your story! He wanted to help in some way. Isn't that nice?"

"Wow, this seems to be a day for good news."

"Oh? Are you having a good day, too?"

"Yeah, well, my workload just increased substantially. Some people might not think that's beneficial news, but it is for me."

"Well, I'm happy for you, Michael. I'm sure you can handle it. Listen, why don't we celebrate? How about lunch? I've got a few things to do here, but then I'm free. May I buy you lunch, Michael? Please say yes."

Michael was excited, stunned, and just a little bit disappointed at the same time. "You know, I appreciate the offer, Laurie, but it looks like I'll be driving up to Healdsburg this afternoon. Maybe we could do it another time?"

There was silence for a beat before Dr. Scott answered. "Sure, Michael. I understand. I'm disappointed, but I understand."

"Thank you for that. And I appreciate the kind words. I'm glad the story helped."

"Me too, Michael. You have my number, don't you?"

"Yes, I do."

"Good. I hope you use it."

If Michael hadn't known better, he would have sworn he could detect her fragrance over the phone.

Chapter 21

✳ ✳ ✳

For the next couple of hours, Michael spent some nervous energy piddling around the house, waiting for Annie to call back. He tried to finish a story he was working on for his blog, but his mind kept jumping to different things, including the letter to the editor after Polanksi died. Finally, he gave up writing at all and called Annie again. This time she picked up.

"Hello, Michael."

"Hey, you get my message?"

"Yeah. What's up?"

Michael hesitated for a split second, wondering why she hadn't called him back, but he let it go.

"I'm going to work for the *Chronicle*."

"Really? Doing what?"

"I'm taking over the Forty-Niners beat. Can you believe it?"

"You mean you have a steady job, Michael? That's great. How'd this happen?"

"Well, the lady who had the job was in a car accident, and she'll be out for a while. Bo Kimble wants me to run with it for now. He told me to meet him tomorrow and come ready to work. Whaddya think? Pretty cool, huh?"

"I suppose. Doesn't sound too cool for the woman, though."

"Well, no, but she'll be all right. She just won't be able to work for a while. I'm just—"

"And what does 'a while' mean? How long is that?"

"He thinks I might end up covering the team through the playoffs. Of course, they haven't clinched anything yet, but the way their defense is playing, they shouldn't have any problem getting there."

"Then what?"

"Well, then, hopefully then they'll be in the Super—"

"No, Michael, what do *you* do then? What do you do when the season is over? What do you do when the gal comes back?"

"By that time I'll have wowed 'em at the *Chronicle*. This could turn into something steady, and I'm betting it will."

He waited for a response but didn't get one. "Hello? Annie? You there?"

"Yes, Michael. I'm here."

"And?"

"And I'm happy for you. I really hope it works out. But, I dunno, you've been through this before. I just don't want to see you disappointed again. It sounds kinda iffy is all."

What had started as a thought balloon full of joy for Michael was now leaking fast.

"Damn it, Annie, you're wrong. I just got a call from Doctor Scott, who thanked me profusely for the article I wrote about her and how she's helping kids. In fact, Laurie told me she just received a check from a donor because of the story."

"Laurie?"

"Yeah, well, Doctor Scott."

There was a moment of dead air before Annie spoke again.

"Okay, Michael. Let's hope it works out. Right now, I'm thinking about Sadie's birthday. Dad thought it would be fun to invite the neighbor's kids over for a little party so she could get acquainted with them. You know, make some new friends? We're thinking of having it the Saturday before her birthday. Can you make it?"

"Sure, I'll be there."

"Good. Listen Michael, I've gotta run. Take care, okay?"

Michael started to say something else, but realized his wife had already hung up. He stared at his phone. The "End call" prompt was still illuminated. What if he never disconnected from his end? Would the line to Annie still be there? He was in a mood to celebrate and wanted to share his good news with someone willing to listen.

Five minutes later, Michael punched in some new numbers on his phone. His call was answered almost immediately.

"Hello, this is Doctor Scott. How may I help you?"

Chapter 22

* * *

The restaurant Laurie suggested was called Sophie's. When Michael Googled the address and directions, he smiled when he noticed the restaurant was on Scott Street. Sophie's was tucked in the middle of a trendy shopping center in the Filmore District, where hungry shoppers could waltz inside and take a booth or wait to be seated outside at a nice people-watching table.

After parking his Jeep in the lot adjacent to the restaurant, Michael followed a curving sidewalk up to the entrance. Standing at the outdoor hostess station, a trim young girl with short blond hair was holding menus against her bosom. Her smile seemed to be stuck in the wide-open position.

Michael, like some men, thought "perky" in women was okay as long as you were only talking about their breasts. Thankfully, Michael noticed that Dr. Scott was already seated outside, and with a wave-off to the hostess, Michael headed directly for his lunch date. Scott looked radiant in a short black skirt and high heels. Sunshine gleamed off her bare legs. The sleeves on her light-brown suede business jacket were rolled back off her wrists and she had on a low-cut, blood-red blouse. A thin turquoise necklace completed the ensemble.

Wait…blood red? Low cut? A sweet memory floated just outside of Michael's consciousness.

"Michael, I'm so glad you changed your mind," Scott greeted him as she took off her sunglasses.

"Thank you, Doctor…er, Laurie," Michael stammered, avoiding making eye contact for more than a second. He pulled out a chair and sat down. "I'm glad I could make it."

Like a good bird dog, the hostess had trailed Michael to their table. She slid another menu onto the table and, without breaking her smile, asked, "May I get you something started from the bar?"

Michael looked questioningly at the wine glass in front of Laurie.

"The house Chablis," she answered. "It's good. Here." She delicately lifted the glass to Michael.

After a sip and a nod, Michael confirmed the selection to the hovering hostess.

"Excellent choice, sir! I'll get that started for you right away." She curtsied and bounced away.

Michael and Scott looked at each other for a second, then shared a quick laugh. Scott shook out her hair and leaned back in her chair. She looked at Michael over the rim of her glass. "So, tell me. What's your good news?"

This time, Michael didn't look away. "Well, okay, but first, I have to confess, when I first met you, I think I gave you the impression that I already had a steady gig with the *Chronicle*."

"And?"

"Well, I'm just a stringer, or at least I was. Hopefully that'll—"

"Wait. What's a stringer. What do you mean?"

Michael took a deep breath. "Let's see if I remember this right. It dates back to the time when part-time reporters were paid by the amount of space their article occupied, or column inches. These column inches were measured by editors or publishers with a piece of string. Sounds kinda weird, right? Anyway, the reporter was given this string to take to the paper's disbursement department, and the reporter was paid according to the length of that string, or something like that."

"Hmmm. Interesting. How long have you been writing?"

Michael launched into the short version of his work history and explained that he was writing freelance for whomever would take him. He hinted at what his goals were. Scott listened without interruption, and five minutes later, as Michael was wrapping up his story, a waiter arrived with the wine. Refreshingly less bubbly than his coworker, the young man quickly scribbled their lunch order and then floated away.

"So there you have it," Michael said as he raised his glass in a toast. "However, I'm starting for the *Chronicle* tomorrow, and I'm hoping it will lead to a steady paycheck."

"Hear, hear." Laurie clunked her support and raised her glass to her lips. A slow sip later, she smiled at him and set her glass down. "Are you married, Michael?"

The question caught him in midswallow. He coughed his answer.

"Yea…ye-s-s. Well, I think so, anyway."

"You *think* so?" Laurie laughed. "Most people know if they're married or not!"

Michael took a quick drink of water. "Well, yes, I am married. And I have a beautiful little five-year-old daughter named Sadie to prove it. It's just that my wife and Sadie are sorta living with my father-in-law right now. It's, ah, been kind of a struggle lately."

Laurie's smile faded. "I'm sorry. I didn't mean to pry."

"No, no, that's fine. It'll all work out." Michael smiled and raised his glass to Scott. "One way or another, things will work out."

Dr. Scott's smile returned, and she touched glasses with him again. "I'm sure they will, Michael. I'm sure they will."

A moment of comfortable silence fell over them, and they turned their attention to the shoppers passing by. A young couple with a baby in a stroller rolled past, towed by a smiling golden retriever. When the baby suddenly squealed, Michael looked at Laurie. "Okay, Doctor, your turn. What keeps your skies blue?"

"Well, sir, I'm glad you asked." Scott reached down into her purse and pulled out an envelope. "This is the check I told you about. One thousand dollars, made out to Scott Therapies. Thanks to your article."

"That's nice. As I said, I'm glad it helped. You certainly have a worthy cause there."

"And I know just what to do with this. The furnace is old in the place and we need…"

"Are *you* married?"

"Dr. Scott stopped in midsentence. She fanned her face with the envelope before continuing. "…some maintenance done on it. No, I'm not married."

"Ever been?"

The good doctor smiled and slowly nodded. "Yes. It was one of those too young, too dumb, too much fun affairs. It didn't last long."

"I'm sorry. Now it sounds like I'm prying."

She waved him off. "Not to worry. It wasn't meant to be, and I should have seen that earlier. We met on the UCLA campus. I was in my first year in pre-med, and he was a part-time student trying to figure out what he wanted to do with his life. Looking back on it, I'm pretty sure he was more interested in surfing than studying."

"Lots of distractions for young people in Southern Cal," Michael offered.

"That's true. But I may have been his biggest distraction. He thought it was cool that I'm Native American. Navajo. I took him home to meet my parents in Arizona once, and he seemed fascinated with the culture. Or at least, he acted like he was. When we came back and he went to the beach, his surfing buddies asked if we had scored any peyote!"

"Did you?"

Scott threw her head back and laughed. "No. We had to settle for some Mexican weed."

"The good old days, huh?"

"Well, I don't know about that. I suppose there were some fun times," Scott said, her smile waning slightly.

"Children?"

Her smile slipped another fraction. "I have a fourteen-year-old boy. He...he doesn't live with me."

Michael was searching for a way to change the subject when the waiter arrived with their lunch. Dr. Scott quickly regained her self-possessed demeanor, and they both ordered another glass of wine.

* * *

An hour later, they tossed their napkins on the table in unison.

"Wow, I'm full," Michael said, suppressing a burp. "That was delicious."

"It was, wasn't it?"

The waiter arrived right on cue and, after asking if there would be anything else, deftly laid the bill to Michael's left. When Michael went to pick it up, Scott covered his hand with hers.

"Not a chance, buster. I invited you, remember?"

Michael made no effort to move his hand, and neither did she. Their eyes locked, and then, slowly, they both began to smile. Michael blinked first. "Is this one of those Mexican standoffs? You know, the kind involving a paleface and a beautiful Navajo woman?"

"Call it what you want, Michael, but this is mine." She emphasized her statement by adding pressure to his hand.

Finally, he gave in. "Okay, but I get the next one."

"Deal."

* * *

They left Sophie's and walked to Laurie's Cadillac SUV. It was the same color as her hair—shiny black. She opened the driver's-side door and turned to him. "Thank you. I'm glad we got together."

She extended her hand, but when he took it, she leaned in and brushed him with a polite kiss. "Good luck tomorrow. Call me if you want. I'd like to hear how your day went."

Michael drew in a deep breath as she drove away. An exciting new scent settled into his nostrils.

Chapter 23

※　※　※

The next morning, Michael drove downtown to meet Bo Kimble at his office. For much of its history, the paper had been headquartered in the heart of the city, at the *Chronicle* Building on Fifth and Mission. Michael knew that the *Chronicle* had been one of the last major newspapers to install a digital printing system, and although the venerable building with its watchtower had been a landmark since 1865, Michael had never set foot inside it.

Now, he parked his car in an open lot two blocks south of the *Chronicle*, and hoofed it up to the Mission Avenue entry doors. The morning sun bounced off one of the glass doors, temporarily blinding him as he let himself in. He took a few steps into the lobby before pausing to let his eyes adjust. When he regained his vision, he was somewhat surprised and disappointed.

Nothing about the interior of the ground floor suggested that the building had anything to do with the newspaper business. There was an information desk in the center of the lobby, and two elevators just beyond that. A directory showed that all first-floor space was rented by companies such as Yahoo and AOL.

The second floor was more of the same. All newspaper operations now took place solely on the third floor. If Michael was looking for ghosts of Herb Caen and other great writers roaming the halls, he wasn't going to find them here. He walked over to one of two elevators and punched an up arrow.

It wasn't until he stepped off the elevator that the original sense of the workplace became evident. Straight ahead of him was a wide-open area filled with desks, cubicles, people, and computers. The only thing missing was the sound of ringing telephones and cigarette-smoking reporters banging on typewriters. To his left, Michael could see the oak doors and glass panels of several offices that looked out over the worker bees. Bo Kimble was just stepping out of one of these offices when he spotted Michael and waved him over.

"Hey, Mike. Good man, right on time." He turned back to his office door. "Come on in here. You want some coffee?"

"No, thanks, I'm good."

Kimble's office was fairly cramped, with a desk, a computer, a couch, and two leather swivel chairs. Two wide-screen television sets were opposite his desk. Photos of sports stars and writing awards adorned the walls. An old double-sash window afforded a view of the Mission Street traffic below, as well as the roof of the parking garage across the street.

One of the things that Michael liked about Kimble was that he didn't waste time. He usually got right to the point. This morning wasn't any different.

"Sit down, Mike. You'll need to fill out some paperwork, W-2 forms and the usual crap, but first I wanna talk to you about some things, bring you up to speed, so to speak."

"Sounds good. I'm ready."

"As I said yesterday on the phone, you'll be taking over Brenda Taylor's beat as long as the Niners are in the hunt, or until she comes back. This is a very unusual situation, and I'm taking a chance here. I've already pissed some people off by hiring you, but screw 'em. Don't take anything personally. There's some budgetary factors in play here that some people don't understand. To be perfectly frank, I've sold you as a bandage. A bandage to cover the wound as it heals. And when it does heal, we'll probably just peel you off. Okay with that?"

Michael had no choice but to nod and smile.

"Good. Now, things happen fast around here. I may ask you to cover other stuff for us. But I don't want you to freak out. We always have contingency plans in case things go sideways. It just so happens you're one of those contingencies now."

"Sure."

"You overwhelmed yet?"

"No…I mean, yes. Yes, I'm overwhelmed that you called me. I really appreciate—"

"Okay, back to the Niners."

Before he said anything else, Bo went to his office door and closed it. When he returned, he sat down behind his desk.

"Have you heard anything about a barroom brawl involving some of their key players recently?" he asked.

Surprised, Michael answered, "No. Who?"

"Well, Brenda got a tip from one of her sources that after the Dallas game, Marshal Decker and some of the boys got into it at an all-night joint over in Berkeley. Shots fired, that kinda stuff. Her source said that Decker and the left tackle, Jackson, weren't walking very well after they left the club. Brenda was on her way to investigate it when she had her accident. So what I want you to do, Mike, is follow up on that."

"Can you give me Brenda's source?"

"I think it's a guy named Howard. Works as a bouncer at the St. Regis Nightclub there in Berkeley. I say 'I think' because I don't know that for sure. Brenda always keeps her sources close to the vest, which is fine by me. I trust her judgment. I've never questioned her expense account when it comes to things like this."

"You mean she pays her sources?"

"Tips for tipsters, she called it."

"Okay," Michael asked. "How should I follow up? Brenda's in no condition to talk, is she?"

"No, not yet. But a nurse friend of mine who works at St. Francis says they're planning on moving her out of intensive care tomorrow. Now, please don't think I'm being callous or insensitive here, but I'm hoping you can talk with Brenda before Coach McCaffy's press conference tomorrow afternoon. If some of McCaffy's players *were* involved in a shooting, I wanna be the one to break it, or at least bring it up. I'll call my friend tomorrow morning and get an update on Brenda's condition. If she can have visitors, I'll let you know. If she can't, don't worry about it, we'll go to plan B and run a bluff with McCaffy.

"As you probably know, McCaffy's super protective about his players. His weekly injury report to the league is almost laughable; you never know whether to believe him or not. It probably drives the other coaches crazy, to say nothing of the oddsmakers in Vegas.

"Mike, as I said earlier, I know you've covered press conferences on a college level, and personally, I don't think there's a hell of a lot of difference in protocol between collegiate and pro. Outside of the shooting incident, if there was one, you'll probably hear the usual clichés and coach speak. But don't be afraid to cut through the bullshit. I want some juice if you can find it. I want *your* take' I want to know how *you* see it. Give me six inches for the morning edition."

Bo paused for a few seconds, tapping a pencil on his desk. "One of the hardest things to do in sports journalism is to be objective, especially local sports stuff. It's hard not to be biased for certain teams. You're a fan. You wouldn't be in this business if you weren't."

Michael nodded, wondering where Bo was going.

"Take Brenda, for example. Now, I think the world of her, and I hope you will keep this between you and me, but if there was one thing I would criticize about her work, it's that she has a tendency to shy away from asking the hardball questions. There have been times when I've thought she should've gone for the jugular but didn't. Maybe it's because she has such a good rapport with the team. Know what I mean?"

Again, Michael nodded.

"I know that won't be a problem with you, Mike. I've read enough of your stuff to know that you can get down and dirty if you have to. I saw some of that in your piece on Polanksi. If there's a story within a story, I want it."

They spent the next thirty minutes going over the more mundane parts of Mike's job: how much he was getting paid and when. Where to park. The location of the men's room. A description of the office personnel. And what was expected of him. Then Kimble showed Michael Brenda's cubicle.

"You can send your stuff from home, or work here," he said. "Probably do a little of both. I don't care. Just don't get too comfortable. Remember, it *is* Brenda's desk.

"Another thing to remember is that I can always rein a writer in if I have to. I can always deflate a story. It's when I have to look for substance that I worry. Or, as the old saying goes, 'It's easier to temper a fire than to build one.' Think you can handle it?"

Michael's head was swimming, but he sucked it up. "Sure, no problem."

"Okay. Here's your press pass. Go impress me."

Chapter 24

* * *

The next morning, Kimble called Michael and told him that Brenda was still in the ICU and was not allowed to have visitors. Plan B was now in effect, and he was to proceed to Candlestick Park for the press conference at 4:30 p.m. Michael made a mental note to stop by St. Francis when the time was appropriate. If he couldn't meet or talk with Ms. Taylor, he would leave a card, maybe flowers. He didn't want to come off as cheesy, but he wanted to wish her well and convey to her that he wasn't out to take her job.

* * *

Later that afternoon, Michael pulled into the nearly deserted parking lot at Candlestick and felt a twinge of regret for the condemned structure. The stadium had never lived up to its state-of-the-art status, but four generations of the Fletcher family had shared some good times there. Annie and Sadie had enjoyed a Father's Day there not long ago. Michael and his dad witnessed Willie Mays' three thousandth hit there. Michael's grandmother and grandfather, Leo and Irma Fletcher, had been there when the Beatles had played their last concert together. Now, in a few months' time, Candlestick Park would be leveled to make way for a state-of-the-you-know-what mall and residential office complex. Michael knew well the history of the stadium and the teams that played there from the many stories his father and grandfather had told him. He had also learned about it from the research he'd done for an English class assignment while in high school. He had learned that in the mid-1950s, the New York Giants baseball team had become disenchanted with their digs at the Polo Grounds on Harlem River Drive. The once-revered stadium was becoming old and crumbly. The ballpark in New York originally opened in 1911, seated sixteen thousand, and was built for three hundred thousand dollars. But, as the then-modern-day franchise of the fifties had lamented, the venue was no longer adequate. It was done. Plus, more and more baseball games were being televised. Who wanted to look at shabby playing fields and disintegrating stadiums?

Meanwhile, the city of San Francisco stepped up to the plate and offered to build a new stadium if the team would take its young men west. The city would build the structure at Candlestick Pointe, an area on the southwest shores of San Francisco Bay. They would name it Candlestick Park after a long-nosed bird that inhabited the area. Apparently, the powers that be assumed the bird wouldn't mind.

A local contractor who had sold the property to the city was awarded a no-contest bid contract to build said playground. The deal resulted in a grand jury investigation, but the project went forward anyway. Some folks weren't pleased with the investigation or the location of the ballpark. Others didn't care.

At least one person was ecstatic about the whole proceeding, and that was Michael's grandfather, Leo Fletcher. Leo was a newly married man, and supported his bride, Irma, by working as a machinist at the Hunter's Point shipyard in San Francisco. The shipyard was only four miles away (as the candlestick bird flew) from Candlestick Pointe. Leo was a huge baseball fan, and his favorite team was the New York Giants. The Giants were his favorite team mostly because a young man named Willie Mays played center field for them.

When the New York Giants made their move to San Francisco after the 1957 season, they suffered the indignity of having to play at a minor league ballpark while their new home was being built. In 1958 and 1959, the Giants conducted their business at Seals Stadium, a former Pacific Coast League venue, located at 16th and Bryant Street in the city. Actually, the small stadium was considered a jewel by many fans, who enjoyed it right up until it was leveled and made into a shopping center.

The jury was still out on whether anyone would ever call the shopping center a jewel.

Ironically, the Giants won their first game at Seals Stadium by shutting out their former crosstown rival Dodgers, eight-zero. The Dodgers, who had also moved west in 1957, returned the favor two seasons later by beating the Giants eight-two in the Giants' final game at Seals Stadium.

When Candlestick Park finally opened on April 12, 1960, Leo Fletcher was probably more thrilled than a grown man should hope to be. The biggest reason for Leo's happiness was that his son, Ray, was born on that day. Another reason for joy, Leo had discovered if there was a large ship in dry dock at Hunter's Point, he could climb onto the bridge of that ship and enjoy an unobstructed view of Candlestick Park. With binoculars, Leo could see the entire infield.

One of Ray Fletcher's earliest and fondest memories was when his father took him to the shipyard on visitors' day. It was June of 1966. The *USS Enterprise* had just returned from a tour in Vietnam and was dry-docked at Hunter's Point. The ship, not to be confused with Captain Kirk's ride, was nuclear powered, and considered to be America's biggest and baddest warship at the time.

Leo had taken little Ray up to the catwalk that surrounded the ship's bridge.

"Look, son. We can watch the Giants play!" he'd said.

All little Ray could do was squeal with delight. Leo didn't know it, but his son was more impressed by the giant they were standing on.

* * *

As Michael got out of his Jeep, he remembered that the *USS Enterprise* had recently made the news again. The once-mighty warship was now decommissioned and sitting alone in a shipyard on the East Coast waiting to be scrapped. Its run was over. It would soon be turned into whatever old nuclear warships are turned into.

Chapter 25

※ ※ ※

As Michael made his way through the bowels of Candlestick stadium, his footsteps echoed off the concrete floor and walls. There were no roars from the crowd, no PA system announcing a score. The long corridors were relatively quiet as he made his way to the press conference.

Michael was forty-five minutes early, but the conference room was already packed with reporters, and television and radio equipment. The room itself was fairly nondescript, with a worn parquet floor surrounded by concrete walls devoid of any pictures or posters, painted a limey green. Without using his imagination too much, Michael could visualize the room full of gray-haired bingo players or Kiwanis gathered for lunch. The only giveaway that it was used for media purposes was a large Forty-Niners banner draped behind a small stage and podium.

There were a couple of reporters Michael recognized from covering minor league events, but none he felt he could chat up. He took an empty folding chair as close to the dais as he could, checked his gear, and waited.

At 4:25, a PR man took the microphone and, in a dreary voice, reminded the media of the rules. Five minutes later, the coach appeared, chewing gum, as usual, and hustled up to the mike.

Brian McCaffy was only forty-three years old, making him the third-youngest head coach in the NFL. His sandy hair and boyish good looks made him look younger than a lot of his players. McCaffy had worked his way up quickly through the college coaching ranks with winning seasons at three different conference levels before he got the call from the owner of the San Francisco Forty-Niners. Now in his second year at the helm, he was as fiery as ever, but still had a reputation as a player's coach. He was tough but fair. The players liked him and didn't mind busting their butts for him. His conditioning program was one of the most effective around, and it was paying off in dividends, especially in the fourth quarter.

Michael sat through the first ten minutes listening to the give and take before he raised his hand. Nobody had mentioned anything about Decker being involved in an altercation. The coach answered several other questions before he finally acknowledged Michael.

"Thank you, sir," Michael stood up and cleared his throat. "There's been a rumor that a couple of your players were injured in a fight at a nightclub after the Dallas game. Specifically, Marshal Decker and Adrian Jackson. There may have been shots fired. Would you care—"

"What? Wait a minute. Who are you? Where'd you get that crap?" McCaffy nearly spit out his gum.

"I'm Michael Fletcher. I'm with the *Chronicle*. I heard—"

"You're with who? The *Chronicle*?"

"Yes, sir. I'm—"

"Then you should know better. I don't know what you're talkin' about. Next!"

It was Michael's first and last chance to ask a question. McCaffy was quickly looking around the room for someone else to talk to.

When the press conference ended forty minutes later, Michael sat glued to his chair while the other reporters gathered their gear and started filing out of the room. Some were joking and sharing opinions on upcoming games; others talked about a new restaurant that had opened near the stadium. As they shuffled by him, one of the veteran reporters reached out and patted Michael on his shoulder. "Some fun, huh, kid?"

Twenty minutes later, Michael was still sitting in his chair, alone in the room. He had glanced through his notes and put away his recorder. Now, he was trying to piece a story together in his mind. He was staring at his shoes when the idea hit him. Why not write two stories? One would be the one that everybody would expect him to write, the one with the coach's nebulous doublespeak, the expectations of the team, some of McCaffy's quotes and predictions, the usual pabulum. The other story he could write from a slightly different angle. Bo could choose between the two.

Finally, Michael stood up and walked out of the room. As he made his way to the car, he thought about the offer his father had mentioned, the one about working in the shipyard.

Chapter 26

✳ ✳ ✳

The next morning, Michael couldn't wait to read the paper. He had slept well after Kimble had e-mailed him saying "Nice job" on the coverage of the press conference, but he didn't indicate which story would be in print. When Michael unfolded the sports section at the kitchen table, he was delighted to see that they had used the story he had gambled on, the one written from the perspective of a reporter on his first day on the job.

At the top of the column, Michael identified himself as a newbie reporter to the readers, and then took them along with him on his first NFL press conference. He described how nervous he was when he asked the coach about Decker and Jackson possibly being involved in a barroom brawl that included gunplay. He reported how it felt when he saw the veins in McCaffy's neck bulge out when he fired back at him, "I don't know what you're talkin' about! Next!"

Michael described his own pulse rate as he sat through the rest of the meeting, watching the coach take questions from every reporter but him. He explained to the readers how it felt to be the only scribe in the room with his hand still raised when McCaffy declared the conference over.

It was a short column in the *Chronicle*, but it was just as Michael had written it.

As the day wore on, other papers and media took it from there and put their spin on it. The *San Jose Mercury News* ran its own story, headlined, "Rookie Reporter Riles McCaffy. Barroom Brawl? Shots Fired?" TV stations ran a clip of the McCaffy mini-rant, with one of the commentators asking, "Could the good coach be covering up something?"

Kimble had even e-mailed Michael again, saying he thought the story was ballsy, insightful, and a little humorous.

Of course Michael paid attention to the social media as it twittered furiously. It might have been coincidence, but not long after the "rumor" roared through the sports cyberwave, the oddsmakers in Las Vegas changed the point spread on the Niners' game against Denver. San Francisco went from a six-and-a-half point favorite down to a three-point favorite.

Later that afternoon, the article also triggered a call from his former neighborhood pal.

"Hey, Mikey. It's Dan. Dan Kelly. I just read your article on McCaffy."

"Yeah?"

"Boy, what a piece of shit!"

Michael knew he'd taken a chance with the story, and he knew Bo had taken an even bigger chance by running it. He figured there would be some criticism, but he was hoping what there was of it might be constructive.

"No need to sugarcoat it, Dan," he said. "Tell me what you really think."

"Wha...oh no, no," Kelly laughed. "I mean McCaffy! *He's* a piece of shit."

"Oh."

"Don't get me wrong, he's a good coach and everything, he just doesn't have time for the average Joe."

"Well, he's got a lot on his plate. Maybe—"

"Man, that had to be embarrassing for you. I bet you felt like crawling in a hole somewhere, huh?"

"No, not really, but I'm beginning to feel that way now. Whadda you want, Dan?"

"I just wanna know if there is anything to that rumor of a brawl. Did those guys really mix it up somewhere?"

"Why do you care? Are you asking as a cop?"

"Oh, no, nothin' like that. I just wanna know if you got any inside info. Are those guys hurting? I gotta protect my fantasy football league you know, ha ha."

"Well, I can't answer your question, Dan, because I really don't know yet."

"Well, whadda you think of the spread? Got a chance?"

The conversation was beginning to make Michael uncomfortable. "Sure, look for an upset."

"Really? Wow, that could mean—"

"Look, Dan, I gotta get back to work."

"Yeah, me too. Hey, Mikey, it was good talkin' to you. Let's stay in touch."

"Yeah, sure."

"Oh, listen, my kid's playin' at that new field again. Maybe I'll see you there? They won last time, you know. They even covered the spread! Ha!"

* * *

Two days after the story was printed, Kimble called Michael with another assignment. It was early Saturday morning, and Michael was just finishing his breakfast.

"Any chance you could cover the Sharks game today?" It was Kimble's way of saying, "Good morning, Mike. How are you? Do you have a minute?"

There was something niggling at Michael's brain. Something he was supposed to do. He couldn't come up with it, so he swished his mind clear and answered, "Ah...sure. No problem."

"It's an early afternoon game against the Oilers, and I'm sure you're aware that San Jose hasn't won many games since Polanksi died. I know you saw some of his teammates at his funeral, and I'm hoping you might have a feel for who was affected most by his passing. See if you can get a postgame interview with whomever that might be. Human interest angle sorta stuff. I may want to use your story tomorrow. Probably make it more interesting if they lose again, but we can go with it either way. I'm thinking about three columns' worth. Can you get that done for me?"

"Of course...oh, and by the way, I read some of the letters to the editor after Polanksi died. Well, this one reader took exception to the media glorifying overpaid athletes. Kinda like our culture was responsible for his death or something."

"Yeah, I remember that one. Had some merit to it, I thought. Why, what about it?"

"Oh, just wondered. There was something about numbers and symbols too."

"Mike, you should see some of the stuff I get. Not close to printable. Really whacked. You'll go crazy if you pay too much attention to it."

"I suppose."

"So, go get me something to print, or I'll have you whacked."

Chapter 27

※ ※ ※

The HP Pavilion, or the Shark Tank, as the locals called their hockey rink, was a forty-minute ride down the 101 for Michael. Due to a scheduling conflict, the Sharks had agreed to move the time of the opening face-off up to 1:30 p.m. to accommodate a Britney Spears concert later that evening. The Tank could seat fourteen thousand hockey fans, but ten minutes before the game, from his vantage point in the press box, Michael guessed the place to be less than half full. He reasoned an early game time and the lingering effects of past lockouts probably had something to do with the poor turnout. Throw in a losing record, and it was easy to understand the weak draw. The thought crossed his mind that Britney would fare better.

Michael hadn't been to many hockey games, either as a reporter or a fan, but every time he went to one, he vowed to attend more in the future. Just walking into a hockey rink was unlike walking into any other sports venue. The thing that always struck him the most was the brilliance of the ice. And even though it was probably a comfortable seventy degrees inside the rink, his brain would send him a message, subliminal or not, that there was a chill in the air. The fans who were at the Tank kept their jackets on and talked quietly while they awaited their gladiators. To Michael, it seemed that hockey fans were the kind of people who drove four-wheelers and wouldn't mind a sticky tavern floor.

At 1:28 p.m., the two centers for the teams met at center ice to begin the game. One of the referees slowly skated backward around the center circle before joining the men in the huddle. There were couple of nods from everyone, and suddenly the ref tossed the puck down as if it was a hot coal.

The two centers immediately began stabbing at the puck, their sticks clacking against the ice and each other as they tried to control the puck long enough to send it out of the circle to a teammate. In this case, the puck bounced out to an Oiler, who took two steps and banked a pass off the boards to his forward, who was immediately slammed back into the glass by a Sharks player. The Oiler forward retained control of the puck long enough to pass it back to the Oiler's center. The center fought off a couple of defenders and then dropped the puck off to Pat Ulin, his left forward. Ulin went skating by his center as if his feet were on fire. He flew through the neutral zone with a defender right behind him, crossed the blue line, and was about twenty feet in front of the goal when he went into a quick, short glide, loaded up on his front leg, and fired a shot. The puck sailed over the goalie's right shoulder, clanked off the post, and rebounded back in front of the goal. Both Ulin and his defender tried to change course, but their momentum took them right toward the net. An Oilers player who was trailing the play tried to flick a backhand into the net; unfortunately, the net was no longer in place, as it had been knocked from its posts by its collision with Ulin and friend, who now had their gloves off and were whaling away at each other against the backboard.

Time was called with 19:30 showing on the first period clock. *Whew.*

Michael thought about how he could describe the first thirty seconds of the game; *Exquisitely brutal? Breathtaking? Fast? All of the above?*

* * *

Mercifully, for the Sharks anyway, when play resumed, the pace of the game slowed somewhat. But by the end of the first period, the Sharks looked as if they'd had all the breath knocked out of them and were trailing two-zero. They showed some spark at the beginning of the second period, but couldn't sustain it. Where the Oilers were fast and slick, the Sharks looked as if they were wearing snowshoes, slow and sick.

When the horn sounded, ending the second period, the Sharks were probably lucky to be still only down two-zero. Some diehard fans stayed until the end of the game, waiting for something to cheer about, maybe a few more brawls. But there were only a few minor skirmishes and none of them was tooth shattering. When the final horn sounded, the Sharks had been shut out, three-zip.

Michael made his way down to the locker room in hopes of getting a quote or two from the coach, Alex Catlin, and then talking to one or two of Polanski's former teammates. Michael quickly found that Catlin was far more approachable then the Niners' McCaffy. In the coach's office, four other reporters had gathered to quiz Catlin. Within minutes, the coach had given Michael enough to write about, including how Catlin felt about his job status. "I think we're all skating on thin ice right now, no pun intended. But if we can get refocused, we should be fine," he said. When another reporter asked Catlin if he was going to make any changes in the lineup, he answered with a laugh. "Can you skate?" he asked.

Michael left the coach's office and wandered toward the players' locker room. He spotted one of the players who had helped with Polanski's eulogy. It was Craig Hudson, one of the Sharks' forwards. He was shirtless and was pulling on a pair of jeans in front of his locker when Michael approached him.

"You got a minute?" Michael waved his handheld recorder.

Hudson glanced at Michael and shrugged. "Sure, why not?"

Hudson hadn't bothered to shave and, with what looked like about a two-day stubble, he could have passed for a shorter version of George Clooney.

Michael introduced himself and, in a show of empathy, said, "It looked like you were skating hard out there today. Tough loss."

Hudson finished with his pants and reached into his locker for a shirt. He gave Michael another look. "Yeah, tough loss. You are...who again?"

"Fletcher. Michael Fletcher. With the *Chronicle*."

Hudson resumed dressing while Michael resumed sucking up.

"It looked like you guys had something going at the start of the second period. You were getting a lot of shots on goals. But then you got that interference call. Any thoughts on that penalty?"

"Yeah. It was bogus. I was pushed from behind. That goal shoulda counted, no question. We had some momentum going. Woulda only been down a goal. Bullshit call."

Michael asked a couple more innocuous questions, and then he asked the one he'd come for. "How is your team coping with the loss of Troy Polanksi?"

Hudson took a breath before answering. "It's been tough for everybody. But whadda you gonna do?

We just have to move forward, play the best we can."

"Do you think the NHL's drug policy is tough enough?"

Hudson looked at Michael. "If you're insinuating Troy might be alive today if it was, I'd have to say you're barking up the wrong tree."

"Why? What do you mean?" Michael checked his recorder's audio level before pushing it back in Hudson's face.

"Troy didn't do drugs. He didn't need them. He was a natural athlete."

"The autopsy report showed—"

"I don't give a shit what the autopsy report said. I grew up with Troy. I've known him since I was twelve. We played junior hockey together. I knew him like a brother. He hated drugs. He didn't like people that did them."

Hudson sat down on the bench, reached into his locker, and pulled out a pair of snakeskin cowboy boots that looked as if they might cost five or six hundred dollars a foot. He pulled on one of the boots, stomped it into place, and then looked at Michael.

"Okay, there was one time he told me he snorted coke before a game. But he said it just made him nervous and jittery. It threw his timing off. He asked me to please shoot him and whoever gave him the shit if he ever did it again. I believed him."

Confused, Michael asked, "Could he have hid it from you? For example, if he were taking steroids, I mean?"

"I suppose he could have. But he was deathly afraid of the side effects, so it doesn't make sense that he'd do them either."

"Side effects?"

"Yeah. Like liver problems. You know his father died of liver disease? Troy was always worried about it being in his genes."

"Interesting."

Hudson pulled on the other boot and stood up. "Yeah. Plus, Troy considered himself a ladies' man. He couldn't understand why guys would take steroids if there was a chance of getting acne and having their nuts fall off."

"Good point," Michael mused. He was already writing the piece in his head when he thought of something else. "How would you describe Troy's relationship with his agent?"

"Weinstein?"

"Yeah."

"It's funny you should ask that."

"Yeah, how so?"

"Troy told me he was considering dumping him."

"He tell you why?"

"Yeah, said he thought Weinstein was too greedy and had conned him."

"Conned him? How?"

"Well, Troy didn't mind the money he got for playing hockey, he just wished he would have paid more attention to the peripheral shit Weinstein had written into his contract. Endorsements, TV commercials, appearance fees, stuff like that. Troy just wanted to play hockey, but Weinstein had him lined up to do all the other crap, constantly pushing him. We all know hockey players don't get the same kinda money other pro athletes get, but still, we do okay. Troy didn't want or need the extra money and distractions that came with the 'whoring,' as he called it. Weinstein seemed to thrive on it."

"Isn't that an agent's job? To get his client all the money he can?"

Hudson slung a light coat over his shoulder, indicating he was ready to wrap up the interview. "Yeah, I suppose so. But anyway, I gotta go." Hudson patted Michael on the back and made a move toward the double doors that led to an exit. He stopped as he got to the doors. "Actually, there was another reason Troy was considering breaking it off with Weinstein. Something that he had just learned about his agent."

"Oh?"

"Does the name Jack Stewart ring a bell?"

Michael considered the question. "No. Should it?"

"You being a newspaper guy and all, I thought you might know the name. Jack Stewart was one of those guys who were busted down in Florida a couple a years ago. They were running a gambling ring out of a barbershop, betting large money on everything, including peewee football. Even some of the coaches were in on it."

"Oh, yeah, I remember something about that. But what's that have to do with Weinstein?'

"Maybe nothing, but Stewart is Weinstein's brother-in-law."

Hudson flipped Michael a two-fingered salute and disappeared through the doors.

Chapter 28

* * *

Any thoughts Michael had of zooming home and pounding out his article faded as soon as he hit the 101 northbound. Light rain showers had turned into a steady downpour, and traffic was sluggish at best. Michael picked out a traffic lane that looked like the steadiest and let his thoughts return to his interview with Hudson. He would have to pick and choose what he could use in the main body of his story. Although he would have loved to mention Weinstein's relationship with a criminal element, that wasn't the focus of his story. The story was supposed to be about Polanski's legacy.

Still, the image of Weinstein and his buddy at the dedication ceremony was still crystal clear in Michael's brain.

Scouting for future clients? Or making book?

And to insinuate that Weinstein's relationship with a known gambler was improper would be treading on libelous grounds. But Michael also knew that that's what editors were for.

With his Bluetooth plugged in, Michael called Bo. As usual, his boss wasted no time.

"Whadda you got, Mike?"

Michael gave him the storyline of the game, and then briefed him on the interview with Hudson.

"Wow, that's interesting," Bo said. "Hudson's saying Polanksi was clean? We can probably use that. Of course, it could be like you say, Polanksi coulda been on the juice and doing coke easy enough without Hudson knowing. Still, we can stir the pot a little.

"The gambling connection thing with his agent is good too, although the story itself is dated. You might research it a little more, if you want."

"Love to."

"Anything else?"

Michael hesitated, not sure of his place, but then said, "This Polanksi situation reminds me a little of the Lavorini deal."

"In what way?"

"Polanski's teammates say he hated drugs, right?"

"Yeah. So?"

"The story I read about Lavorini's death said he had an abnormal amount of alcohol in his system when he died. But everything that I remember or knew about Lavorini was that he didn't drink at all. It made him sick."

Kimble didn't say anything for a moment. Then he said, "Hmmm. Interesting. Yeah. Well, anyway, thanks for covering the Sharks today. I'll look for your story."

"Okay. Sure. I'll get to work on it as soon as I get home," Michael said.

"I appreciate it. Hope I didn't spoil your weekend."

"Oh, no. I wasn't doing anything…oh, shit!"

"What? What is it? Hello? Mike, you run off the road?"

"No. I just remembered something I was supposed to do today. Damn!"

"Well, drive safe, Mike. I'll talk to you later."

"Sure, if I'm still alive."

* * *

On the rest of the drive home, Michael wondered what he would say to Annie. By the time he pulled into his driveway, he had come up with something. The truth.

Michael turned off the ignition and punched in Annie's number. She answered on the first ring.

"Michael, where *are* you?"

"Oh, I'm really sorry, honey. I had to go to San Jose to cover the Sharks game. The boss sorta threw it at me at the last minute. I guess I spaced it. I'm sorry, I really am. I could run up there now, but I still have to write the column to make tonight's dead—"

"Ah, damn it, Michael."

Two of Michael neighbors walked by and nodded to him. He went on with what must have looked like a conversation with his steering wheel.

"Well, it's not like I missed her *real* birthday or anything. It was just a party with her little friends, right? She probably had more fun without me there anyway."

"You're missing the point, Michael! You *promised* Sadie you'd be here. You said you'd bring Scooter! We thought we'd see you today!"

"Yeah. I know. I'm a shit. Look, I'm sorry. I really am. I…I just forgot okay? I've been really busy lately. Which is a good thing, you know? By the way, did you read my article in the *Chronicle*? About my first day on the job?"

"No, Michael. I didn't."

"Well, Bo loved it. He said it was the kind of progressive writing he's looking for. And tomorrow I'll be at the Stick, in the press box, no less. The Niners could finally get back to the playoffs after—"

"Oh Jesus, Michael. Never mind that now. Please tell me that you'll be here for your daughter's birthday on Wednesday."

Michael didn't take the bait. He resisted the urge to remind Annie that she was the one who had taken their family to the country.

They said their good-byes coolly. Michael sat in his Jeep for a good five minutes. *At least I have a story to write*, he thought. That would take up the rest of his day. His Saturday night was a different matter. He wondered how Dr. Scott was spending hers.

Chapter 29

By early Sunday morning, the weather system that had brought Saturday's rain had moved on and left the Bay Area to dry out. An hour before game time, blue skies were the backdrop for Candlestick Park, and the Stick was already three-quarters full and filling up fast.

On the field, both teams were going through their stretches and warm-up drills. San Francisco wore their home colors of red and gold, while Denver dressed in their traveling blue and orange. Footballs spiraled high in the air as punters practiced their thing. Wide receivers ran abbreviated sprints. Television crews checked and rechecked their equipment. Even the cheerleaders were getting loose.

From his perch in the press box, Michael could feel the energy welling up through the stadium. He also felt a knot of nerves settling in his gut. It was at moments like this when Michael had to remind himself of something an old professor had told him: "It's okay to have a little nervous energy as long as you use that energy to your advantage."

Some of the members of the media Michael remembered from previous events were gathered in the press box. Other writers politely acknowledged him, and then went back to their prep work. Juan Rodriguez from the *San Jose Mercury News* introduced himself and inquired about Brenda Taylor.

"Last I heard, she was responding pretty well," Michael answered. "Might be able to go home in a couple of days. She'll probably have to do rehab for a while."

"That's tough. She's a nice gal."

"Yeah, she is," Michael said, as if he knew her well.

"Well, good luck." Juan nodded. "Say hi to Bo for me. And if I can help you with anything, just ask."

* * *

At 1:08 p.m., the players, referees, and sixty thousand fans in the stadium were ready for some football. In the center of the field, on the Niners' logo, team captains from both teams, as well as Sam Dornam, the honorary coin flipper, met for the coin toss. The players fidgeted and bounced on their toes like fighters getting ready to rumble. The head field judge joked with Dornam while they waited for television to come back from selling fifty million viewers cars and toilet paper. Finally, after what seemed like a lifetime for those standing in the middle of the field, the red light on the television camera illuminated again, and the coin was flipped. San Francisco won the toss, but it would be about the only thing they would win all afternoon.

San Francisco deferred the call to Denver, who elected to receive the opening kickoff. Thirteen seconds later, Denver was ahead six-zero thanks to a 101-yard return for a touchdown. It was the first time in eight years that a team had run a kickoff back on the Niners.

After an ensuing touchback, San Francisco took the ball on their twenty-yard line. Their first play from scrimmage was a short slant pass over the middle that fell incomplete. On their second play, the Niners' running back, Matt Williams, coughed up the ball on their own twenty-one-yard line. Denver took over and quickly completed two passes to get to San Fran's three-yard line. With first and goal, Denver ran their fullback straight up the middle and right over Marshal Decker for their second touchdown. With just a little over three minutes gone in the first quarter, Denver was on pace to score 130 points.

On San Francisco's second possession of the game, their offense managed a first down thanks to a questionable call of pass interference against Denver. A three-and-out later, San Francisco punted the ball back to Denver, and the rout was on.

As the onslaught continued, Michael paid close attention to Marshal Decker. By the end of the first quarter, Decker had yet to make a tackle and was getting blocked out on just about every play. He didn't appear to be gimpy, but he certainly hadn't shown any of the speed he was renowned for. When Denver ran a crossing pattern over the middle, their receiver was two steps past Decker before he could react. Then, to make matters worse, the pass intended for Denver's tight end was off target and hit Decker in the back of his helmet. The football fell to the ground, untouched. Officially, Decker was given credit for breaking up the pass, but the crowd knew better. For the first time in his life, Marshal Decker was getting booed.

By halftime, Denver was leading, thirty-five to three.

The fans praying for San Francisco to turn things around in the second half were quickly disappointed. Denver intercepted the first pass, leaving many to wonder if maybe God was a Broncos fan. Denver continued the pounding and didn't let up. Marshal

Decker did manage one tackle for a loss and immediately jumped up and pounded his chest, leaving many to wonder if there was a God at all. San Francisco finally put together a couple of drives late in the fourth quarter, but by then, the game was out of reach. Final score: Denver, forty-nine, San Francisco, seventeen.

After the game, Michael followed a few of the reporters down to San Francisco's locker room, where it was understandably quiet. A few players offered shrugs or one-syllable answers as the media gathered around them. Others declined to be interviewed at all. During the press conference, Coach McCaffy looked extremely uncomfortable and fielded questions as briefly as possible. He left the podium after suggesting that all his players and coaches do a little soul-searching before the next game.

Michael could only write about what he had seen on the field, which was nothing but a good ol' ass kicking. He juxtaposed the statistics for both teams, which clearly showed San Fran on the short end of every category except the coin toss. "The Forty-Niners' offense looked totally confused," he wrote. "The defense? Totally defused. By halftime, Denver was leading thirty-five to three, which, for the mathematically challenged, put the Broncos on pace to win by around nine touchdowns. Marshal Decker was not a factor, and after the game, he slinked off the field with one tackle for his efforts. This team was beaten in every facet of the game, including coaching."

Michael closed his article with some questions: "Has the Forty-Niners' stake to the playoffs been played out? Is their claim worthless? Inquiring minds want to know!"

Monday morning, a banner above the *Chronicle's* front page read, "Niners, Missing In Action."

Tragically, those four words were about to become more than just a metaphor.

Chapter 30

* * *

Michael's experience as a beat writer for a major sports team was still in its infancy, but he had a pretty good idea that to be successful in the job, he'd better have his finger on that team's pulse, even if it was Monday, usually an off day for the players.

Of course, any day was usually an off day for Michael, which probably had something to do with his decision to go to the Niners' practice facility and hang out.

After a twenty-minute drive from his house, Michael parked his Jeep in a nearly empty parking lot near Candlestick Park. He walked the short distance to the one-level stucco building that housed the coaches' offices, training facility, and workout rooms. He flashed his press pass at a disinterested security guard at the door and let himself in. There were a few people wandering along a green-carpeted hallway that stretched the length of the building, but they all looked like maintenance personnel or office staff. The first room that Michael came to on his right was a glassed-in weight room. He tried not to gawk as he sauntered by, but he couldn't help but notice the few big men in the room. Their sweaty skin looked as if it had been stretched over cobblestones, and they all appeared to be grinning while lifting weights the size of small locomotives.

Michael continued down the hall, but a few steps later, a set of swinging double doors on his left suddenly burst open and a small, silver-haired man, dressed in a white T-shirt and pressed white pants, pushed his way into the hall, nearly colliding with Michael.

"Whoa! Sorry 'bout that," the man said. His face was flushed, and he had an armload of what looked like dirty towels.

"Hey, no problem," Michael offered.

"Didn't expect anybody around today," the man said as he steadied his load and began walking down the hall.

Michael quickly caught up with him and matched his stride. "Yeah, pretty quiet today, huh?"

The man looked at Michael as if he was trying to remember if they had ever met, and then noticed the press pass around his neck.

"Oh, yeah. Fletcher. The new guy from the *Chronicle*, right? I think I saw you after the game yesterday."

"Oh, Yeah. Tough loss, huh?"

"Got that right. So, whaddya doin' around here today? Not a lot of people to talk to. Mostly just coaches watchin' film. Few guys workin' out. I got a coupla guys on the table, that's about it."

"So, this is normal for the day after a game? After a loss?"

The man stopped and looked at Michael as if he was an imbecile. "Normal? No, it's not normal. Normally, we don't lose."

"Oh, yeah, sorry. I'm just trying to get a feel for things. I'm a rookie, remember?"

Finally the man smiled and said, "That's okay. We're all rookies at some point, right? But yeah, what you're looking at is pretty much how it is after a game. Although Decker didn't come in like he usually does. He likes to watch the game film, you know, same as the coaches. In fact, I think this is the first time he's ever missed comin' in on Monday. The man does like to look at himself. Nobody's heard from him, though, not even his pal Jackson."

"Oh?"

"Yeah. But I don't think anybody's worried about it. I heard one of the coaches say, 'He's probably just takin' a bow. Takin' a day off like everybody else.'"

The man looked at Michael and said, "But between you and me, friend, I'll guarant-goddamn-tee you, if Decker doesn't show tomorrow, there'll be plenty of folks around here worried."

Without another word, the man turned to his right and disappeared through another set of swinging doors.

Chapter 31

※ ※ ※

The next morning, Michael was at the practice field at nine o'clock...but Decker wasn't. Thirty minutes into the players' stretches, murmurs began rolling quietly around the field. On a one to ten scale for concern, the level was still fairly low. Maybe a three. Possibly a four. But when Decker hadn't shown by the afternoon's session, the needle rose to a seven, and calls were made.

At three-thirty, Michael went back to the *Chronicle* to prepare a story for Wednesday's edition. It was 4:38 in the afternoon when his cell phone rang.

"Hey, Mikey, Dan Kelly. Thanks a lot for the tip on the Oakland game. You sure called that right. I owe you."

Michael immediately regretted answering the call. "Forget it, Dan. It was just a hunch. I'm sorry, I don't have time to—"

What Kelly said next changed Michael's mind about the call. "Now I might have something for you. It's about Marshal Decker."

"I'm listening."

"I'm talkin' to you anonymously here, okay?"

"Sure. If that's what you want."

"Client privilege, sorta thing, okay?"

"I said yes," Michael snapped. "Whadda you got?"

"Well, the Eighth Precinct is responding to a call as we speak. They're in route to the San Francisco Yacht Club. Someone found a body aboard the *Deck Mate*."

The name of the boat didn't register, but Michael's antenna was on full amp. He waited for Kelly to continue.

"Mike? You there?"

"Yeah, I'm here, Dan."

"That's the name of Decker's boat, isn't it? The *Deck Mate*?"

Bo was just coming out of his office when Michael stopped him and told him about the phone call.

"What? You think it's legit?"

Michael looked at Bo and shrugged. "Something's goin' on. And, well, you know, nobody's seen Decker since the game on Sunday."

Bo turned and walked back into his office. He waved Michael in behind him. "I better call the boss on this one." Bo picked up the phone on his desk and was about to punch in some numbers when he stopped and looked at Michael.

"Or better yet, why don't you get going over to the marina as fast as you can? I know the boss will want to send somebody else over to cover this too, but I'll…ah, I'll let her know that you got a tip and were already on your way."

Michael was almost out the door when Bo called to him, "Mike?"

"Yeah?"

"Drive careful. I don't want you winding up like Brenda."

* * *

It was dark when Michael arrived at the marina. Red and blue lights flashed from a medic-one vehicle and the half-dozen police cars surrounding the entrance to Pier D. Police radios squawked their idioms as a small crowd gathered in the parking lot. Some boat owners were standing on the decks of their vessels, red and blue lights bouncing off of their faces…and their cocktails.

The *Deck Mate* was berthed three slips away from the seawall. She was stern-to, and all of her interior lights, as well as her running lights, were on. A police boat had taken a position just off the *Deck Mate*'s bow, its spotlight illuminating the waters around the yacht. A gurney belonging to the medical examiner was being rolled down to the port side of the boat. Police were busy yellow-taping off the area and talking into the radios strapped to their left shoulders.

It seemed strange to Michael to be the first correspondent at the scene of a such an event, but he also knew that as the situation developed, the parking lot of the San Francisco Yacht Club would be jammed with every news agency around. He had covered sporting events where fights had broken out among the press and security and police had intervened.

Michael knew enough to stay out of the way of the emergency personnel, but he also knew to look for whomever might be authorized to give a statement to the press. A cop with several chevrons on his sleeve was standing guard at the entrance to the dock below him. Two plainclothes detectives flashed their badges at the cop, and then hustled down the ramp.

With his press credentials clearly visible, Michael took his cue and approached the sentry. He noticed that the cop's name was McLeary.

"Good evening, Sergeant. Anything you can tell us?" he asked.

"Not at this time. Sorry. We need to keep this area clear." McLeary made a motion for Michael to stand aside.

Michael pressed on in the cop jargon that Dan had used. "I understand that you're investigating a possible ten-oh-nine?"

The cop raised an eyebrow.

"That's what I heard on my scanner, anyway." Michael shrugged nonchalantly.

This time, McLeary shot Michael a look that he probably reserved for ambulance chasers. "You know the drill. You know I can't tell you anything right now," he said coolly. "An officer will release a statement as soon as we know for sure what we have. Now, move aside."

Michael took up a position along the railing overlooking the slips. He was about fifty yards from the *Deck Mate* and could see what looked like camera flashes going off intermittently from the main salon area of the boat. Every porthole and hatch was open, as if the boat was being aired out. As he watched, a cop emerged from the cabin carrying a portable barbeque. He sat it down on the rear deck, and then went back inside the boat. Michael was lost in speculation when suddenly his phone shrilled from his shirt pocket. What had once seemed like a buoyant blues piano riff now seemed intrusive and incongruous. Michael made a mental note to change his ringtone.

"Hey, Bo."

"What's goin' on?"

Michael brought his boss up to speed. "I think it's safe to say that there is at least one body aboard Decker's boat, otherwise we wouldn't be seeing the medical examiner's team here. Nobody's saying who it is yet, although—"

Michael stopped talking when he saw a short black man stepping off the *Deck Mate*. "Ah, wait a minute, Bo, I might have something. Call you in a minute."

Michael watched the figure walk from the boat and then up the ramp. The man muttered something to McLeary and then continued to walk, head down, toward a lone silver Mercedes parked outside the ring of emergency vehicles. As the man neared the car, a tall, attractive black woman got out of the passenger's side and stood by the door. Michael slowly made his way toward them, keeping a respectable distance. The two embraced, and Michael could see the man's shoulders start to shake as he began sobbing against the woman. Michael stopped and looked away. *What the hell am I doing? I'm a sports reporter, for Christ's sake. To hell with Bo and his mantra of getting the almighty story. Leave these people alone!*

When Michael looked back at the pair, they were holding each other at arm's length, tears running down their faces. Then the woman looked over the man's shoulder and noticed Michael standing just outside their ring of privacy. She dabbed a handkerchief to her face and composed herself.

"Do you…do you need something?" the woman sniffled.

Michael made his decision. "I'm…ah, I'm sorry to intrude. My name's Michael Fletcher. I'm with the *Chronicle*—"

The man suddenly spun around. "You guys don't waste any time, do you?" He wiped his eyes with his sleeve and glared at Michael. "My cousin is dead, okay? Is that what you wanna hear?" He took a step toward Michael, obviously agitated. "I just identified his body, okay? Have you ever had to identify a body, Mister Writer-Man? Huh? Have you?" He took another step toward Michael, but the woman grabbed his arm.

"Come on, honey, let's go home." She led him back to the car and opened the passenger-side door.

"Goddamn bastards," he said as he got in the car. The woman closed his door and walked around the front of the car to the driver's side. She had her hand on the door handle when she looked at Michael. "I'm sorry. He didn't mean it. He's just upset."

"I understand. I'm sorry too."

She smiled weakly and started to open her door.

"Miss?"

"Yes?"

Michael hesitated a split second, not knowing how to phrase his question. He decided to use the past tense. "Was his cousin Marshal Decker?"

There was no smile this time, just a sad nod.

Chapter 32

※ ※ ※

Back at the *Chronicle*, Michael typed the last period of his story. He was thirty minutes past deadline, but he knew that the paper was extending its deadline, not just for him, but also for the other *Chronicle* reporters and national media sources. Information was still being gathered. Speculation was that Marshal Decker had died from accidental asphyxiation; however, foul play had not been ruled out. The official cause of death had yet to be determined.

Michael hit "Send" and rubbed his eyes. Being at a death scene was spooky thing. It was tragic. And then to write about it?

Michael leaned back in his chair and put his feet on the desk.

A week on the job, and he'd been asked to write a piece on how the death of a hockey player was affecting the team, and now, about the death of one of the best players in the NFL. Toss in the coverage of Polanski's funeral, and Michael could only hope that there wasn't a trend forming here.

As he stared at the ceiling, he wondered how many people already knew about Marshal Decker's death through social media. *No doubt about it, social media is a powerful tool*, he thought. No time frame, no deadline. News zapped around the planet almost before it happened.

"A peso for your thoughts?"

Michael immediately sat up straight in his chair and looked behind him. Len Wrighton was standing at the entrance to his cubicle, a cup of coffee in his hand. Michael had yet to meet him, but certainly knew of him.

"A peso would probably cover it." Michael laughed as he stood to greet his visitor. He stuck out his hand and said, "Hi, I'm Michael Fletcher."

"Yes, I know. I've been meaning to come by and introduce myself. I'm Len Wrighton."

"Yes, I know," Michael echoed awkwardly. "Here, have a seat." He offered the writer the only other chair in his cubicle, an old, wooden, straight-backed affair that was probably new when Wrighton was as well.

"I enjoyed your article about your first day at work," Wrighton said as he accepted the chair and sat down. "Nice angle. Very interesting."

Michael squirmed a little. "Thank you, sir. I…I appreciate that."

Wrighton crossed his legs and perched his coffee cup on his knee. The man made the old chair look comfortable.

"Hard to believe another athlete has died."

"Yes, sir. Makes you wonder."

"About what?"

Michael squirmed a little more. The man had a friendly but direct approach. "Oh, I don't know. Three different accidents? In what, six months?"

"You don't think they were accidents?"

"I don't know. Have to be awfully coincidental, I guess."

"Hmmm, do I detect a young nose with an itch to investigate further?"

Michael laughed and shook his head. "Right now I'm just trying to keep up with what's goin' on around here."

"You were out at the marina tonight, weren't you?" Wrighton asked.

Michael drew in a breath and let it out slowly. "Yeah."

"Pretty sad, huh?"

Michael nodded his head in agreement, and then changed it to a sideways motion, as if to indicate none of it made any sense to him. "Yeah, it's too bad. What a waste."

"Did you know him personally?" Wrighton asked.

"No, I didn't. But I met his cousin tonight. He was taking it pretty hard."

"How about you? How are you doing?"

The question surprised Michael. "Me? I'm fine. I guess."

"I understand that you knew Larry Lavorini. I just wondered how this latest thing affected you."

"Well, to be honest, I'm not used to writing about tragic events. I hope it doesn't become a habit. I'm pretty sure I'd rather be covering the Forty-Niners in the Super Bowl this year."

Wrighton laughed. "Well, a lot of folks around here hope you get the chance to do just that. Especially with the team moving south next year." He paused to take a sip of coffee. "But this can be a cruel business, my friend. We don't always get to write about the things we want to."

"Oh, I didn't mean it to sound like that, I just meant—"

Wrighton held up a hand to let Michael know he understood. "Not to worry, son. We all learn to take the good with the bad. It's just that in the newspaper business, bad can be good."

"Excuse me?" Michael smiled and waited for an explanation.

"Bad news sells. Tragedies make the front page."

"I suppose so," Michael said, "but I don't know if I'm cut out for that kind of reporting. I don't know if my skin is thick enough." Michael told Wrighton about the incident with Decker's cousin. He didn't mention Weinstein's suggestion that he drive out to the Golden Gate Bridge and wait for jumpers.

"You can't take it personally. You know that," Wrighton said.

"Yeah, I know. I...I guess...I don't want people to think I'm an ambulance chaser, is all."

Wrighton nodded. "Good for you, son. But there's a difference between chasing an ambulance and investigating one. You uncover something that helps the story, you'll be seeing your name in many a byline."

Michael began to feel a little more at ease with Wrighton, enough to play devil's advocate. "What about Princess Di? I wasn't very old when she died, but didn't the paparazzi contribute to her death?"

"Touche," Wrighton said as he held up his coffee cup. "We in the media are supposed to take pride in not being part of the story, and for the vast majority of the time, that's the way it is. Kind of like a referee or an umpire. You don't notice them until they miss a call. But unfortunately, sometimes a few of our brethren become overzealous. Having said that, I'll also say we need reporters on the scene. We need pictures to help us tell the story. Discretion is sometimes a thin line."

Michael felt as if he was in the company of a legend and should take advantage of that by mostly remaining quiet.

"But, in a way, the Princess Diana tragedy serves my point," Wrighton continued. "Her death was on the front page of every newspaper in the world. One of the biggest days, circulation-wise, that there's ever been."

Legend or not, Michael jumped in. "With all due respect sir, do you think that would be the case today?" He tried to make it sound as if he really didn't know the answer.

"Certainly. Why wouldn't it?"

"Well, ah…with social media and all."

"Michael, I appreciate your honesty. Nice to see in a young pup. But I'm not going to sit here and pretend I don't see the elephant in the room. Facebook, Twitter, blogs, hell, the atmosphere is jammed with news-bearing electrons zipping around the globe nonstop. Will a lot of people know about Decker's demise before tomorrow morning's edition comes out? Of course they will. Everyone is connected to an electronic leash these days. Radio and television breathe twenty-four-seven. You'd have to be living with some lost lizard tribe in the Amazon jungle not to know about what's going on in the world today.

"But you know what, Michael? There's still a ton of people who want the latest story substantiated in a newspaper. For example, the tsunami in Thailand in 2004, that killed two hundred and fifty thousand. Or the nuclear disaster in Japan in 2011. Millions of people knew about those events long before they read about them in the newspapers, but still the papers flew off the shelves. Why? Because people want to know the details. They want pictures. They want more. For a lot of people, a newspaper confirms the rumor."

Wrighton looked at his watch and stood up. "Well, I've taken enough of your time. This story on Decker is going to keep you busy for quite a while. I better let you get to it."

Wrighton was almost out of the cubicle when he stopped and looked back at Michael. "Oh, there's something else that social media lacks compared to a newspaper."

"What's that?" Michael asked.

"You can't wrap fish in it."

Chapter 33

* * *

The Forty-Niners canceled Wednesday's practice and held a news conference at 1 p.m. Michael was there, pen and paper at hand, along with a mob of other writers and news media. The owner of the team, Josh Milner, gave a short speech extolling Marshal Decker and bemoaning how tragic it is when a life is cut short. He mentioned how much the team and the rest of the world were going to miss Marshal. Coach McCaffy reiterated Milner's words about what a fine young man Decker was. The coach proclaimed that the team would henceforth wear a black armband on the left sleeve of their uniforms and dedicate the rest of the season to their former linebacker. The coach also announced that the team would keep to its schedule and play next Sunday's game. "He would want us to play," McCaffy explained.

* * *

On his way back to the *Chronicle*, Michael tried to compose his feature in his head. He would have no problem writing about the news conference—there were plenty of quotes and announcements to fill the column—but he knew that the key part of the story was still missing: the autopsy report. And by all indications, that report wouldn't be available for another twenty-four hours.

Michael was pulling his Jeep into the parking lot at the *Chronicle* when his phone rang. It was Annie. What compositions Michael had spinning in his mind vanished instantly. He suddenly remembered—it was Sadie's birthday!

"Hi, hon, I was…I was just gonna call you."

"Is everything okay?"

"Oh, sure. In fact, I…ah, I was just about to head your way."

"Good. Don't forget Scooter, okay?"

"No, no, I won't."

"Okay, love you, see you soon."

* * *

Michael explained his predicament to Bo and promised a column before deadline. Bo seemed to be bothered by something, but Michael didn't have time to sit down with him and find out what it was. *Probably has something to do with Decker*, Michael thought. The Decker story was bothering everybody.

On his way home to pick up Scooter, Michael stopped at a Walmart, threw down his Visa, and left with a pink and white girls' bicycle. Michael wasn't sure about the training wheels, but decided it wouldn't hurt to have them. He bought a bright-red bow and tied it to the handlebars.

Within an hour and a half after talking with Annie, Michael and Scooter crossed the Golden Gate Bridge. The fog that had enveloped most of the city in the morning had given way to hazy sunshine. Temperatures lingering in the sixties made for a beautiful fall afternoon. A little more than an hour later, Michael and Scooter turned onto the dirt road leading up to the Ireland farm.

Halfway up the road, Michael saw Annie walking toward the house. She had a bundle of letters and a newspaper in her hand, apparently having just picked up the mail. She turned when she heard the Jeep coming and shaded her eyes with the newspaper.

Michael rolled his window down when he reached Annie. Scooter's head was already out the back window, and she was whimpering and going slightly ballistic as she recognized Annie.

"Hey, good-lookin'. You need a lift?" Michael said.

Annie cooed over Scooter and nuzzled her for a moment. Then she smiled and placed her hand on the edge of the driver's window. "How are you, Michael?"

"Fine, and I'm also dandy, if you must know."

Annie's smile widened a bit. "Well, we don't get many dandies up here, that's for sure."

Michael was relieved to see Annie in a good mood, and for a moment it seemed that all might be well between Mr. and Mrs. Fletcher.

"How's Sadie? She having a nice birthday?" Michael asked.

"Oh, yeah she's fine. She'll be happy to see you and Scooter. Right now she's riding the wheels off the new bicycle that Dad got her for her birthday. She really likes it."

Michael's spirits dropped, and he swallowed hard. He could see a small trail of dust just beyond the barn.

"Why don't you go on up and surprise her?" Annie said. "I'll walk up and join you guys in a minute."

It took some doing without stopping the Jeep, but while he drove up the road, he reached behind him with one hand, untied the red ribbon, and slid a sleeping bag over the bike from Walmart.

Sadie saw her father drive up and park by the barn. "Daddy! Daddy! Look what I got from Grandpa!" Sadie beamed as she stood up on the pedals of her new, training-wheel-less bike and raced hard around in a tight circle. Michael watched his daredevil daughter for a couple of seconds but finally had to give in to Scooter's demands. Michael opened the Jeep's door, and Scooter jumped hurriedly over Michael s lap and ran straight for the little girl.

It was a poignant moment for Michael, but he knew he was doing the right thing. Scooter looked terrific in her new red ribbon.

Michael noticed the flash from a welder coming from the barn as he drove up. Now, standing in the doorway with a helmet perched on top of his head, Jesse Ireland smiled and waved at Michael.

"You're just in time, Mike," he said. "Can you give us a hand for a minute?"

Sadie was hugging and petting Scooter. Scooter, in turn, was licking and nuzzling Sadie. The two were giggling and whimpering, respectively, and Michael knew that they would be preoccupied for a minute or so.

"Sure, Jesse," Michael said as he headed toward the barn. The two men shook hands and went inside. A tractor was backed up to a disk, and a ground wire from the welding machine was clamped onto a side rail of the disk. Sitting behind the wheel of the tractor was a dark-haired, young, Mexican man.

"Michael, I don't think you've met Joaquin Espinoza, my foreman?" Jesse asked, waving his arm toward the man on the tractor. When Michael shook his head no, Jesse introduced the two.

"Hello," Joaquin said brightly. His complexion was smooth and unblemished. When he smiled, he displayed perfect white teeth. It struck Michael that Joaquin was a very handsome guy, almost pretty.

"Nice to meet you." Michael nodded at the man, guessing his age to be about twenty-five.

Michael looked around the barn, which was now doubling as a machine shop, and noticed several pieces of equipment that he hadn't seen before. "Looks like you're staying busy around here."

"That I am, son," Jesse laughed. "That I am." He rolled up the welding leads and took off his helmet. "In fact, I just contracted for another five tons on some new acreage. I'm not sure where all this is coming from or where in the hell it's goin', but I'm certainly gonna roll with it. The demand for our grapes is the highest it's ever been. Knock on wood."

"Well, you put out a good product," Michael said. "I can vouch for that."

"Thanks." Jesse smiled, walked back to the disk, and stood on one side of it.

"Here, Mike, you stand on that side and help me lift this thing. Joaquin, you back her up when we're ready."

The foreman started the small tractor and waited for Jesse's signal. Jesse looked at Michael. "Okay, on three. Ready? One... two..." On three, the two men lifted the tongue of the implement while Joaquin smoothly backed up the tractor. Together, Michael and Jesse positioned the disk onto the three-point hitch.

"Always easier when you've got help." Jesse winked at Michael, and then stepped away from the equipment.

"Okay, Joaquin," Jesse said. "You're ready to roll."

Joaquin nodded, and then said something in Spanish. To Michael's surprise, Jesse answered in kind. After a brief conversation, Joaquin waved and drove out of the barn.

"I didn't know you spoke Spanish," Michael said to Jesse as they watched Joaquin drive away.

Jesse laughed. "Well, I'm working on it. *Pero, es nessario practicar cada dia*, or something like that."

"Huh?"

"It's necessary to practice each day. Joaquin has been staying in the small cabin just up from here. I think he enjoys teaching us his language."

"Us?"

"Yeah. Me and Annie. Oh, and Sadie. Joaquin is teaching her a little bit too."

And then, as if on cue, Sadie came racing through the door on her bicycle with Scooter barking happily behind her. Sadie stopped and giggled, and then girl and dog tore off the same way they'd come in.

Jesse smiled at Michael. "If I could bottle that, we'd have world peace!"

"Hear, hear."

"Speaking of bottles," Jesse said, as he wiped his hands on his pants, "I better select one for dinner. You have a preference?"

"Ah, no. I mean…I…I won't be able to stay. I have to get back to the city."

Jesse looked puzzled. "Annie said you'd probably stay here tonight?"

"Oh. She…she did?"

"Yeah."

Michael took a breath. "Damn. I wish I could."

"Work?" Jesse asked.

"Yeah. You know, the Marshal Decker thing?"

"The football player?"

Michael considered Jesse pretty savvy about most things. He tried not to think of his father-in-law deep in the Amazon jungle.

"Yeah, the football player. He's dead. They found him on his boat yesterday afternoon. Looks like he was barbecuing something inside the cabin. They're doing an autopsy today, maybe even as we speak."

Jesse just shook his head.

"It's…it's one of the reason's I have to get back to the city," Michael said weakly. "We're expecting a press release from the medical examiner's office anytime now."

Jesse pulled on a ball cap that advertised fertilizer. "Sadie'll be disappointed you can't stay longer. Birthday cake and everything, you know."

"I know. I'm sorry, but this is front-page stuff. This is a very big story."

"Not to Sadie it isn't," Jesse said over his shoulder as he headed toward the door. Annie came around the corner a split second later. The two nearly collided.

"What isn't to Sadie?" Annie asked, almost smiling.

Jesse looked at his daughter and ignored her question. "I thought since it's Sadie's sixth birthday, we should have a six-year-old Chardonnay with dinner tonight. That okay with you?"

Jesse was already turning toward the house before Annie said to his back, "Sure, that's fine."

Annie watched her father walk toward the house for moment before looking back at Michael. "What isn't what to Sadie?"

The atmosphere was heading south in a hurry.

"The story about Marshal Decker. I told your dad I had to get back to the city to cover it. I said it was a big deal."

"Oh."

"You understand, don't you?" The words were hardly out of Michael's mouth when he realized how pathetic they sounded.

"You're not staying for dinner?"

Michael suddenly felt weary and defenseless. "Sorry."

Neither one of them said anything for a second or two until Annie said, "I noticed the ribbon around Scooter's neck. Is that what you brought Sadie for a birthday present?"

"Yeah."

"Well, at least you did something right today." Like her father, Annie turned and walked out the door.

Chapter 34

✳ ✳ ✳

Michael stayed at the Ireland farm long enough to have cake and coffee on the veranda in the backyard. For Sadie's sake, everyone stayed upbeat and sang happy birthday to her as she blew out the candles on her cake. Scooter hovered nearby, vigilant for any crumbs that might fall to her licking level. When a squirrel dashed across the lawn, Scooter bolted after it and chased it up an oak tree.

Sadie squealed with delight and gave chase herself. The three adults sipped their coffee and watched in smiling silence. Finally, Jesse took the opportunity to invite Michael to his farm for Thanksgiving.

"I assume you'll be here for dinner next week, Michael. One of my neighbors raises American turkeys. You know, the white ones? I bought one from him, and he'll dress it for us. I'll pick it up next Wednesday. Just don't tell Sadie where we got the turkey, okay? She thinks my neighbor raises them for pets!"

"Oh, sure thing. Thank you. I'll be here."

For many families throughout America, Michael thought, *Thanksgiving means, among all the other traditional things, several hours of football on TV. The games can provide a common denominator for friends or relatives that haven't seen each other in a while. The games have even become a backdrop for dinner.*

But not so at the Ireland farm. At Jesse's place, the TV stayed off so family could talk to each other without being distracted.

Michael knew that if he was going to report on football played on Thanksgiving Day, he would have to settle for recording the games on his TV and viewing them later. Actually, Michael preferred it that way. He could zip through the commercials.

Michael took a quick look at Annie, but she was still watching her daughter and dog.

The squirrel eventually made his escape to another tree, and Sadie and Scooter began skipping and panting their way back to the table. It occurred to Michael that he should ask Jesse if it was okay for Scooter to stay at the farm.

"Of course she can stay," Jesse answered. Sadie plopped back down in her chair just in time to hear the end of their conversation.

"If Scooter can stay, why can't you, Daddy?" she asked. Jesse and Annie grew quiet and let the spotlight fall on Michael.

"I've got to get back to the city, sweetheart, it's my job." Michael fumbled. "I've...I've got to write a very important story. People are counting on me." Michael shot Jesse and Annie a look, but the two turned away. "You'll understand when you get older," he said.

"I'm pretty old now, Daddy."

"I know you are, sweetie."

"I'm six."

"Yes, you are, honey."

"I'm old enough to count too, then...aren't I?"

Chapter 35

Michael's drive back to the city was long and lonely. He thought about his daughter and how happy she seemed to be out on the farm. He thought about Annie and where his relationship with her might be going. He knew Scooter wasn't with him, but he glanced in the back seat for her anyway. He wondered about Joaquin. Finally, in an attempt to ward off the depressive nose dive he was headed for, Michael turned on the Jeep's radio. He had a lot of work to do before his day was through and needed to get his mind right, or at least get it back to neutral. He needed to lay out his game plan.

The radio station was tuned to a country station and was playing an Emmylou Harris ballad. Unconsciously Michael's thoughts began to shift along with his mood. Unfortunately, the next song, "She Thinks My Tractor's Sexy," sent his mind right back to the Ireland farm. Michael hit the seek button on his radio, but before it settled on another station, Michael's phone rang.

"The autopsy report just came in," Kimble said, not bothering with a hello. "Carbon monoxide poisoning. We don't have an official police report yet, but at this point it looks like Decker was doing some indoor barbecuing by himself."

"Wow. You'd think he would have been smarter than that."

"You'd think. But every year, we hear about somebody dying that way. Usually in the winter. Like it's too cold to cook outside, so they bring the grill indoors."

"That's suicide," Michael said.

"That's right."

"You don't think...?"

"Nah. One bad game? No, the kid had everything goin' for him but brains. But hell, you never know. Where are you now?"

"I'm about twenty minutes from the office."

"Good. Come see me when you get here."

* * *

Michael went straight to Bo's office but found it empty. *Just as well*, he thought, *best to go to my desk and get started on my column.*

He was walking toward his cubicle when it hit him. *My cubicle? My desk? My column?* He looked around the small space. The certificates, diplomas, and awards on the partitions; the framed pictures of people, headlines, and historic events that made the pages of the *Chronicle*—none of them had his name or face on them.

Michael slumped down in his chair and stared at his computer screen. He was lost in the moment when Bo came waltzing in. Wordlessly, Bo leaned over the desk and studied the blank screen for a moment. Then he straightened up and slapped Michael on the shoulder. "I'll need more than that."

Bo walked out of the cubicle and disappeared into the hallway.

Of course it's blank. I just got here! It's my daughter's birthday, for Christ's sake!

Other than a stare down between writer and computer, nothing happened for good minute or so. But slowly, the reality of the situation began to settle in through the other side of Michael's brain. And then finally, like a wet dog, he shook himself and got to work.

* * *

Two hours later, Bo walked back into the cubicle and pulled the old wooden chair over to the desk. The chair groaned a little when he sat down. Michael couldn't remember if it had made that noise for Len Wrighton or not.

"Good work, Mike," Bo began. "Interesting stuff about Decker's father and family history."

Michael shrugged off the compliment. He wondered if Decker's cousin would read the article.

"I liked the way you explained how carbon monoxide can kill. Maybe save a few lives, who knows?"

Michael shrugged again and asked, "Anything on the police report?"

"No, not yet. But an FBI agent came by my office earlier today."

"FBI? Whadda they want?"

Kimble studied the floor for a moment. "They're interested in your story about the nightclub thing, with Decker. They wanna know where you got the information about a shooting. They wanna know your source."

"*My* source? I didn't—"

Kimble held up his hand. "I know, I know. I explained everything to the agent. He'll probably want to talk to you anyway."

"I wonder what they're after?"

"Good question. But we have nothing to hide. Even if Brenda doesn't disclose her source, I'm sure the feds can find out on their own. They've probably already talked to some of the players. This isn't like Deep Throat or something."

Michael looked thoughtful but didn't say anything.

"Deep Throat," Kimble said. "You know, Watergate?"

"Yeah, yeah, I know. I'm just wondering if the FBI thinks there's a connection between the shooting, assuming there was one, and Decker's death."

"I don't know. But the agent did ask me a question that I thought was odd; he wanted to know where we get the point spread for games. I don't know if he was screwin' with me or not; I mean, he's the FBI for God's sake. He knows where we get our numbers. Sure, we post predictions on the games, but it's not like we just throw out the line ourselves."

Both men were silent for a minute, and then Michael asked, "Do you think there's a connection between Decker's death and the other guys, Lavorini and Polanksi? You think they were really all accidents?"

"Don't you?"

Remembering his conversation with Wrighton, Michael didn't want to appear naive or overeager, but still he wanted to answer truthfully. "I dunno. If Decker was shot, maybe it was more than just a barroom scuffle, I suppose someone *could* have been trying to kill him then, huh?"

Kimble smiled. "Unfortunately we don't deal in suppositions here. Just the facts, ma'am. Just the facts."

Michael nodded.

"Lenny would've laughed at that."

"I'm sorry?"

"Just the facts, ma'am. It's what Sergeant Joe Friday used to say on an old television series called *Dragnet*."

"Oh. Before my time, I guess."

"Before mine too, really. Anyway, I appreciate your imagination, fits right in with the perception of a liberal media. But if the Giants or A's lose a baseball player soon, I'll know you're on to something."

Michael smiled, and then had a thought. "Can Brenda have visitors yet? I'd like to meet her. Pick her brain a little, you know. Maybe ask her about the tip she got on the shooting incident…if that's all right with you, I mean."

"Sure, have at it. She'd probably welcome the company. I should check on her too, let her know you might drop by." Bo looked at his watch, yawned, stood up, and stretched. "Well, my friend, it's been a long day. I'm gonna get outta here. How 'bout you?"

Michael took his cue and began shutting down his computer. "Yeah, I'm done. I guess I'll head for home myself."

Kimble was halfway to the door when a thought occurred to him. "Hey, Mike, you wanna stop at Sal's for a drink before you go home? I'm buying."

Michael was about to turn down the offer, but then it hit him: home? Hell, he didn't even have a dog at home anymore.

"Yeah, sure. I'll have a drink with you."

"Good. Park in the lot behind the place. I'll see you there."

Chapter 36

※ ※ ※

There were only two people sitting at the bar when the two newspapermen walked into Sal's. A lanky man with red hair was behind the bar with one foot on the ice machine, reading the sports pages. He noticed his new customers and quickly folded the paper.

"Evenin', Bo, how ya doin?" he said.

"Good. Red, I'd like you to meet a new coworker of mine. This is Michael Fletcher."

"Nice to meet you. What'll you have?"

The question was directed to Michael, not his boss. Caught off guard, it took him a second to make a decision. He looked behind Red at the selection of beer bottles lined up along the mirror. Finally, he saw an oldie but a goodie.

"I'll have an Anchor Steam."

"Very good." Red nodded and turned to get the beer.

As he did so, Bo slapped some keys down on the bar and turned to Michael. "Okay, let's grab a booth."

Kimble guided Michael to the back room and slid into the first booth they came to. "Save Red a few steps," he said. "No waitress tonight."

It seemed they had barely settled in before Red showed up with drinks on a tray. He quietly placed a cocktail glass with clear liquid and a maraschino cherry in it in front of Kimble. Michael's beer followed, accompanied by a frosted mug. The barkeep bowed slightly and left.

"Manhattan?" Michael asked.

"Rob Roy."

"I didn't hear you order."

"Don't have to when Red's working," Bo said, and raised his glass. "Cheers."

Michael quickly poured a small amount of beer into the frosted glass and lifted it in response. "Cheers." He set his glass down first. "It looks like you've got a routine going here. Did I see you give him your car keys?"

"You did."

"And?"

"And Red keeps them behind the bar near the front door."

"And?"

"And when I go to leave, I make the walk from here to the front door. Red either gives me the keys or he keeps 'em. You might say I've given him Power of Bartender Attorney."

Michael laughed. "Has he ever exercised that power?"

Bo looked at his drink for a moment before he answered. "Just once. About three years ago."

Michael waited for him to elaborate but Bo changed the subject. "So, I hear Wrighton stopped by to see you."

"Yes, he did. Interesting man. He gave me his theory on train wrecks."

"Huh?"

"Well, you know, how tragedy sells newspapers." Michael explained the conversation he'd had with the veteran writer.

"He's right, of course," Kimble said. "Did you know he started working at the *Chronicle* about the same time the Zodiac Killer was making news? The guy that was killing people at random and then sending cryptic messages to the paper? Thumbed his nose at the paper and everyone else. It was like, 'Okay, here's the clue; try to catch me. I own you.'"

Bo turned and pointed across the room. "There's an old headline clipping above that booth over there." When he turned back, he looked at Michael and said, "Never did catch him, you know."

Michael took a sip of beer. "Maybe he's still in business. Got a thing against athletes?"

"Don't think so," Kimble said. "He'd be awfully old by now."

"Far as I know, there's no age limit on killers." Michael countered.

"No. But, as far as *I* know, nobody's been murdered. At least, that's what they're saying so far."

Both men were silent for a moment. Then Kimble said, "God, could you imagine the headlines if they do find out these athletes were murdered? That'd sell a few papers. Just like in New York City in the midseventies, when the Son of Sam was knocking off a bunch of people. They caught that guy, though."

Bo looked at Michael and laughed. "As my buddy Wrighton would say, 'Where's a good killer when you need one, huh?'" He drained his glass and then looked over his shoulder toward the bar. "Or better yet, where's a good bartender when you need one?"

* * *

Over next two hours, the conversation drifted off to other things: sports, politics, religion, and of course, women. Bo did most of the talking and drinking, while Michael paced himself and did most of the listening. Through the course of conversation, Michael learned that Bo's wife had left him after thirteen years of marriage. They had no children, which Bo hinted was part of the problem, but Michael guessed there was more to it than that.

Bo Kimble had a reputation as a workaholic who usually worked late every day. He tried to take Mondays off, but more often than not, you could find him at the *Chronicle* then too. Michael remembered something else Bo had told him the first day they met: "I feel sorry for guys who get this newspaper shit in their blood. Constant deadlines can take their toll on marriages and relationships if you're not careful. Takes a special woman to put up with it."

When it came time to leave, Bo wobbled a little as he stood up, and then threw some money on the table. "Tomorrow's another day. Let's get outta here."

Both men walked toward the front door, where Red was waiting. "Cab, Bo?"

Bo swiveled his head and looked at Red. It took him a blink or two to focus, but then he answered. "Guess so."

Red smiled. "Good call."

As the bartender turned to his phone, Michael stopped him. "I'll drive him home."

Red and Bo both looked at Michael as if he'd just said something stupid.

"I…ah…I mean, if that's okay?" Michael stammered. "With… with you guys."

Red studied Michael for a moment, and then looked at Bo as if to get his opinion on the matter.

Bo shrugged. "Well, if it's okay with my attorney, I'm good with it. 'Sides, it'll save me that huge cab fare in the morning."

Red tossed the keys across the bar and smiled. "Goodnight, gentlemen."

* * *

Bo wasn't kidding when he said he only lived a few miles from Sal's. Five minutes after leaving the bar, Michael pulled up to the curb near the Alamo Square area of San Francisco. A row of Victorian townhouses lined the block, all about the same shape and size, with modest garages. The houses were all painted different colors, but tastefully so, as if the same *artiste* had been contracted to do the whole neighborhood.

"Mine's the dark burgundy house with no lights on. The empty-looking one," Bo said.

The hollow inflection in Bo's voice didn't escape Michael's attention. "You want me to pick you up tomorrow? We could grab some breakfast."

"Naw, I'll walk. Pay my penance, as it were. Besides, I need the exercise." Bo patted his stomach, belched, and let himself out of the Jeep. "Thanks for the ride, Mike. I'll talk to you tomorrow."

Michael watched as Bo slowly trudged up the flight of stairs. Like a proper date, Michael didn't leave until Bo had safely let himself in the door.

Fifteen minutes later, Michael pulled up to his own dark, empty house.

Chapter 37

* * *

Three days after Marshal Decker died, Michael visited Brenda in the hospital. Her condition had been upgraded to "good," and she was due to be discharged in a few days. When Michael entered her room, she was sitting up, poking at some food on a tray in front of her with her left hand. Her right arm and shoulder were in a sling, and the left side of her face was bandaged and swollen. Even with all of her bandages, Michael could see she was attractive, an African-American woman maybe in her late thirties or early forties. Michael had brought a bouquet of forget-me-nots and a copy of the morning newspaper with him.

"Good morning. Brenda?"

She smiled and waved a fork at him. "Come in, come in. You must be Mike Fletcher, hey?"

"Yes ma'am. I am. I hope I'm not bothering you?"

"No, but I'm a little dopey yet, so 'scuse me if I mumble some. Bo said you might stop by. Thanks for the flowers. I hope that's the *Chronicle* you have there."

"Sure is." Michael set the flowers down on a nearby table and looked around for a place to put the paper.

"Here," Brenda said and nodded to a chair by her bed. "Pull up a seat. Read to me if you have time. But first, tell me what's goin' on. How's the job workin' out?"

Michael immediately liked the woman and felt at ease with her, even under the circumstances. He quickly filled her in on his thoughts and impressions, and then made sure she knew his intentions as well. "I hope you can come back to work soon. I could learn a lot from you, I'm sure," he said.

"Thank you. It's nice of you to say that, but we'll have to see how my rehab goes." She nodded at the paper and said, "So, what's the latest on Decker?"

"Well, that's what I'd like to talk to you about," Michael said as he unfolded the paper to the front page. "The police just issued a statement saying that Decker's death was accidental, due carbon monoxide poisoning."

"Sad."

"Yes, it is, but..." Michael scanned through the story until he found what he was looking for. "Here, in the article it says, 'Although foul play has been ruled out in the incident, police continue to investigate a possible shooting that Decker may have been involved in just days before his death.'"

He looked up from the paper to see Brenda smiling. "What?"

"Bo said you think there's a link between this case and the other athletes that died. 'Cause of the shooting, I'm guessing."

Michael shrugged, "Maybe. What do you think?"

"I'm thinkin' you're off course, Mike, and I'll tell you why. You know 'bout my Howard? My sometimes-anonymous source?"

"Yeah, Bo told me."

"Well, he came by to see me yesterday. Told me how that whole thing went down with Decker. It seems our linebacker got in an argument over a pool game with a Dallas Cowboys fan and some other cowpokes. Things started to get nasty, lotta shovin' and jivin'. When one of the cowpokes grabbed a pool cue and held it up like Barry Bonds waitin' on a fastball, one of Decker's entourage pulled a gun from his waistband, or tried to anyway. The gun went off a little early and the fool shot himself in the hip. The bullet also hit Decker in his ankle."

"Wow. So, he *was* shot though, huh? And the cops don't know any of this?"

"Not yet. But they'll find out soon enough. Word'll get out. I'm surprised it hasn't yet."

"And you're pretty sure that's what happened? That Howard is a reliable source?"

"Oh sure. If Howie said that's what happened, then that's what happened. Besides, he says he's got the surveillance tape showin' it all. Slow motion, even. Howard said when the gun went off, the shooter doubled over, lookin' like Lee Harvey Oswald being gut shot by Jack Ruby."

"Do we know who the shooter is?"

"Like I said, it was one of Decker's pals; don't know his name yet. Pretty sure it wasn't Jose Canseco, though."

Michael laughed and nodded.

"Hope I didn't burst your bubble, Mike. I just don't think there's any more to the story."

On the drive home from the hospital, Michael wondered if he'd ever had a bubble to burst in the first place.

* * *

Two days later, Brenda's prophesies proved accurate. Decker's story began to fade and was no longer front-page news. His story value was replaced by the usual suspects: terrorist attacks, a looming national fiscal crisis, a planned teacher's strike, and more hijinks from the Kardashian kids.

Thanksgiving was only days away, and the papers were beginning to fill up with holiday ads. If there was anything in the paper about Decker's death, it was now regulated to the back of the sports pages. But even then, sportswriters were weaning away from the story and refocusing on San Francisco's football team and their chances of making the playoffs. The loss of San Francisco's star linebacker certainly didn't help their chances, but it seemed a good bet that they would still be playing past the end of the regular season. Life, for the remaining people on the planet, was going on.

Chapter 38

※ ※ ※

By the time Sunday's game rolled around, all the ingredients were in place for a roaring, redeeming football game. A few high, puffy clouds dotted blue skies, with temperatures in the upper sixties. The American flag above the stadium moved slightly in conversation with a light southerly breeze. A sellout crowd stood for the National Anthem, which was sung a capella by a local group with chilling fervor, followed by a moment of silence for the Forty-Niners' fallen warrior.

Even the coin toss at midfield to start the game brought roars when San Francisco won the flip. The Niners deferred and kicked off, and finally, the game was underway.

After a touchback put them on their own twenty-yard line, Buffalo's first offensive play from scrimmage was a quick slant pass in the area of Decker's replacement, Tommie Wilkens. It was good for a nine-yard gain. Second play was a run off tackle toward Wilkens again. It went for six yards and a first down. Another pass on first down netted twelve yards. It was Buffalo's way of saying, "Sorry about your loss, but bidness is bidness."

The Bills continued to take the ball upfield with surprising ease until San Francisco called a time-out with 12:24 left in the first quarter. It was the earliest noninjury time-out that McCaffy had ever called in his life.

The Niners' defensive coordinator tweaked some coverage schemes to get Wilkens some help, but the tone had been set. The Bills were going to continue to attack Wilkens's coverage assignment until San Fran figured out a way to stop them.

Unfortunately, for the Niners, when they did make the necessary adjustments, the Bills countered and worked away from the double coverage.

When all was said and done, it was a very boring game. The redemptive story that San Francisco's fans were hoping for never materialized. The home team lost, seventeen-three. The postgame interviews were somber and depressing. A few of the players said they'd be ready to play by next week, but they didn't sound very convincing. Most of the sportswriters, along with Michael, would write the game off as something akin to post-Decker blues.

* * *

Two and a half hours after the game, with his column finished, Michael walked out of the *Chronicle*. He was still in the same funk that he had been in when he had walked into the building. It seemed like the depression in the Forty-Niner's locker room had permeated his clothing, almost as if he had been in a room full of cigarette smokers. He wondered if his column would stink.

Michael got in his Jeep but didn't turn the key. He didn't know where to go. As he sat there, he noticed a peace sign that had been spray-painted on a brick building across the street. His mind drifted back to the Ireland farm, and he visualized Sadie and Scooter racing through the barn. He remembered what Jesse had said: "If I could bottle that, we'd have world peace."

Michael looked at his watch and decided it wasn't too late to call Annie.

His call was answered on the first ring, but not by his wife. "Hello? Who's speaking please?" Sadie said in her sing-song voice.

"Oh, hi, sweetie, this is Daddy. How are you?"

"Fiiiiine." She drew the word out as if it had more than one syllable

"How come you're answering Mommy's phone?"

"Mommy is in school right now. Joaquin is our teacher. He says it shows respect to learn someone else's language. Listen, Daddy, I can count in Spanish...uuuno, doughs, twaasee...

"That's great, hon. Can you put Mommy on the phone, please?"

"Okay. I mean, *si*."

Sadie giggled and then yelled, more into the phone than away from it, "Mommy, Daddy's on the phone."

Michael could hear Mexican music in the background. Several seconds passed before Annie came on the line. She sounded winded.

"Hello?"

"I hear you're learning Spanish."

Annie laughed. "Well, I'm trying to remember some of my high school Spanish."

"Where are you?"

"Well, right now, we're at Joaquin's. You know, up from the house?"

Michael heard Sadie laughing in the background. He pictured his daughter playing with the handsome Mexican. "Shouldn't Sadie be in bed?" Michael looked at his watch again.

"Soon." The timbre in Annie's voice had changed. It was a few seconds before either of them said anything. Then Annie said, "Why did you call, Michael? To check on Sadie?"

"I called," Michael said, "to see how my wife and daughter are. That's okay, isn't it?"

"We're fine," Annie said, too quickly. Michael could hear her take a deep breath before letting it out slowly. It was her way of regaining her composure. Michael had heard it a number of times.

"I'm sorry."

"Me too."

Then, in a more conciliatory tone, Annie filled Michael in on a few of the things that had been going on. She said her father had been working really hard lately and was even thinking about putting in another vineyard. She was worried about him not having enough help. Annie shifted gears and told Michael that Sadie's homeschooling was going well and that she was happy playing with the neighbor's kids.

Michel knew Annie was just making small talk, but he appreciated it. He was glad they could talk without arguing. He was trying to decide if this was the time to ask his wife what her intentions were when she beat him to it.

"I need to get back to the house soon," she said.

"Yeah, it's getting late. You better go."

"No. I mean…you know, our house, in the city."

"Oh! You're coming home?"

"Well, yes, I, uh, I need to pick up some stuff."

Chapter 39

* * *

As usual, the newspaper hit Michael Fletcher's front drive at 5:15 a.m. And as usual, Michael heard the *thwack* from his bed, and then rolled over for another hour of semi-sleep. When he did roll out of bed to begin his day, it started with bathroom study, which usually took ten to fifteen minutes, depending on the magazine du jour. Then he put on his work clothes for the day: sweats, socks, and the moccasin slippers that Sadie had bought for him the previous Christmas. From there, it was off to the kitchen to power up the laptop that occupied the table. Make coffee. Retrieve the paper. Toast two slices of cracked wheat bread con peanut butter. Scan headlines, then read the sports pages.

On this particular morning, when Michael opened the gate to the backyard to fetch the paper, he reminded himself he needed to clean up Scooter's deposits. At least old turds were easier to deal with, he rationalized. Still, he knew he would've cleaned up all the turds in Tahoe to have his dog back.

Because there was a threat of rain in the forecast, the paper was wrapped in a thin plastic cover with a blue rubber band around it. When Michael picked up the paper, he suddenly had an early morning epiphany: the cover and the rubber band would have had to have been put there by hand. Did the distribution department have to hire extra help on rainy days just to put rubber bands around the paper? Was the local economy affected? He thought of Len Wrighton. He would have to tell the writer that there was another advantage that print media had over social media: a free rubber band that you could put in your catch-all drawer for later use.

Back inside his house, Michael turned on the TV set in the living room, a habit he had just recently picked up, mostly for the company it provided, he supposed. He tuned the TV to an all-music channel that featured easy-listening instrumentals. He adjusted the volume to low and then settled in at his workstation at the kitchen table. This time, he didn't bother with the front-page stuff, but went straight to the sports section.

The Forty-Niners were, of course, the lead story. Michael's story. And like the rookie that he was, it was still a thrill for Michael to see his name in the byline. He sipped his coffee and, with some trepidation, read what he had written twelve hours before. Satisfied that there were no typos in his column on the first read-through, he read it again to see if the essence of the story was still there and if he still agreed with it. He tried to imagine he was an just an average sports fan at an airport, waiting for a flight and reading the sports pages.

Finally, he imagined that he imagined too much. The only thing that he did feel right about was that what he had written looked better in a newspaper than it on a computer screen. Len Wrighton would be proud of him. He picked up the rest of the paper and began scanning through it.

Michael had just turned a page in the Calendar of Events section when *boom*, his scanning abruptly stopped and locked on a photograph.

There were two people in the picture holding a check the size of a small car. On one end of the cardboard facsimile, in all her miniskirted glory, was Dr. Laurie Scott. Holding up the other end of the check and exposing his pearly whites was none other than Carl Weinstein.

Michael immediately felt a pang of…jealousy? Anger?

The caption below the picture read, "Dr. Laurie Scott is all smiles as she accepts a donation from the Weinstein Sports Agency. See accompanying story for details."

Michael quickly found the short segment that went with the picture. It mentioned Scott's therapy facility and the work she was involved in. It quoted Scott as saying, "While we don't rely solely on donations or grants, they are a big part of the success we've had in our physical therapy program for kids. Our goal here is to help every child we can. The Weinstein Agency has generously stepped up to help us accomplish those goals, and for that, I am extremely grateful."

The piece also included a quote from Weinstein: "I believe children are our future. We must help them and give them every chance in life to succeed. I've been fortunate in my business career, and I'm just glad to help out in any way I can."

Sure you are, you creepy bastard. You're probably just trying to get into the good doctor's pants. Probably got a bet on it with someone.

Michael looked at the picture again and at Scott's miniskirt. He tried not to imagine Weinstein and Scott wining and dining together.

The article concluded by saying there would be a benefit luncheon tomorrow, at the downtown Sheraton. Proceeds would go to help Dr. Scott's facility as well as a local Boys and Girls Club. The public was cordially invited to attend.

Cordially invited? Michael thought. *Of course they're cordially invited. What else would they be? Uncordially invited? Sorta invited? Reluctantly invited?* He threw the paper down in disgust.

It was at times like this that Michael would stew for a few moments before he realized he was being silly. What the hell did he care what Dr. Scott was doing?

One of the methods Michael used to alter a bad mood was to go outside and throw the ball for Scooter. He stood up to do just that before he realized that that wasn't in the cards. For an instant, Michael's mood was in danger of plunging further into funk. He knew he had work to do, including writing his blog, but he needed to get his mind right first. He needed something physical. It still wasn't raining, and he thought about washing his Jeep, but felt that was too easy. He needed to sweat. Since he was already dressed for a run, he decided a brisk jog around the neighborhood would fit the bill.

He traded slippers for sneakers, grabbed his headset, and went out the door. After a series of quick stretches in the driveway, he set the music volume and took off running.

Usually, when he went for a run, he would circle the neighborhood in three-block chunks, thereby running on level ground. But today, with the sound of the Subdudes pulsating through his earbuds, he was marching to a different drummer. Instead of turning after three blocks, he went straight, which took him down Ferguson Avenue. It would mean a grueling uphill return, but he welcomed the challenge. He started down the hill in short, measured strides.

Unfortunately, after about a half a mile, Michael's downhill speed began to get away from him. When he tried to slow his pace, his right foot landed awkwardly, and for a split second, his right knee seemed to bend backward. He let out a yelp and went crashing down onto the concrete. He rolled twice before coming to a sitting position. He sat motionless for several seconds. He was still breathing hard, and it took a few moments for him to catch his breath. One of the earbuds was dangling across his chest and still emitting sound. Slowly, he removed the other earbud and shut off the music.

A passing motorist slowed to see if he was alright, but Michael waved him on. From his sitting position, he made a quick assessment of the situation. His knee hurt like hell, and he felt a small scrape above his left eye, but nothing seemed to be broken. More embarrassed than hurt, Michael struggled to his feet and tried to regain his composure. His first steps were tentative and painful, but a least he could put some weight on his left leg. He took a deep breath and slowly began to gimp his way back up the hill. That's when the rain started.

* * *

By the time Michael reached his house, he was completely soaked. His sweatpants and hoodie had absorbed every drop of rain that hit him. He felt like one big, soggy sock. He limped past his rain-washed Jeep and let himself into the house through the back door. He peeled off his wet clothes, left them in a heap on the kitchen floor, and headed for the bathroom.

He stayed in the shower until the hot water ran out.

Chapter 40

* * *

After his shower, Michael swallowed some ibuprofen, limped to the kitchen table, and set up his laptop. With his knee wrapped in an ice pack, he was able to get his writing duties out of the way. Later, he made his way around the house, doing some chores, including his laundry. Still, something was nagging him, and he knew what it was. He grabbed a beer out of the fridge and settled on the sofa in the living room, where he made the call.

"Hello?"

"Hi. Laurie?"

"Oh, hi, Michael. How are you?"

He could imagine her smile. "Well, I've had better days, but I have a beer in my hand now, so I'm guessing it'll get better."

"Care to share?"

"My beer?"

Michael heard a throaty laugh before she said, "Hmmm, that's not a bad idea. But I was thinking more of how your day has been. Details?"

If Michael had wanted to keep an edge to his voice, he was out of luck. Twenty seconds into the conversation with Dr. Scott, Michael's angst melted. He told her of his jog and the agony of his climb back uphill in the rain.

"Oh no," Laurie said with concern in her voice. "Are you going to see a doctor?"

"I think it's just a sprain. I'll see what tomorrow brings. Besides, I'm talking to a doctor right now."

"Who? Oh…yeah." Dr. Scott laughed. Then she lowered her voice and said in her most official voice, "Well, Mr. Fletcher, I would be happy to take a look at your leg. Hopefully we won't have to amputate. Would you like to stop by my office for a consultation? You may bring your beer if you wish."

It was Michael's turn to laugh. "That's tempting, Doctor, but I tend to shy away when amputations are mentioned."

"That's a good sign, Michael. Means you probably didn't suffer a concussion during your fall."

They had some more fun with Michael's situation before Michael finally mentioned why he had called. "I saw your picture in the paper today. You and Mr. Winedick."

"Winedick?" Laurie laughed. "Oh, that's funny. You do mean Weinstein, don't you?"

"Yeah, whatever."

"Michael, if I didn't know better, I'd say you and Carl aren't exactly chums."

"Carl?" The edge had returned to his voice. "Well, there's just something about him, I guess. I dunno."

"Well, I think I know what you mean, but he has been very generous to me and the foundation."

"I'll bet."

"Michael? Are you jealous?" Dr. Scott asked teasingly.

"No," Michael said, a little too fast. He decided not to mention Weinstein's brother-in-law yet.

She gave it another second, and then added, "Because if you *are* jealous, Michael, I'm flattered. But no, Carl Weinstein isn't my type." Again, Dr. Scott lowered her voice and whispered conspiratorially, "He wears too much cologne."

"I'm sorry. It's none of my business," Michael said, relieved.

"Not to worry, Michael. Actually, I was hoping it was—your business, that is."

"Excuse me?"

"Well, I was wondering if you wanted to attend the luncheon. I'm not sure it deserves a follow-up in your paper or not, but it *is* for a worthy cause. Sam Dornam will be there, and he's bringing some ex-jocks who belonged to the Boys Club when they were younger. I'm assuming they'll make a few speeches and presentations. You were a member of the Boys Club when you were growing up, weren't you?"

"I was, yes."

"Well, there you go. Please tell me you'll be there. It's in one of the meeting rooms at the Sheraton on Union Street at noon. I'd love to see you again."

Michael tried to sound casual. "I suppose I could swing by. It might be worthy of an inch or two in the paper. I'll check with my boss."

"Wonderful. I'll save a seat for you at my table."

Michael knew he should leave it at that, but before he hung up, he asked, "By the way, Doctor, what is your type?"

"My type? Hmmm, let's see…"

Michael could visualize Dr. Scott thinking and unconsciously wetting her lips with the tip of her tongue. Finally, she answered.

"I like men who embrace the elements."

* * *

Michael's mood was greatly improved when he made his next call to Bo. Bo quickly acknowledged that he, too, had noticed the picture of Dr. Scott in the paper.

"She's the one you did the piece on about kids and physical therapy, right?" he asked.

"That's her."

"Good-looking woman. I wouldn't mind being in her care." Bo paused for a second. "But yeah, if you want to go to the luncheon, go ahead. See if you can find out what some of the old ballplayers are doing now. If it doesn't make the Green section, maybe Jack can use it in Society. I'm sure he would give you credit for it."

"Okay, thanks."

"One other thing, Mike. I noticed Weinstein was handing her the check in the picture. You think he'll be there tomorrow?"

"I'm not sure; why?"

"Just wondered if you'd had a chance to look at him a little more. You know, his brother-in-law and all. Something about that man bothers me."

"*Everything* about that man bothers me, Bo. Can you be more specific, or is this just your nose-for-news intuition flaring up again?"

"Listen, my young friend, this old nose has sniffed out plenty, and it's not done yet. And if you stick around long enough in this business, you'll learn when to trust those intuitions too."

"And sell a ton of papers."

"If you're lucky, yes."

"And maybe Weinstein will turn out to be the son of the Zodiac Killer?"

"Fuck you, Mike."

Chapter 41

* * *

The next morning, Michael awoke feeling as if he had spent the night in his clothes dryer. Every muscle and joint in his body ached. His first steps to the bathroom were hesitant and accompanied by tortured syllables. Besides the welt around his left eye, the bathroom mirror showed more abrasions on various parts of his body. He knew that if he was going survive past the bathroom stop, he'd better plan on a bathtub filled with hot water. He would deal with thinking or moving his limbs after a good soak. The whole thing reminded him of a hangover. Then he remembered the beers he'd had after he talked with Bo last night. *Hmmm...does this qualify for hair of the dog measures?*

While he soaked in the tub, he let his mind wander. He pictured Joaquin in his cabin, teaching Annie Spanish.

It shows respect to learn someone else's language.

Well, la-de-fucking-da.

By the time the water in the tub had cooled, he had made a mental note to research the Navajo language.

* * *

Later, in the kitchen, some toast and coffee gave Michael reason to be optimistic. Backed by two Advils and some exploratory stretches, he slowly gained confidence. He decided against the breakfast beer, and by midmorning, he was able to shave and dress himself. He even found the time to look up the word "hello" in Navajo. He wasn't sure of the pronunciation, but it looked like "ya-at-eeh."

* * *

At 11:15 a.m., Michael was out the door and climbing into his Jeep. Now, most Jeeps are built a little higher off the ground than most cars, which is a good thing if you're out in the woods, but if you're in the city, feeling a hundred years old, and trying to pull yourself into the cab, that extra height can be annoying. Ask anyone with a bad back.

After a brief struggle, Michael finally settled in behind the wheel and was about to start the engine when it hit him. *Cologne!* "Son of a bitch!" At least he was speaking in complete sentences now. With steely resolve, he hoisted himself back out of the Jeep and went back inside the house to the bathroom. He scrubbed his face until he was sure there was no trace of fragrance left.

Thinking he had a handle on things, Michael returned to his Jeep. Unfortunately, that's when things really headed south. When he tried to start the engine, it just turned over…and over…and over.

His gas gauge showed a half a tank. He pumped the accelerator and tried again. Same thing. Nothing. The "Check engine" light glared at him. He got out and popped the hood. He really wasn't sure what he was looking for—or at, for that matter—but everything looked to be in place. He wiggled a couple of wires and tapped what he thought might be a carburetor or something important. He left the hood up and crawled back behind the wheel. At least he was figuring out the best system for getting in and out of the Jeep.

After ten minutes of on-and-off trying to start the Jeep, the battery started to lag. Michael gave up and semi-stormed back into his house. If he was going to make it to the luncheon at all, he was going to have to call a cab. He would deal with his Jeep later. Maybe it would fix itself while he was gone.

* * *

When the cab finally dropped Michael off at the curb of the Sheraton, he was about forty-five minutes late. He grabbed his camera bag and recorder and limped through the main entry of the hotel. A concierge in the lobby pointed toward a long hallway and described the room Michael was looking for. Halfway down the corridor, Michael heard applause coming from behind the closed double doors labeled The Redwood Room. As the applause died down, Michael cracked one of the doors just wide enough for him to peek inside. The room was full of men and women sitting at linen-covered dining tables. Their attention was directed toward a small stage and podium at the far end of the room.

Apparently, they had been applauding Sam Dornam, who was walking off the stage and waving at the audience. Michael took this opportunity to enter the room, but as soon as he pulled back the door, a hinge squeaked loudly, and half of the people stopped what they were doing to look his way.

Smiling meekly, Michael slipped quickly into the room and stood silently against the wall by the door. Two seconds later, the door clicked shut loudly enough for a few more people to turn their heads back again.

Fortunately, Dr. Scott was one of the people who looked his way. She was sitting at a large, round table just in front of the small stage. There were five or six people at her table, and to Michael's relief, none of them was Weinstein. He also noticed that the seat next to her was vacant. Scott stood up smiling, said something to her tablemates, and hurried over to him.

"Hello, Michael. I'm so glad you could make it."

"Ya-at-eeh."

"Excuse me?"

"Ya-at-eeh? Doesn't that mean, hello in Navajo?"

Scott laughed. "Oh, yes. Ya-at-eeh. Very good, Michael. I'm impressed."

Her pronunciation was completely different from his. *Oh well...mission accomplished*, he told himself.

She slid her arm through his with the intention of escorting him to her table. "Come on, shi ak'is, let me introduce...oh, no. I forgot about your leg."

"Aw, it's okay. I'll live...I think." Michael laughed. "But what did you just call me? Sounded like shithead?"

"No, no. I said shi ak'is. It means friend." They took a couple of tentative steps together, and Scott asked, "You okay?"

"Yep. No problem." After a slight pause, Michael gave Scott a once-over and then said, "And I would ask you how you are, Doctor, but I can see that you're, er...fine."

Scott smiled off the compliment, but Michael's diagnosis was accurate. She was wearing her trademark black short skirt and matching heels. An emerald-green linen jacket covered a low-cut, cream-colored blouse. Her jet-black hair hung loosely over her shoulders.

"You lead the way, lady. I'll follow," Michael said.

As Michael limped along behind her, he couldn't help but look at her legs and noticed how the muscles in her calves delicately defined themselves with each step she took, winking at him. Left, right, left, right, left, right. The thought occurred to him that the first lemming over the cliff was most likely a female with great legs.

Scott introduced Michael to the people at her table and then filled him in on what he had missed. She reiterated how the theme of the luncheon, "Instilling Character in Kids," had been carried through with each guest speaker. She flavored her comments about the different athletes, donors, and speakers in attendance with colorful anecdotes. While Michael listened, it occurred to him that Dr. Scott was pretty much writing his story for him, and all he had to do was to scribble down what she was saying.

Laurie Scott's beauty seemed to be matched by her brains and charm. At one point, Scott went over to another table to bring back Sam Dornan and a couple of ex-Forty-Niners for a quick interview so Michael wouldn't have to hobble over himself. She stopped a passing busboy and asked if he would mind taking a group photo of their table. The young man was beaming with pride and probably would have married Scott right then and there if his mother would have let him.

"I should be late more often," Michael joked to Scott as the event began to wear down and people began to leave. "You've done most of my work for me here."

"Anything for the cause, Michael." Scott smiled. "If it benefits kids, it benefits the world."

"Think globally, act locally type of thing?" Michael asked.

"I suppose you could say that," Scott said thoughtfully. "But if we need to change our culture, and I think we do, we need to start with kids. Too many old farts in Washington are so set in their ways, they can't see the need or the urgency for cultural change. Take the gun control issue and our 'righteous' Second Amendment, for example. They think if we just kick the can down the road some more, it'll go away. No need to change good ol' America. Bullshit."

"Wow. I pushed a button, didn't I?"

Scott laughed and placed her hand on Michael's forearm. "I'm sorry. I've strayed off the sports pages again, haven't I?"

"Not at all," Michael shrugged. "It just shows you care."

Scott's eyes softened and she looked tenderly at him. "Thank you, Michael. I do care, you know."

Scott's hand slid down Michael's forearm, and she took his hand in hers. Michael wasn't sure what the gesture meant, but he made no effort to disengage his hand. A moment passed before she patted his hand playfully and said, "So, Mr. Fletcher, tell me, why *were* you late to our little event? Was it because of your injuries? Don't tell me you had something more important on your agenda?" Before he could answer, she let go of his hand. Michael wasn't sure if he was relived or disappointed.

"If you must know, I was late because my Jeep wouldn't start. The 'Check engine' light has been on for a few weeks, so I'm guessing that has something to do with it."

"Ya think?" Scott laughed. "Why do men ignore that stuff? You probably don't stop for gas until you're just about out, right?"

Michael shrugged, guilty as charged.

"So how'd you get here?" Scott asked.

"I took a cab. Which reminds me, I better call for one now. I need to get home so I can send the boss the pictures and story about this little affair."

Michael immediately regretted his choice of words, but if Scott noticed, she didn't show it.

"Oh, don't be silly. I'll give you a ride." She took his hand again and smiled. "It'll be my pleasure."

Chapter 42

* * *

Riding with Scott in her Cadillac *was* a pleasure for Michael, but it wasn't enough to keep the pain in his knee from flaring up. By the time they pulled up next to his house, Michael was in obvious discomfort, and the good doctor knew it. She offered to take him to an urgent care facility, but he wasn't having any of it.

"I'll be fine once I get to my medicine chest in the bathroom. Besides, I need to make some calls about my Jeep and then get to work on your story."

Scott shook her head. "There you go again, pulling that guy crap. Okay, Mr. Caveman, I'm not an orthopedist, but at least let me look at your knee. What's it gonna cost you?"

She had a point. As usual, Michael's financial situation was tenuous, and temps at the *Chronicle* weren't covered by health insurance.

"Mmmm…I dunno, Doctor. What do you charge for a house call?"

"Does the house have wine in it?"

"It does."

"Then you're covered."

* * *

Once inside, Michael showed Scott into the living room and told her to make herself comfortable. "I'll be right back," he said as he headed for the bathroom. "I've got some aspirin here somewhere."

Before he disappeared into the other room, Scott called to him, "I'll open the wine if you want. Just tell me where it is."

"There's an open Cabernet on the kitchen counter by the fridge," Michael mumbled as he rounded the corner in his bedroom.

"What? Where?" Scott asked.

Michael stopped, stuck his head back around the corner, and said loudly, "Glasses are in the cabinet above the stove."

While Michael did his thing, Scott rummaged around the kitchen. She was standing in the living room with two glasses of wine when he re-emerged from his bedroom.

"Well, this is a switch," Michael said. "It's usually the patient who's kept waiting."

"You have a nicer waiting room than I do," Scott said as she handed him a glass.

"Thank you, Doctor. Cheers." They clinked glasses and each took a sip.

"Hmmm…excellent," Scott said, smiling at Michael. "You have good taste, sir."

"Why thank you, kind lady. It seems the more I learn about wine, the more I'm interested in it."

Michael's palate was unreliable at the moment due to the mouthwash he had just gargled in the bathroom, but he wasn't about to mention that fact.

"Please, sit," he said as he gestured toward the couch. He punched the television remote and out on the soft instrumental music channel, then settled on the couch beside her. They talked comfortably about the day's events for a while, and then he apologized for butchering "hello" in Navajo.

"Man, just lookin' at the language in print is confusing," Michael said. "It looks like Russian, or…or Arabic. Something that can't possibly be translated, or make sense. A bad formula in physics, maybe."

"That's funny," Scott said, although she wasn't smiling. She shifted gears and asked, "So how's the job working out?"

"Well, I feel I've been baptized by fire. First, when I had to ask Coach McCaffy about his star linebacker getting shot, he really chewed me a new one. I can't blame him, though; just trying to protect his players. He hides a lot from the media."

"Kinda hard to hide an injury if the player's ankle's sporting bandages, I would think?"

"Huh? Oh, yeah, but the real hard part for me was when they found Decker's body. I was the first reporter on the scene. That was not fun."

Scott's face clouded. "No, I don't suppose it would be. I'm sorry."

Michael shrugged and took a sip of wine. "And dealing with people who think that I chase ambulances and lust for blood turns me off."

Scott pulled one bare leg under the other and turned to face Michael. Her skirt rode up a few inches on her thighs. "Well, you'll just have to learn to ignore them."

"Yeah, I know. But sometimes they wear so much cologne you can't."

Scott laughed and punched Michael in his bicep.

"Ow, damn!" Michael grimaced and rubbed his arm. "Okay, I have to say I enjoy working for Bo, although I think that he thinks I'm a little young and innocent. Naive, maybe."

"You are, Michael." Scott laughed. "I like that about you too."

"Oh, come on. Naive? Just because I think that there could be a connection between the deaths of those athletes? I think you'd have to be naive to *not* think that."

"Do you have any theories? Any motives?"

"No. Not yet. But…well, I don't want to bore you with it. Could just be coincidental, I guess."

"I suppose. Kinda creepy, though, if you ask me." Scott uncoiled from her position, stood up, and placed her glass on the table next to her.

"More wine?" Michael asked.

"Not until I look at that knee of yours. I may have to amputate, remember?"

"Well, *I'll* need more wine if you do." Michael handed his glass to Scott and kicked off his left shoe. He tried to gently pull his left pant leg up and over his knee, but the swelling in his knee prevented him from doing so. Scott placed Michael's glass next to hers on the table and surveyed the situation.

"You'll have to take off your pants, sailor."

"You didn't bring an examination gown?" Michael asked meekly.

Scott spotted an afghan shawl on the recliner. She threw it to him. "Here, cover yourself. I'll turn around."

Michael obediently complied. When he lowered his pants, he was surprised to see how much his knee had discolored since morning. "Okay, Doc. I'm ready. Give me the bad news."

Scott turned around and looked down at his knee. "Wow. You did a number on it."

"That's all I get for my money?"

Scott laughed and slid down on her haunches in front of Michael. "You might be sorry you said that once I start probing around. You might want a bullet to bite on. Lean back."

Michael leaned back and braced himself for pain. He thought it better to not watch what she was doing in case something popped out of place. Michael kept his eyes trained on a picture on the far wall. He flinched when Scott put one hand under his knee and the other hand on his ankle. She slowly lifted his ankle and leg while her fingers felt the tendons behind his knee.

"Any pain when I do that? Scott asked.

"Of course there's pain when you do that," Michael said, still looking away. "And there's pain when you *don't* do that. There was pain when we started. Remember?"

"Don't be a smartass. You know what I mean."

Scott moved one hand from his ankle up to the inner part of his thigh while her other hand moved down to the side of his calf. She leaned forward and gently pushed her hands in opposite directions. "Anything?"

"Nope."

"Good." She switched hands and repeated the motion. "Now?"

"Nope."

Scott moved both hands to his kneecap and began to gently probe the injured area. Hoping the worst was over, Michael allowed himself a peek at what was going on. Scott's head was bent over his knee, and she was intently studying his skin as she touched him. Her hair had fallen over one shoulder, and a few strands lightly brushed against his inner thigh. Michael's viewpoint also afforded a look down Scott's blouse. The lower half of her breasts were encased in a sheer, rust-colored bra, while the top portions swelled smoothly upward.

Frantically, Michael realized that something else was beginning to swell upward. *Oh, God, not now...go away...go away, please!* He looked quickly at the ceiling. *Politics... taxes... North Korea... Dennis Rodman.*

Help did arrive, but not in the way Michael could have imagined.

Michael's heart jumped to his throat when he heard the front door open. A split second later, Scooter came bounding into the living room, wagging her tail and barking her pleasure in anticipation of seeing her master. Annie closed the door and called from the foyer. "Michael? It's me." She was two steps into the living room when she froze. In the blink of an eye, her brain snapped a picture of everything in front of her: the long-legged, dark-haired beauty kneeling in front of her husband on the sofa, his pants down around his ankles. The wine bottle on the kitchen counter. The glasses on the table.

Annie threw her arms in front of her face and looked away like someone trying to avoid the flash of an explosion. Then she made a sound like she was going to throw up. "Auh-g-gu-waa, nooo!"

Michael tried to stand up, but Scooter knocked him back to the sofa. Scott quickly jumped to her feet, smoothing her skirt. Suddenly, Scooter started barking and growling at Scott. Scott tried to compose herself and mitigate the situation by introducing herself. "Hello. I'm Doc—"

Annie screamed, "Scooter! Come! Now!"

"Annie! Wait!" Michael said as he stood up, tossed the afghan aside, and began pulling up his pants. "It's not what you—"

"Scooter!"

Scooter was still barking at Scott when Annie turned on her heel and headed for the door. "Goddamn you!" was the last thing Annie said before she stormed out of the house, viciously slamming the door behind her. Scooter stopped barking and started whining. Before Michael could get halfway across the room, he heard the screech of tires as Annie's Volvo roared away.

It was all over in less than a minute. Neither Scott nor Michael knew what to do or say. They both stood, stunned, in the middle of the living room and looked at each other. Scooter wasn't sure what was going on either and froze in place. The only sound in the house came from the soft music channel.

Finally, Scott spoke, "Michael, I'm *so* sorry. I...ah...I assume that was your wife?"

Michael smiled weakly and nodded. When he tried to say something, his voice squeaked, and he had to clear his throat before he could talk. "Yes, ahem...that was her."

Scooter resumed her wagging and looked hopefully at Michael.

Scott sucked in a deep breath, and then blew it all out. "Whew... well, damn it. I *am* sorry. Is there anything I can do, Michael? I'll call her if you want me to."

"No, that's okay. I'll...er...I'll sort it out."

"I better go," Scott said as she picked up her shoes. She slipped her heels back on and stepped over to Michael. Scott tenderly touched his cheek. "You're a good man, Michael."

Michael smiled bravely at Scott. "Thank you for your help." His shoulders sagged as he finally moved and walked Scott to the door.

There, she hesitated, smiled once more, and then walked to her car.

Michael moved slowly back into the living room, found the remote and clicked off the music. He stared at the couch and tried to imagine what the scene must have looked like through Annie's eyes. His heart rate had barely slowed down. He took a deep breath and considered his options for damage control. His first thought was to drive out to the farm and plead his case to Annie with the facts: *Scott is a doctor who was examining my knee. Nothing happened between us. I have never been unfaithful to you.* He could swear on a stack of Bibles that that was all true. *Nothing but the truth, your honor. I did not have a sexual relationship with that woman.*

Bill Clinton would be proud.

Then he remembered the situation with the Jeep and he realized that driving to Santa Rosa wasn't an option. He knew Annie probably wouldn't answer his phone call, but he had to try. Maybe he would leave a message laughing the whole thing off: "*Hi, honey. Boy, I bet you're mad. Well, heh, heh, I can't blame you! That must have looked like something was going on! But you see, I hurt my knee jogging—you know how I like to jog…Well, anyway, I was at a luncheon and Dr. Scott was there…*"

Michael picked up the wine glasses and walked to the kitchen. He tried to tell himself that once Annie simmered down, she would understand. His rationale changed immediately when he saw the open bottle of wine sitting on the kitchen counter. The one from Annie's father. To be opened only on a special occasion.

Chapter 43

* * *

Michael started the next morning with a phone call to his mechanic. Despite all that had happened the day before, he'd still had the wherewithal to write his story and send it to the paper. His next act was to call the local garage and make arrangements to have his Jeep towed. He was desperate to get his ride fixed before the long, four-day holiday started.

"Your cam sensor is bad," the mechanic told him.

"My what is what?" Michael hadn't slept well and was hoping things might be better. At least he had his dog back—for another day, anyway.

"Your cam sensor. It sends a signal to the computer in your car that your camshaft is turning."

"Ah…okay. Is my camshaft turning?"

"Oh, yeah, it's fine. We just need to change out the sensor. We could have it done by this afternoon. Probably run you about hundred and fifty. I noticed your battery is pretty old. You probably should—"

"Let's just change out the sensor for now," Michael said. "That'll get me back on the road, won't it?"

"Yeah."

"Okay, I'll deal with the rest later."

Michael called Annie's phone but it went to voicemail, so he left her one. He gave her a short description of his injury and what had happened with Dr. Scott. He then texted her an even shorter version ending with "c u tomrow."

Annie would have to talk to him once he showed up the farm for Thanksgiving. His next phone call was to Bo Kimble. The Niners were flying to Phoenix after Thanksgiving to prepare for their Sunday game against the Cardinals. Michael would be making his first trip with the team, and Kimble wanted to go over some traveling do's and don'ts with him. Kimble answered on the first ring.

"Hey, Mike. Good stuff on the luncheon yesterday. I wondered what Kyle Jordan was doing since he hung up his jockstrap. Good to see him involved with the kids like that. He was a hell of a wide receiver in his day."

"Yes, he was. Good interview, too." Michael decided to steer the conversation away from the luncheon. "Hey, Bo, my Jeep's in the shop right now and won't be ready until this afternoon. I figured I'd grab a cab to the practice this morning. You still want me to come by the paper when I'm done? Or can I zap you the piece?"

"All right, just send it to me. Traffic is gonna be a mess today anyway with everybody trying to get outta town early. Why don't you come by the office around nine Friday morning, and we'll go over your travel plans? I think the team's flight leaves around three-thirty that afternoon."

"Gotcha."

"By the way, I noticed the point spread for Sunday's game is going down again. The oddsmakers must know something. Keep your eyes and ears open."

"Will do."

Chapter 44

✳ ✳ ✳

Michael remembered the first time he had been to the Ireland farm. It was soon after he and Annie had returned from their Hawaiian honeymoon. They had spent a couple of days unwinding at their place before Annie decided she would drive up to the farm and spend a quiet evening alone with her father. Michael would drive up the next day. Annie had wanted her father to know how happy she was and how her mother would have approved. She wanted her dad to know how much she loved her new husband. How smart he was. How considerate he was.

It had been a hot summer day, and it hadn't rained around Santa Rosa in weeks. The grapes in the fields looked thirsty. Michael was humming and tapping his fingers on the steering wheel as he approached the farmhouse. What he knew of Jesse Ireland, he liked. He was eager to get to know his father-in-law a little better and, hopefully, impress him.

He was also anxious to be with his bride again after going twenty-four hours without seeing her. He hoped their bedroom wouldn't be too close to Jesse's. Annie and Michael hadn't had anything close to a fight yet, so they wouldn't be able to call it makeup sex. Or could they? Making-up-for-no-sex-last-night sex?

He remembered how he had screeched to a stop on the circular drive just as Jesse was coming out of the barn. He remembered the cloud of dust that had followed the Jeep and how it had settled over his father-in-law's face.

Welcome to the country, son.

Now, on Thanksgiving Day, it was cool and cloudy, with a chance of sprinkles later in the afternoon. Michael drove up the lane slowly, not for fear of creating dust, but out of trepidation. Annie hadn't returned his messages. How would she act when she saw him? What about Jesse? Would they even let him stay for dinner?

Michael pulled into the drive and parked the Jeep. He opened the door and let Scooter jump out over his lap. The dog barked happily a couple of times and looked around for signs of life. Finding none, she bounded for the front door of the farmhouse. *Good scout.* Who can be mad when there's a friendly dog wagging its tail at you?

Michael was halfway up the walk when the front opened. *Jesse.*

"Hello, Michael. Glad you could make it." He bent down and scratched Scooter's ear.

Seems cordial enough, Michael thought. "Hey, Jesse. Ah…happy Thanksgiving." Michael raised a bouquet of flowers and a bottle of wine as a salute. Michael had been bringing a bottle of wine for Jesse ever since his first Thanksgiving dinner at the Ireland farm. Michael had been uncomfortable bringing wine to someone who made it for a living, but Annie had convinced him it was perfectly acceptable. And it was. In fact, it became a tradition at the dinner table for Jesse to do a blind taste test of the wine that Michael brought before anybody could raise a fork. Jesse would carefully sip the wine, nod, and then give his assessment.

"Fruity…opulent…toasty…silky…unoaked…earthy. A chateau de blah, I would guess." More often than not, he was right on the money.

Jesse acknowledged Michael's salute and waved him into the house. "Scooter, you stay outside for now."

As soon as Michael stepped inside the foyer, he smelled the aroma of cooking in the kitchen. "Mmm, smells delicious," he said. *So far, so good.*

"We put the turkey in early," Jesse said. "Should be ready in an hour or so."

With his heart in his throat, Michael followed Jesse through the living room, past the dining area, and into the kitchen. Empty. An L-shaped granite countertop jutted out into the far end of the kitchen, with a stool on either side of it. The family room beyond the counter was void of humans as well. There was kindling and wood in the fireplace, ready for a match. The flat-screen television was dark. There didn't seem to be anybody else in the house. If Annie and Sadie were upstairs, they were being very quiet.

"Annie and Sadie should be back anytime now," Jesse said, as if reading Michael's mind. "They just went up to Joaquin's. He's got a new puppy now, you know?"

"No, ah…I didn't know."

"Yeah, cute little shit," Jesse said as he took the flowers from Michael and laid them in the sink. He looked at the bottle of wine in Michael's hand. "Should that be chilled?" As per tradition, the bottle's label had been taped over.

"Yeah, I'll—"

All of a sudden, they heard squealing and laughter coming from outside. Both men turned to the kitchen window and saw

Sadie barreling through the backyard gate. She was chasing a light-colored, floppy-eared, mongrel puppy, who in turn was chasing Scooter. When they all got to the middle of the lawn, they started running in a circle. After about three laps, Scooter tired, stopped running, and rolled over on her back. The puppy pounced on Scooter, who playfully used all four feet to push her attacker off. Sadie rolled on the ground with them, giggling in delight.

Unfortunately, the puppy, as puppies will do, became too aggressive and nipped Scooter where he shouldn't have. Scooter ended the playing with a sharp snarl and bared her teeth at the puppy. Sadie jumped up and spanked Scooter on the nose. "No, Scooter! Bad dog! Bad dog!"

Michael hustled to the family room slider door and let himself out. "Sadie! Don't do that!"

Sadie snapped her head around and saw her father coming toward her. "Daddy! Scooter bit Amigo. Scooter bit him!"

"No, she didn't, sweetheart. I saw it. It's okay. Scooter didn't hurt him. The puppy has to learn. They're just being dogs."

Sadie hung her head and looked as if she was about to cry.

Michael knelt in front of his daughter. "Hey, Pumpkin, it's okay. They'll be playing with each other again soon, you just watch."

"What's going on?" Michael looked up and saw his wife standing by the gate. Joaquin stood behind her. He was smiling. She wasn't.

"Oh, hey!" Michael stood up and faked a smile. He glanced down at the puppy. "New dog, huh?"

Annie brushed past him and took Sadie by the hand. "Come on, honey. Let's get cleaned up; then we'll check on the turkey."

At least I haven't been run off yet, Michael thought. *It looks like I'm staying for dinner, anyway.*

Joaquin was still standing by the gate, still smiling, when Jesse hollered from the kitchen window, "You guys want a beer?"

Looks like Joaquin is staying too.

Jesse stood in front of the refrigerator with his hand on the door handle. He looked at Michael and his foreman. "We've got Corona, Bud Lite, and Anchor Steam."

Anchor Steam? That was another good sign. *Did Annie do the shopping?*

Joaquin chose a Corona. Michael went with the Anchor Steam. He resisted the urge to ask if there was a chilled glass that came with it.

"There's an opener in that drawer," Jesse said to Michael as he popped the top on a can of Budweiser.

Jesse raised his Budweiser. "Salud!"

Joaquin answered, "Bueno suerte!"

Michael hesitated, and then shrugged, "Yeah. Si."

The three men were still standing in front of the refrigerator when Annie and Sadie entered the kitchen. "Shoo! All men out of the kitchen, now," Annie ordered.

Jesse and Joaquin turned and ambled off toward the family room. Michael followed them for a few steps but stopped at the edge of the kitchen counter. He set his beer down and pulled up a stool on the family room side so he could face the kitchen. Behind him, he could hear Jesse and Joaquin talking about wine production.

Annie had the oven door open and was poking the turkey. Sadie was standing by her side, watching with great interest. Annie jabbed the bird once more and said, "Sweetie, would you get the silverware out of the drawer for me?"

Michael jumped up. "Sure. Which drawer?"

For the first time that day, Annie looked directly at him. He had seen that look before, only this time, Annie wasn't dripping wet with beer.

Sadie stood where she was and looked at her mother, then at her father. When neither said anything, she said, "I know where it is, Daddy. I know." She skipped over to the silverware drawer. "You know what else, Daddy?"

Michael sat back down.

"No, what else, Pumpkin?"

"Joaquin is going to let me ride his horse."

This time it was Michael shooting a look at Annie. "Whoa, wait a minute. What's this all about?"

Annie closed the oven door and wiped her hands on a dish towel. "Joaquin has offered to show Sadie how to ride, that's all."

Michael stole a glance at the family room, but both Joaquin and Jesse were engrossed in conversation. "She's a little young, don't you think?" Michael said, looking back at Annie. "She could get hurt."

Annie's pained smile looked as if she had just sucked on a lemon. "Well, you know a good doctor, don't you? I notice that you're not even limping."

"Annie, look, I need to talk to—"

"I won't get hurt, Daddy, I promise." Sadie's had her hands full of silverware and did a quick pirouette as if to prove her agility.

Michael looked at his daughter and let out his breath. He couldn't help but smile at her innocence. He remembered what Jesse had said about Sadie that day in the barn. He thought of the NBA player who had changed his name to World Peace. Of course, *he* was an idiot. If there was anybody on the planet who could exemplify the true meaning of harmony, Sadie Fletcher was a much better example.

"Okay, honey, we'll talk about it later." Michael looked at Annie. "Maybe after dinner, okay?

Chapter 45

* * *

When the call to eat was made, everybody shuffled into the dining room and gathered by the long oak table, waiting for seating instructions. Annie brought the turkey out of the kitchen and placed it in the center of the table.

The antique table was exquisitely adorned with all the usual suspects: green bean casserole, mashed potatoes, gravy, cranberry slices, a three-bean salad, and of course, the turkey.

"Wow, look at that, would you?" Joaquin said, obviously impressed.

"I set the table!" Sadie said proudly.

"Where do you want me?" Jesse asked Annie.

"Here," she said, and patted a seat. "Your usual, Dad. Head of the table."

Jesse Ireland pulled out a chair and sat with his back to the window. Annie quickly sat down next to her father and motioned for the others to sit. Before Michael could make a move, Joaquin took the seat next to her.

"I wanna sit by Grandpa!" Sadie jumped into the other seat next to Jesse.

Michael felt like the loser in musical chairs.

After Jesse delivered his critique of the wine, it was time for another tradition: holding hands in a silent prayer. All thoughts would be on Janice Ireland. With Sadie's hand in his left and Annie's in his right, Jesse bowed his head. It was the signal for others at the table to do the same. Sadie quickly reached to her left for her father's hand and Michael instinctively reached to his left for…Joaquin's?

For Michael, it was an uncomfortable twenty seconds before Jesse proclaimed, "Amen."

Annie quickly dabbed her eyes with her napkin and then reached for the turkey. "Okay. Let's eat."

Everybody began passing plates and filling up their own. During the first part of dinner, conversation was light and centered on Sadie. When Joaquin asked her what she wanted to be when she grew up, she said, "A cowboy!"

Annie and Joaquin immediately looked at each other and burst out laughing. Annie briefly laid her head on his shoulder as if they were sharing an inside joke. From where Michael was sitting, it looked as if Annie's eyes were sparkling as much as Joaquin's teeth.

Michael tried to join the conversation and levity.

"Are you sure you don't want to be a cow*girl*, Sadie? You know, so all the cow*boys* will chase after you? Heh, heh."

Michael might have just as well have farted at the table.

Sadie looked puzzled. Finally she looked up at her father and said, "No, Daddy. I wanna be a cowboy, like Joaquin."

It got very quiet around the table. Everyone suddenly became interested in their food. After a few moments of silent eating, Jesse cleared his throat. "So…eh, Michael. How's the job coming?

Must be pretty exciting being around all those football players and sports stars, huh?"

Michael's respect for his father-in-law moved up another notch.

"Well, it's definitely keeping me busy, that's for sure," Michael said. "I'm flying to Phoenix tomorrow with the team. Some big games coming up for the Niners."

Michael's words hung in the air. Nobody added to them. Again, the only sounds from the dining room were the clinking of silverware. Michael looked to his left. "You like football, Joaquin?"

"Yes, I do, but—"

Michael saw a chance to redeem himself in his daughter's eyes.

"Well, I tell you what, my friend, if you'd like to go to a Forty-Niners game, I'm pretty sure I can score you a couple of tickets." Michael was just blowing smoke. If he had to, he'd buy the tickets.

The foreman rubbed his jaw and squirmed. "Oh, thank you, but I meant I like *futball*—you know, soccer? That's what we play in Mexico. Soccer." Joaquin flashed his pearly white smile at Michael. "It's not as brutal as American football."

Michael stared at the young Mexican. He wanted to scream, *So, what do you call torturing and killing bulls on Sundays? A day at the beach?*

Instead, a breath or two later, Michael tried to match Joaquin's smile, "Oh…sure. But have you ever been to an NFL football game?" he asked.

Joaquin's smile faded as he touched the scar above his left eye.

"I'm afraid I have. Oakland Stadium. The Raiders were playing the Chargers."

"And…?"

Joaquin looked around the table, not sure if he should continue. Finally, he looked back at Michael and said, "It wasn't a good experience."

Michael didn't like the way the conversation had turned, but he was in too far now to disengage gracefully. "In what way, may I ask?"

Annie eyed Michael, and then jumped in. "Maybe he doesn't want to talk about it, Michael. Not everyone has to like sports, you know?" The sparkle in her eyes was gone.

"No, it's okay." Joaquin put down his knife and fork. "After the game, as my brother and I were leaving the stadium, a couple of drunk Raiders fans jumped us in the parking lot. They took exception to the Chargers hat I was wearing. Probably not the smartest thing to do—wearing the hat, I mean."

"No, probably not," Michael agreed.

"That's ridiculous," Annie looked at Michael. "You should be able to wear any damn hat, or anything else you want to, without getting beat up for it. That's as bad as being in a gang."

"No, I can't argue with you there, but—"

"Professional sports is getting more out of whack all the time," Annie continued. "Every day we hear about some jillionaire jock being arrested for something. Did you know that an NFL player is arrested every four point eight days? And it's not just DUIs anymore. Did you know that?"

At least she's talking to me. "Wait a minute. Where did you hear that, about an NFL player getting arrested every four-point-something days?"

"I read it somewhere…I think."

Annie folded her arms against her chest and glared at Michael. "It's no wonder there's all those drunken Neanderthals in the stands these days. Look who their role models are!"

Before things could escalate further, Jesse stepped in again. "I think the problem is, those Neanderthals are probably drinking cheap wine." He held up his glass and admired it. "If they had any sense, they'd been drinking a fine Cabernet from Ireland's Acres." He smiled at Michael. "How 'bout some more turkey, son?"

The rest of the meal went without anyone speaking of sports. Just as dessert was being served, Michael's phone chirped from his pants pocket. Nobody seemed to notice, so he discreetly took a peek. It was a text from Bo. "Did you see that catch by Jonston?" Bo would seldom abbreviate anything, even in text.

Michael assumed Bo was talking about the Detroit Lions' wide receiver, Errol Jonston. He was about the only bright spot on an otherwise dismal team. Michael wondered if Bo was at Sal's or at home alone watching football. He almost envied his boss.

After dinner, Michael tried to get Annie alone several times, but each time, she brushed him off. "Not now, Michael, please. Let's not spoil Thanksgiving, okay?"

Michael knew when he was beat. He hung around for another thirty minutes, and then thanked his host and said his good-byes. He hugged his daughter and promised to visit again soon.

Nobody seemed to notice when Scooter followed him to the Jeep and jumped in.

Chapter 46

✳ ✳ ✳

Friday afternoon at 3:30 sharp, fifty-three football players, five coaches, three trainers, three equipment managers, one travel coordinator, and Michael began boarding a chartered Boeing 737 at San Francisco airport for the flight to Phoenix. By design, the travel coordinator, a pretty, red-headed gal named Suzy, was the first to board the aircraft through the forward cabin. She had a briefcase in one hand and a carry-on slung over her shoulder. Michael had been instructed to follow her and did so as she made her way to the aft section.

"Back of the bus for us, huh?" he said lightly.

Suzy laughed and said over her shoulder, "Yeah. It gets a little bumpy back here, but we've got the last rows to ourselves, lots of room to work, if you want...plus, we're close to the bathrooms."

When she reached the last row, she stopped, set her briefcase down on a middle seat to her right, and popped open the overhead bin. She gestured to Michael to make himself comfortable in the seats across the aisle from her.

After stowing his gear, Michael sat down, leaned over the aisle seat, and watched the rest of the team come aboard. He wasn't surprised to see that there weren't any linemen heading his way. He had been briefed earlier that the big boys sat in first class. "Have to have wide seats for wide loads," Kimble had said. Of course, with almost eight tons of human flesh aboard, it also made sense to have the beef in front of the aircraft. It would help keep the plane from stalling.

There was another unwritten rule, probably unwritten by a lineman, that punters and place-kickers weren't allowed to sit in an emergency exit seat. The running joke was, in case of trouble, it would be best if the person sitting in that seat was actually strong enough to open the door in an emergency. Of course, if the place-kicker had hit a fifty-yarder with no time left on the clock to win a game, he could sit wherever he wanted to on the flight home. He could probably fly the damn plane if he wanted to.

An hour into the flight, Michael got up from his seat and started up the aisle, notebook in hand. He was hoping to talk with a few of the players whom he hadn't spoken to yet, maybe get a nugget or two that he could use later.

The mood throughout the aircraft was light but not reckless, more one of subdued confidence. Coaches mingled with their respective players, drawing a few laughs and going over different game scenarios. The time for screaming and pounding each others' helmets would come soon enough.

Michael was halfway up the aisle when a flight attendant emerged from the forward cabin rolling a beverage cart his way. Michael spotted an empty row of seats by the emergency exit and ducked in to let her pass. When she stopped to serve a couple of players, he sat down and waited.

He was looking at his notes when he overheard parts of the conversation directly in front of him. Two of the trainers were discussing last week's game.

"We'd have won that game if Deck...Buffalo got lucky... could've stopped.... Tommie played well enough, but...Decker was the player everyone looked...accident..."

When he heard "shot," Michael leaned forward.

"...it was unintentional. The guy shot himself too, you know. Almost funny now, but the way Decker played after the incident, I think it bothered him more than he let on."

"What was funny was how he tried to hide his wound. Put some sort of makeup on it, I think. Like we wouldn't notice?"

"Yeah, no shit. Jackson said he kept his ankle bandaged while he was on his boat, but he made sure to take it off before going ashore."

"Speaking of tape, I think that new stuff they sent us is shit..."

The conversation shifted to trainer speak, and Michael sat back in his seat. Something buzzed around in his head. *Something about Decker. Something about a bandage.* Then it hit him. The conversation he'd had with Scott on the couch at his house. *Kinda hard to hide an injury if the player's sporting bandages.* He wondered if he should bring up the subject with the trainers, but in the end, he decided against it. He was slowly gaining some trust and rapport with the players and coaching staff, and they had already voiced their desire to move on. *Decker is dead. Let him rest in peace.*

When the aisle was clear, Michael felt free to move about the cabin and did so. He chatted up a few players but kept the conversations brief. He didn't want to distract anyone from their preparations and thought that he would be able to gain more insights on the flight home, especially if they won. Players would let their guards down more after a win. They would all weigh less. He envisioned some dancing on their toes like a young Muhammad Ali.

By the time the plane touched down in Phoenix, Michael was feeling pretty good about himself and the team's chances of ending their two-game losing streak.

* * *

By the time the game started at 1:25 p.m. the next day, San Francisco was still the favorite, giving seven and a half points.

By the time the game ended three and a half hours later, San Francisco didn't have any points to give anybody. They'd gotten their butts kicked and were shut out, seventeen-zero. Their record had fallen to seven-five. To make matters worse, two of their starting offensive linemen had suffered serious injuries.

The postgame interview with McCaffy was short and not sweet. Basically, it consisted of, "We didn't execute on offense and missed assignments on defense. Thank you. Goodnight."

And the personal equity that Michael might have gained on the flight to Phoenix all but disappeared on the trip home. No one offered much as to why the team was in a slide, but when Michael asked one of the wide receivers the question, his answer was, "All I know for sure is, we haven't won a game since you started writing about us. Maybe you're the reason we're losing."

The man was obviously joking…wasn't he?

And then another player chipped in, "Yeah, Maybe you're a cooler."

"A cooler?"

"Yeah. Like in that movie, with, oh, what's his name…great actor…uh…Macy. Yeah, William Macy."

This got the attention of a player across the aisle. He looked up from his magazine and leaned over. "I saw that flick. Really good. Macy works in a Las Vegas casino as a cooler, a guy who's such a loser, the joint pays him to stand close to anyone who starts winning a lot. Right?"

"That's it. No shit."

A cooler. Hmmm. Sumbitch.

The somber flight home was made even worse by the news that the Seattle Seahawks had won their game and were now leading the West Division by two games.

Now, with only four games remaining in the regular season, the Niners would probably have to win out to extend their season…and Michael's career in sportswriting.

Chapter 47

* * *

Monday morning arrived with a chill and light mist in the air. From his bedroom, Michael heard the neighborhood coming to life. A car door slammed, and an engine started. The newspaper hit the driveway. *Thwunk.* A dog barked. Commuters were stirring, but Michael made no move to join them. He had stayed up late writing his piece for Bo and now planned to stay in bed as long as Scooter would let him. He hadn't slept well, and bits of dreams still skittered through his brain. *Cooler! A loser! Why don't you go out to the Golden Gate and judge some dives? You ever have to identify a body? Ambulance chaser!*

When he finally did roll out of bed, he took care of Scooter, and then started for the bathroom. That's when he noticed some things were missing from the house: Annie's hats from the rack by the back door. An umbrella. The two cookbooks by the stove. A shawl. Annie had been there...or they'd been robbed by a very strange burglar. He checked Sadie's room, and some of her things were gone, too.

He called Annie but got her voicemail. He left a message for her to call him. He was still in damage-control mode and was anxious to see if the situation had thawed at all.

Finally, he went out, picked up the paper, and brought it inside. With coffee and toast as his companions, he sat at the kitchen table and opened to the sports pages. An Associated Press piece was headlined, "Forty-Niners Lose Third Straight. Playoff Picture Cloudy."

No shit.

Four weeks left in the season. Four weeks left in the year. Four weeks left to write a story…to write the *story about…whatever.*

He was thinking about driving up to the farm when his phone rang.

"Mike? Bo here. Hey, listen, we didn't get a chance to talk much about the game last night or how your flight was. Any chance you could come by Sal's tonight? About five?"

"Sure. No problem."

"Good. There's some other things I'd like to talk to you about in person."

* * *

There were the usual number of customers scattered throughout Sal's when Michael walked in. A few of the regulars sat in their designated stools at the bar, arguing mildly about something. Red was ringing up some totals at the cash register. Michael was surprised to see Len Wrighton seated with Bo at one of the tables in the back room. As Michael passed by the bar, Red looked up into the mirror. "Hey, Mike. Can I bring you an Anchor Steam?"

"Oh, yeah, sure. Thanks, Red."

Wrighton and Bo were engaged in what looked like a serious conversation and didn't notice Michael as he approached their table.

"That's bullshit, Lenny, and you know it." Bo had an unlit cigar stub in his right hand, pointed at Wrighton. He had his left hand around a half-full Rob Roy.

"Well, Bo, you *are* an expert in bullsh—" Wrighton stopped and smiled when he saw Michael. "Oh. Hello, Michael. You're just in time. Please, sit. "

Michael pulled out a chair and sat. He waited for the two men to resume their conversation, but they just looked at him without saying anything.

"What? Did I interrupt something?" he asked.

Bo waved his cigar in the air. "No, no. Nothing new, anyway, Mike. I was just putting up with this old fart's usual tirade. He's antisports, you know. Be careful what you say around him."

Wrighton lifted a martini glass to his lips, took a sip and smiled. "I am *not* antisports, and you know it," he said softly. "Sports are fine. In fact, I'd like to see more kids involved in sports, especially with all the talk about child obesity these days. Let 'em run around the playground and burn off all the fat they can."

Bo pointed his cigar stub at Wrighton again. "We weren't talking about playground stuff, Lenny. We were talkin' about professional sports and your disdain for it. What happened to you, Lenny? You used to be interested in what was goin' on in the sports world."

Wrighton raised an eyebrow. "My disdain, dear comrade, isn't for sports per se; it's for the way our society is evolving around sports. We're sending our kids the wrong message by paying athletes tremendous salaries while tolerating their indiscretions."

"Wow, you sound like my wife," Michael said, and then immediately regretted saying it.

The conversation stopped momentarily as Red arrived at the table and placed a chilled beer glass in front of Michael. The bartender poured half the bottle of Anchor Steam into the glass, forming a perfect head of foam, set the bottle down, and then slipped away.

"Wait a minute, my friend," Bo said to Wrighton. "Indiscretions? You've told me that when you were growing up, your favorite baseball player was Mickey Mantle."

"That's true. He was, but—"

"But nothing, Lenny. Unless you're talkin' about the butt Mantle used to chase around when he was playing ball. He *was* a married man, you know. And the booze and partying? Mantle would be so hung over on game days, the Yankee trainer had to pump him full of amphetamines just so he could find center field. You don't think players had indiscretions in your day? Ha!"

Wrighton nodded acquiescently. "Your point is well taken, sir. However, if you'll indulge me, you've provided an opportunity for me to make a point, to wit: in 1965, Mickey Mantle was the highest-paid player in baseball. He made one hundred thousand dollars, and—"

"Which probably seemed like an ungodly amount at the time, right?" Bo interjected.

Wrighton raised his index finger, imploring Bo to shut the hell up for a second. "And," he continued, "bread cost thirty cents a loaf, stamps a nickel, newspaper a dime. Gasoline was about thirty-two cents a gallon, and a new car was around twenty-five-hundred dollars. You could park that new twenty-five-hundred dollar car in the garage of a new twenty-five-thousand dollar house."

Bo couldn't resist. "Is it gonna take you another twenty-five minutes to make your point? I gotta pee."

Wrighton deadpanned a look at Michael. "When you tire of your servitude to this Neanderthal, please come see me. It would be a pleasure to work with someone other than a half-wit."

Michael smiled diplomatically and sipped his beer. He realized that there were three generations of opinions seated at the table.

"Okay, oh wise one," Bo muttered, and waved a hand. "Please, do continue."

"Thank you." Wrighton acknowledged Bo but kept his eyes on Michael. "Now, if you multiply the example prices of the 1965 commodities I gave you by the power of ten, you'll see that most of those would fit into today's range of prices. For example, if you multiply the price of a loaf of bread in 1965 times ten, you get three dollars, which is about the cost of a loaf of bread today, right? Do the same with gasoline and you'll get three dollars plus for a gallon. Somewhat low in today's economy, maybe, but you get the picture. Same with 1965 car and house prices. Twenty-five thousand sounds about right for a car today, and if you lived anywhere but San Francisco, you could probably find adequate housing for two hundred fifty thousand dollars."

Wrighton paused and looked back at Bo. "I only use the power of ten formula to help those with multiplication issues."

Bo snorted. "Fuck you and your formula, Professor. Make your point."

"My point is, most things have risen equally across the board since 1965. The glaring exceptions? Professional athletes' salaries. Multiply Mantle's '65 salary times ten and you get one million dollars. Nice salary, you say? Sure it is, unless you compare that to the two hundred and seventy-five million the Yankees were paying Alex Rodriguez. Two hundred and seventy-five million!

I'm not sure what the length of his contract was, but still, that's an absurd amount of money to pay a grown man to play a game. It took Mantle all season to make one hundred thousand dollars. Rodriguez made that in two times at bat, for Christ's sake."

Wrighton's countenance had morphed into that of a cranky Morly Safer. "You want another example?" Wrighton said as he pushed his drink aside. "How about Joe Namath? You remember him, right? Well, I had just begun working at the paper when 'Broadway Joe' was arguably the best quarterback in the pros. I think he signed a three -ear contract for four hundred seventy-five thousand dollars. Again, a nice wage at the time, but tell me, Mister Sports Editor, how does that compare to, hmmm, let's say Peyton Manning's remuneration of close to twenty million a year?"

"I'm not sure, but I bet you can tell us." Bo tilted his head back and drained the last of his Rob Roy.

"You bet I can." Wrighton took out his smarter-than-hell phone and punched in some numbers. Five silent seconds later, he laid the phone on the table. "Twenty-eight thousand," he said smugly.

Bo took the bait. "Twenty-eight thousand what?"

"Twenty-eight thousand dollars. That's roughly what Manning made each time he attempted a forward pass in 2013."

Wrighton picked up his phone again, punched in something else, and then declared, "Actually, based on an average of thirty-five passes a game, it comes to twenty-eight thousand, five hundred seventy-one dollars and forty-two cents per attempt. Not completions, mind you. Attempts."

Wrighton looked across the table at his coworkers. "That sounds reasonable, doesn't it, boys? I mean, the thirty-five passes per game average, that is."

Chapter 48

※ ※ ※

Michael's intentions were good when he offered to buy Len Wrighton another drink; he just wasn't aware that in all the years the reporter had been coming into Sal's, the man never had more than two drinks during any one visit. He remained true to that tradition when he politely refused the offer and made it clear it was time for him to head home.

"There is a perception in our society that all of the great writers of our time have been of the character to take a drink from time to time," Wrighton said as he stood up from the table. "Having had mine, I'll bid you gentlemen adieu."

Bo and Michael said their good-nights to Wrighton, and then watched in silence as the venerable writer glided past the bar and out the door.

After a moment, Bo looked at Michael and nodded toward the bar. "Let's get closer to greatness, shall we?"

Red wordlessly acknowledged their move with two fresh drinks seconds after Bo and Michael scooted their stools into position.

"Well, I guess you pushed Mr. Wrighton's hot button, huh?" Michael said.

"He's got his opinions, that's for sure." Bo laughed. "He's also got a tremendous memory, and he's a stickler for stats. He could probably tell you exactly how much he weighed at birth and how many inches long he was. Probably tell you how long his wee-wee was, too. He did bring up some valid points about salaries and such, but the bastard always leaves before I can counterpunch with the positive side of sports. Charities, scholarships, teamwork… but, hell, I'm preaching to the choir, right? You know."

They chatted awhile about Wrighton, and then Michael cut to the chase.

"You said you wanted to talk to me about the game and some other stuff. What's up?"

Bo fidgeted with the stem of his glass. "Brenda has been recovering faster than anybody thought she would. She'll probably be able to come back to work in a couple of weeks."

"Oh?"

"Yeah, before the end of the football season."

"So I'm out of a job pretty soon?"

"Maybe. We'll have to sorta play that by ear. But for now, figure on covering the beat just like you've been doing."

Michael took a deep breath and stared at his beer.

"Look, Mike, you've done a great job for us. You've got your foot in the door now, and you can put the *Chronicle* on your resume, if it comes to that. I just wanted to prepare you, okay?"

"Thanks. I appreciate everything you've done for me. For giving me a shot."

"Yeah, well, you're welcome. But listen, you're not done yet. I've got a couple of other assignments in mind for you while you're still on the payroll."

"Really?"

"Yeah, the boss likes the features you've done for us. She also liked your stuff on concussions in the NFL and the pending settlement."

Michael gave Kimble a doubtful look and said, "Well, 'pending' is the key word there. Some of the victims' families are suing for more than what the NFL is offering. Especially the families that lost loved ones due to suicide."

"Like Junior Seau."

"Yep. Like Junior Seau. The autopsy on his brain showed CTE."

Kimble shook his head in sympathy and said, "The sad thing is the number of other cases like Seau's. Remember Jovan Belcher, the former Kansas City Chiefs linebacker, who fatally shot his twenty-two-year-old girlfriend and then later shot and killed himself in front of one of his coaches? They say he suffered CTE damage too.

"So I'm guessing there'll be lawsuits up the yin-yang. Who knows, maybe Decker's family will sue. You know, they could claim he took too many shots to the head and couldn't remember the consequences of barbequing indoors. Hell, O.J. Simpson's lawyers coulda said, 'His head took the hits, you must acquits.'"

"Acquits?" Michael laughed. "You think Red's gonna let you drive home tonight?"

Kimble smiled. "Okay, bad joke."

"Well, if anybody is thinking of suing professional football," Michael said, "they should be aware that the NFL's settlement will not compensate any player diagnosed with CTE before January 1, 2006, or after July 7, 2014."

"Good eye, me boy," Kimble said. "That's why I'd like you to dig into it some more. All this has been in the news, of course, but not to the degree I think it should or could be. Are there things about this story that are being left out? I dunno, but see what else you can come up with, okay?

"And you might include what Brett Favre said recently, you know, about how if he had a son, he didn't think he'd want him playing football. Bob Costas said something like that too. Course, Favre may have taken too many knocks to the noggin along the way himself."

Michael gave it some thought, and when Kimble didn't say anything more, he asked, "Think we should look at high school and college football some more too?"

"Couldn't hurt. Brenda might be able to help with some of the research; she's already working on some stuff for me about the next big scandal in the NFL, which most likely will be about painkiller abuse."

"Painkillers, huh?"

"Oh, yeah, big time. But that's another story. Right now, see if you can find any more on concussions and the settlement."

"Sure. How soon you want this?"

"As soon as you can. I think there's a movie in the works about all this stuff; maybe we can steal some of their thunder."

"Okay, I'll do what I can."

"Thanks, Mike."

Bo took a quick drink, looked around the bar, and then leaned in close to Michael. "You ever dig up anything on Weinstein?"

"No, but I must admit, I haven't really spent a lot of time on it. Kinda wish I had've, though." Michael took a long drink of beer and said, "Maybe I should just go up to the asshole and say, 'Excuse me, Mr. Winefuck, are you involved in any hanky-panky in the Bay Area? The good folks at the *Chronicle* suspect you might be involved in a tots-n'-tort program. Would you care to comment on that?'"

Bo faked a serious thought for a moment. "Hmmm…I like it. Maybe you should leave the paper out of it for now, though."

Michael laughed. "And maybe I should just leave this bar for now, before I come up with any more crazy ideas."

"Did you ever ask Dr. Scott about Weinstein?"

Michael's expression froze into a drunk-staring-into-a-cop's-flashlight look.

Bo smiled. "Don't worry, I don't think she's involved in anything, ah…you know, shady. But I got the impression from you that she was kinda chummy with Weinstein."

Michael shook his head so hard his eyeballs couldn't keep up. "According to her, there's nothing there. Just some nice donations for her work from time to time."

"And you believe her because…?"

"Cologne."

"Huh?"

"Cologne. *His* cologne. He slathers it on. She says she hates that."

Bo took a moment to think about it. "That'd do it, all right. Why do guys do that?"

Michael smiled and sipped his beer.

"Anyway," Bo continued, "I'm thinking while you're working on the football injuries story, you could interview Dr. Scott, find out if kids are getting hurt more than the general public knows about. Get her opinion on things."

Michael nodded. "Hmmm, that's a good idea."

"I thought you'd like it." Bo grinned.

"And while I'm at it, you want me to get whatever information I can on Weinstein, right?"

"Subtly, of course."

"Of course."

Chapter 49

The following week, Michael was fully engrossed in his research when his cell phone rang. It was Dan Kelly.

"Hi, Mikey, D.K. here."

"Yeah, Dan. What's up?

"That's what I wanna to ask you. What the fuck's up with the Niners, man? I can understand them losin' a little on the defense, but they're stinkin' it up in every department now. What's goin' on?"

For a second, Michael thought about telling Kelly that he would most likely be out of a job soon, but decided against it. "It might be my fault, Dan."

"What?"

"You ever hear of someone being a cooler?"

"What's a cooler?"

"Someone who's such a loser that he brings everyone around him down."

Kelly laughed. "There you go again, my friend, bein' a funny son of a bitch."

"Yeah, well, that's just a theory. I was really just—"

"So, wait a minute....you're sayin I should be betting against the Niners? Or just taking the under?"

"Like I said Dan, they've had some injuries."

"Yeah, yeah, yeah. The old injury card. Bullshit."

Michael was just about to hang up when he had a thought. "Say, Dan, how old is your boy? How long has he been playing football?"

"What? My boy? He's twelve. Be thirteen next August. What's that got to do with anything?"

"Just wondering. You ever worry about him getting hurt?"

"Naw, he's tough. In fact, he got his bell rung pretty good the last game of the season, but still didn't want to come out of the game. He was kinda woozy for a couple of days afterward, but like I say, he's tough. He'll be in shape for summer tryouts, I guarantee you that."

"You take him to a doctor?"

"Oh God, no. It wasn't that bad. You get knocked down, you get back up. Simple business. Besides, I don't want people thinkin' my kid is injury prone, you know."

"What does your wife think?"

"She doesn't. She drinks. We've been divorced for a couple of years now. I got custody of the kid."

When Michael didn't say anything, Kelly asked again, "So, anyway, my man, how do you see it playing out next Sunday? With San Fran, I mean?"

Michael sighed and said slowly, "Well, Dan, you know what they say, 'On any given Sunday...'"

"Hmmm, are you saying Jacksonville has a chance?"

"Jesus, Dan. I'm not saying—"

"Okay, okay. I think I get your drift. Well, anyway, I better let you go. Thanks, Mikey. I'll talk to you later."

Michael held his phone out and looked at it like Aristotle contemplating Homer.

Drift?

What drift Kelly was talking about, Michael had no idea. He also had no idea why a father wouldn't take his injured son to see a doctor.

With that thought in mind, Michael punched in Dr. Scott's number. His call went to voicemail, so he began to leave a message asking Scott if she'd like to get together, maybe for coffee or lunch or something. Talk some therapy. Then, thinking it sounded too much like a date, he tried to mitigate what he'd just said, mumbled something about football injuries and kids, and in the end, left a rambling, awkward, message.

Damn it, Michael thought after he tapped his phone off. *Why can't someone invent a take-back device that lets you redial and erase what you just said if you want? To be fair, there could be a time limit on it, say, like, ten minutes. If you change your mind about something you've said or want to delete something, you have ten minutes to do so. Hmmm…*

Michael was still contemplating his invention when his phone jarred him back to reality. It occurred to him that he still hadn't changed his ringtone.

"Hi Michael, it's Laurie. I was on the other line when you called. What's up?"

Oh, good. Maybe she'll just delete the message.

"Bo has asked me to do a feature series about football injuries in the NFL, mostly involving concussions. As you know, it's a hot subject right now, and I'd like to follow up with what's goin' on in kid's sports as far as injuries go. I'd like your opinion, you know, from the physical therapy side of things."

"Well, I'm not an expert on head injuries, but if I can help in any way, I'd be happy to do so."

"Good. Would you have time to meet with me? Ah, you know, at your convenience..."

"Sure. I'd love to, Michael. I'm looking at my calendar right now. Hmmm...what about tomorrow? My last appointment is at two-thirty. Would you like to meet here, at my office, at threeish?"

"Sure, works for me."

Michael would be at the Niners' morning practice, and then cover the Wednesday media day interview session. He figured if McCaffy didn't run practice past the usual two and a half hours, he should be able to be at Scott's office by three.

As soon as he hung up the phone, Michael began jotting down ideas on how he would bring Winestein into the conversation the next day. He would probably start with the stats he had dug up about football injuries to kids and wing it from there.

At some point, he would most likely tell Scott about his job status. Then, while trying to think of other issues he could raise with Scott, Michael's mind wandered back to the last time they had seen each other—the scene at his house. What had been raised with her then. Before the good-guy side of his brain could step in and block out such thoughts, an image of her rust-colored bra popped into his head.

Chapter 50

✳ ✳ ✳

The next day, Michael wrote up a rough draft of his column and was on his way to Scott's office by 2:15 p.m. In contrast to his earlier visit with Scott in her office, when it had been just the two of them, this time was a different story. As soon as Michael walked through the front door, a young girl sitting at the front desk greeted him. Her black hair was clipped short in a Dutch boy. She was wearing a "Save the Whales" T-shirt, and when she spoke, Michael noticed a stud in the middle of her tongue.

"May I help you, sir?"

"Yes, I'm Michael Fletcher. I'm here to see Dr. Scott. I have a threeish appointment."

The girl smiled and jumped up from her desk. "Oh, please have seat. I'll go tell Laurie you're here."

The girl walked down the hall and around the corner. Michael wondered how she kept her stud clean. Maybe she brushed it when she brushed her teeth? And how come she didn't lisp?

Michael walked over to the window that looked out into the workout room. There were at least a dozen people scattered around the room, all engaged in some form of exercise. Their ages could be defined by their hair, from silver and gray to spiked purple. Two women of the gray era churned and chatted away on adjacent treadmills while a weatherman pointed out an occluded front on the flat-screen television above their heads.

Across the room Dr Scott was standing next to a young man who was dressed in shorts and a sweatshirt and holding clipboard. The two of them were closeley watching a girl about twelve-years- old go through some rehab work. Scott looked as if she was ready for a workout as well. She was wearing black and silver Nike workout pants and a blazing red tank top. Black Adidas with three red diagonal stripes powered her feet. Her hair was pulled back in a ponytail.

As Michael stood by the window watching, the girl from the front desk walked over to Scott and the young man. Scott turned an ear to the girl, and after a second, looked over her shoulder and smiled toward the window. She held up five fingers to Michael and mouthed "Five."

Four minutes later, Scott rounded the corner and hurried up to Michael, who was still standing by the window. Her face was flushed. "Hey, Michael. Good to see you."

Before he could respond, she grabbed his hand and said, "Come on, let's sit over here."

She led him to a desk directly behind her receptionist. She pushed out a chair, and then walked behind the desk and flopped down hard on her chair. "Whew! What a day!" She tossed her cell phone onto the desk, raised her arms behind her, and leaned back in her chair. She was in full stretch when her phone shrilled.

Scott slumped forward and looked at the caller ID on the phone. Then she looked at Michael. "Sorry. I need to take this."

Michael stood up and discreetly wandered back over to the window, took out his cell phone, and pretended to listen to it. He put it away when Scott waved him back over.

"Sorry about that," she said. "So, tell me again, what are you writing about? Head injuries? Concussions?"

"Yeah, I'm doing a feature on—"

"Excuse me, Laurie?" It was Whale Girl at the front desk. "Mrs. Callaway is on line one. She wants to reschedule her son for next Friday?"

Scott looked quickly at a calendar on her desk. "Okay," she said loudly. "But we'll have to work him in. We're busy all day. Tell her to have him here by eight-thirty." Then she smiled at Michael. "So, where were we?"

Before he had a chance to answer, another young man with a clipboard walked up to the desk. "Excuse me, Laurie. Mr. Slater thought he was scheduled for a massage today, but Alisa isn't here. You want me to handle it?"

"Deep tissue?"

The young man looked at his board. "No"

"Okay. Take care of it. But be sure to log your time accordingly."

Scott watched the trainer walk away, and then turned back to Michael. A phone rang. Scott leaned forward and drilled her eyes directly into Michael's. "Tequila."

"Excuse me?" Michael blinked.

"Tequila," Scott repeated. "It's five o'clock somewhere, right?"

Scott stood up and grabbed a light jacket that matched her pants from the coat rack behind her desk.

She pulled on an Oakland A's baseball cap and took some dark sunglasses from her purse. She could have passed for a celebrity about to play in a charity softball game.

"Come on," Scott said. "I know a great little place just up the street. Rosie's. They make the best margaritas this side of the border. Plus, they don't care if I'm dressed in my gym jammies or not."

Michael thought she looked fine.

Scott quickly briefed her receptionist, put her arm through Michael's, and waltzed him out the door.

Chapter 51

※ ※ ※

Scott drove the two of them to the restaurant and parked her Caddy on the street almost directly in front of a large, red, neon sign outlining a lovely senorita with a rose between her teeth.

Inside, the lunch crowd had thinned. Only a few couples remained in the high-backed booths that ringed the inside perimeter. Two busboys were busy picking up lunch remnants from the half-dozen empty tables that were situated in the middle of the restaurant. Two men sat at the bar along the far wall, joking with the bartender. Tecate and Corona beer signs decorated the stuccoed walls. Soft Spanish melodies lilted softly through hidden speakers.

A smiling young Mexican waiter in a stylishly wrinkled white shirt appeared and guided Scott and Michael to a booth. According to the name tag on his vest, he was Felix. Felix was either growing his first mustache or had just knocked back some root beer. Scott had her order of margaritas in before the young man could deal out two menus.

After Felix left, Scott and Michael settled in. They looked at each other in silence for a moment. Scott took off her cap and shook out her hair. The large elephant that both of them were trying to ignore had just pulled up a chair.

Finally, Scott tried to address the situation. "So...how was your Thanksgiving, Michael? How is, ah...how's your family?"

Michael nodded, understanding what Scott was really asking. "They're fine, I guess. Annie's still upset about the, um, you know, the scene at my house?"

It was Scott's turn to nod. "I don't blame her."

"Yeah, well, her dad's foreman joined us for dinner. Sadie was there too, of course, and some of the dinner conversation was a little awkward. Annie's dad was cool, though. I'm pretty sure he knows things aren't one hundred percent between Annie and me, but he was a gracious host, and he kept things rolling. A referee at the ready, if you will."

"I take it your wife and her dad are pretty close?"

"Yeah, they're pals. After Annie's mother died, they became even closer."

"That's good that your wife has someone to talk to."

"She's got someone to talk to, all right. In Spanish. His name is Joaquin."

Scott cocked her head. "Joaquin?"

"Yeah. Her dad's foreman."

Michael took a deep breath, and then steered the conversation away from his wife. "But my daughter, Sadie, she's doing well. Growing like a weed. Seems like every time I see her, she's grown six inches. Course, I don't see her every day like I used to."

Felix's timely arrival with chips, salsa, and two margaritas saved the conversation from sliding further south.

* * *

After dipping, sipping, and savoring for a couple of minutes, Scott said, "Okay, Michael. I've regained some of my senses and lost the ones that needed losing. How may I help you?"

Scott seemed relaxed and loose. Michael's plan of subtly working Weinstein into the conversation went right out the window. "How well do you know Carl Weinstein?" he asked.

Scott's demeanor remained unchained. If anything, she seemed amused at the question. "Carl? Why? Is he a terrorist or something?" She sipped her margarita and smiled.

Michael shrugged. "No. Not that I know of. But his brother-in-law isn't exactly Mister Clean, you know."

Scott's facial expression turned quizzical. "No, I don't know. What do you mean?"

When Michael told her the story, Scott was incredulous. "Are you kidding me? These coaches were gambling on their kids' games?"

"Yeah, like I said, it was a huge gambling ring. They operated out of a barbershop in Southern Florida. They bet on everything, including peewee football. I'm sorry, I thought…I thought maybe you knew about it."

Scott looked disappointed. "No, I didn't." She paused for a moment. "You don't think Carl is mixed up in something like that, do you? That's not what you're writing about, is it?"

"No, that happened a long time ago," Michael said as he placed his laptop and yellow legal pad on the table in front of him. "Actually, I won't be writing about too much of anything pretty soon. Bo told me the lady I replaced will be coming back on the job."

"Oh, does that mean…"

"Yes."

"Oh, I'm so sorry, Michael. I know how much it meant to you." She reached over and placed her hand over his. "But will they keep you on? You know, in another capacity?"

"I'm not so sure. I think after I finish these features on football injuries, I'm done."

Neither of them spoke for a minute, and then Michael said, "Of course, if you can give me a really good story, I can still knock their socks off."

Chapter 52

* * *

For the next thirty minutes, Scott sipped a second margarita while Michael sought her opinion on sports injuries to kids, including head trauma and the associated therapy. Scott's acumen on the subject was astonishing. She rattled off statistics from the Centers for Disease Control and Prevention showing a sixty-percent increase over the last decade in children suffering serious head injuries while playing sports or engaged in physical activities.

Although she would preface her comments with "I'm no neurologist," or "I'm hardly an orthopedic doctor, but…," she was quick to respond to all of the issues Michael brought up, including CTE.

"Usually children are not diagnosed with CTE, simply because they haven't been around long enough to take that many hits to the head," she said. "However, a couple of years ago, a seventeen-year-old boy in Ohio died on the football field after making a tackle. His parents graciously allowed an autopsy, and guess what? He was diagnosed with CTE."

Scott took a deep breath before she added, "He might have been young, but if you think about it, he'd already been playing football for ten years."

"What is the medical profession doing, or saying about the situation?"

"Advise and consult…when asked, that is."

"What about spinal injuries to kids playing football?" Michael asked. "Are they increasing? Decreasing? Or can you tell?"

Scott looked thoughtfully at the slush in her glass. She looked at her drink for so long that Michael thought that maybe she hadn't heard the question. Finally, she answered. "Sadly, spinal injuries are increasing as well. You'd think in this day and age, we'd be making progress, but for whatever reason, we're not."

Michael let her words sink in for a moment, and then asked, "Is it the coaching? The training the kids are getting?"

Scott shrugged. "Could be part of it, I suppose. If we have coaches betting on kids' games, who knows?"

When she didn't add anything to her last comment, Michael asked, "What about the parents? Are they pushing too hard? Are they part of the problem?"

"Would you let your daughter play football if she wanted to?"

Michael laughed. "Fortunately, gender raises her pretty head and makes that question moot."

"Not necessarily. There have been occasions when girls were allowed to try out for the football team."

Michael grimaced and dodged the question again. "Yeah, well, in any event, you'll have to ask Sadie's mother. I don't seem to have any control of what my daughter does anymore."

"Damn it, Michael, you know where I'm going with this. If you had a *son*, would you let him play football?"

"Sure I would," Michael responded quickly. "But, well, you know, I…I wouldn't force him to play if he didn't want to."

"Of course not," Scott answered. By the tone of her voice and the spark in her eyes, Michael wasn't sure if she was being patronizing or not. She smiled sadly. "Does your daughter play soccer?"

"Not yet, but she wants to."

"Will you let her?"

"Sure. Why not?"

"Do you know that soccer is the number-one cause of concussions in female athletes? And not just with professionals; we're talking children here too."

"No, I did not know that, but—"

"Did you know that girls are more prone to concussions than boys, even when playing the same sport, like basketball and soccer?"

"Yes, I think I heard something like that." Michael knew he was there to gather information, not to defend himself, but he didn't want Scott thinking he wasn't a good father, either. "Okay, let me give you an example of what type of a parent I wouldn't be. There's a guy I know whose twelve-year-old-son is playing football. In fact, both he and his boy were at the dedication of the new Sam Dornam playing field. Maybe you know him? Dan Kelly?"

Scott shook her head no.

"Well, anyway, this guy's a cop, and maybe he's good at his job, but I'm not so sure about the job he's doing with his son." Michael gave Scott the history between him and Kelly, including Kelly's tip on Marshal Decker, then said, "He thinks I owe him a favor because of the lead he gave me about Marshal Decker being found dead on his boat."

The image of the *Deck Mate* popped into Michael's head, and then another thought materialized. "By the way, I meant to ask you, do you remember saying something about Decker's ankle being bandaged? I think it was when we were at my house?"

Scott took a quick drink. "No. But what has that got to do with children's sports injuries?"

Michael shrugged. "Hmmm, good question. Sorry. Didn't mean to get off track."

"You were talking about the cop's son."

"Yeah, right. Anyway…"

Michael described the scene at the football game between Kelly and his boy. As the story unfolded, Scott's demeanor changed. Her lips tightened, and she shook her head in disbelief. Finally, when he told her how Kelly had handled his son's latest injury, her eyes moistened and she looked away.

"I'm sorry," Michael said. "Maybe I shouldn't have told you about that."

Scott slowly turned back toward Michael. "No, it's fine. I'm glad you did." She drained the last of her drink and looked at her watch.

Michael took it as a cue. "Well. I better let you go. I've got a lot of good stuff here. Thank you for—"

Scott didn't let him finish. "Do you have time to take a ride, Michael? To Moss Beach? We can be there in thirty minutes. There's someone I want you to meet."

Chapter 53

* * *

Scott drove the Caddy west on Geary Boulevard before turning south on Nineteenth Avenue. As usual, afternoon traffic was stop and go, but Scott seemed determined to make good on her ETA at Moss Beach. She dodged in and out of traffic, ran a couple of yellowish-red lights, and at one point cut off an angry, silver-haired gentleman in a vintage Corvette. Three traffic lights later, that same gentleman pulled up next to the passenger's side of the Caddy at a red light. Michael smiled sheepishly at the driver and gave him a thumbs-up, as if to say, "Nice car." The man glared at Michael and raised a middle finger, as if to say, "Fuck you."

The short jaunt south on the 280 Freeway wasn't much better. Michael still didn't know whom they were going to meet in Moss Beach, but decided to keep quiet so Scott could concentrate on traffic. When the Cabrillo Highway morphed back into Highway 1 and the Pacific Ocean came back into view, Scott slowed the SUV and rolled her window down. The weatherman had been wrong about afternoon clouds along the coast, and the sun was still a few hands above the horizon. Scott took off her cap, tilted her head sideways, and let her hair fly out the window into the salty air.

The smell of ocean circulating through the car was enough to stimulate some conversation again, for Michael, anyway. "My folks used to bring me out here when I was a kid," he said. "We'd explore the tide pools and find all kinds of neat things. Of course, it's a federal marine reserve, so we couldn't keep anything we found. Had to leave everything just as it was. My mom called it her happy place."

Scott smiled but said nothing. They rode in silence past a sign proclaiming, "Moss Beach. Population 3,415. Elevation 92.

Michael made another attempt at conversation. "Elevation ninety-two? I don't see where they get that number. Looks like we're pretty close to sea level, if you ask me."

Scott finally broke her silence and said, "Actually, there are some pretty high cliffs where we're going. It's private property, but I'll show you."

A mile later, Scott turned off of Highway 1 onto an asphalt road that twisted and turned its way toward the ocean. On each side of the road, there were a few homes sprinkled in with modest farmhouses. The farmhouses were bordered with one- and two-acre plots of garlic and onions. After they had driven another mile, it was obvious they were about to run out of road…or run into the sea. Down the road on the right, Michael could see a sprawling, flat-roofed building. A hundred yards past the structure, the road ended in a cul-de-sac/parking lot that overlooked the ocean.

As they approached the building, they drove past a redundant road sign warning of a dead end. Just past that, another sign read, "California Convalescence. Private Property."

Scott drove past the building, nosed the Caddy up to the parking lot's guardrail, and shut off the engine. Just a few feet beyond the guardrail, another yellow sign warned, "Caution! Unstable Cliffs. Keep Away." Twenty feet to the right of the sign, a strand of yellow, plastic tape was temporally staked out around an area that appeared to be sloughing away.

Scott looked briefly at Michael before she twisted the rearview mirror and checked her face. With her right pinkie fingernail, she flicked something out of her left eye. Then she snapped open her purse, retrieved a tube of lipstick, and deftly made two quick passes across her lips with it. Satisfied, she fluffed her hair once, straightened the mirror, and got out of the car.

Michael caught up with Scott, and together, they walked past an administration office to the entrance of the main building. As Michael held one of the double doors open for Scott, she said out of the side of her mouth, "We won't stay long."

They walked through a small foyer and into a lobby and an empty waiting area. A nurse in a white uniform sat at a desk across the room, talking on a telephone. Behind her was a set of double doors with round windows like portholes. As Scott and Michael approached the desk, the nurse hung up the phone, looked up, and smiled.

"Oh, hello, Doctor. How are you?" she said.

Scott returned the gesture. "Fine, Paula. Good to see you."

The nurse's smile moved to Michael.

Scott quickly made the introduction. "Paula, this is Michael Fletcher. He's helping me with some research. Would it be all right if he comes with me on the floor? We'll just be a few minutes."

"Certainly." The nurse handed Scott a clipboard with a register on it for her to sign. She took a quick look at her watch and said, "We'll be feeding the residents soon, but that shouldn't be a problem. Take your time."

"Thanks, Paula." Scott scribbled her name on the form and took Michael by the arm. She led him around the nurse's desk and pushed through the set of double doors.

Michael's senses were immediately assaulted as he stepped into another world. The smell of disinfectant filtered through his nose as he followed Scott down the corridor. Half a dozen patients were strapped into wheelchairs outside individual rooms down a long, wide hallway. Some of the interned hung their heads to one side and stared at the black-and-white-checked floor tiles. Others were in more of a prone position and gazed questioningly at the ceiling. Two young men in white, starched uniforms stood talking next to an open door halfway down the hall. As Michael and Scott drew closer, the younger of the two acknowledged Scott in a soft voice.

"Hi, Doc."

"Hi, Sam," Scott replied quietly. "Hey, Jimmy. How's Becky doing?"

"She was fairly responsive earlier," Jimmy said. "I think she's had a good day."

The two men backed away to allow Scott to look inside the room they were standing next to.

Scott stood in the doorway for a moment without saying anything. Finally, she turned back into the hallway and moved away from the door. "Her color looks better."

"Yes, I think her energy level has improved," Sam said. They exchanged a few medical terms that Michael didn't understand, and then the young man said, "Well, we better get back to work. Good to see you, Doc. You know where the coffee is. Joshua is outside."

"Thanks, Sam. We'll catch up to him in a minute."

As Michael walked past the door to join Scott, he stole a glance inside the room. A small, brown-haired girl lay on a hospital bed.

She didn't look much older than Sadie. Her neck was encased in a leather and steel brace. Her eyes were closed. Hand grips attached to pulleys and cables hung over the bed.

Scott let Michael absorb what he had just seen for a moment, then said, "That's Becky. She's sixteen. She's been here for nine months now."

"That girl's *sixteen*?" Michael asked in disbelief. "What happened?"

"She was on the back of her boyfriend's motorcycle when they went off the road just north of here. He suffered some broken bones and abrasions. Her spine was crushed in two places. Neither one was wearing a helmet, although the boyfriend had offered her his. She thought she looked too nerdy in it. The helmet was in her lap when they crashed."

An image of Sadie on Joaquin's horse flashed through Michael's mind.

Scott took a deep breath and said, "But she's not the one I brought you to see. Come, let's go out on the veranda."

Although they'd only been in the institution a few minutes, the thought of fresh air immediately appealed to Michael. Scott led the way down the hall to an exit marked "Courtyard." Before she opened the doors, she briefed Michael. "The boy you're about to meet is a quadriplegic due to a football injury. I'll fill in the blanks later."

Scott pushed open the door, and they stepped outside. The courtyard was meticulously landscaped, with sweet-smelling flowers, small shrubs, and green bushes. Koi ponds lined a winding sidewalk leading to an oval sitting area. A male attendant sat a near a young boy who was propped up on a gurney. The boy's arms were strapped to his sides.

"Look who's here, Joshua," the attendant said as he stood up.

"Hi, Brad." Scott smiled and shook the employee's hand. Then she bent down to the boy and kissed him on his forehead. "Hi, Sweetie," she said. "How are you doing today?"

The boy smiled and blinked twice. He had dark-brown eyes that stayed on Scott for a moment and then shifted to Michael.

Scott took the cue and said, "Josh, this is my friend Michael. He's a sportswriter. He writes for the *Chronicle*. He's covering the Forty-Niners."

Michael's initial reaction was to extend his right hand, but he caught himself in time to turn it into a weak wave and said, "Nice to meet you, Joshua."

Joshua blinked twice.

"Are you, ah...do you like sports? You like the Niners?" Michael asked.

Blink, blink.

"Well, I'll see if I can, uh...get a jersey...or something for you."

Michael's words hung in the air. Nobody said anything for three long seconds. Finally, Scott picked up the conversation. "Which facility did we use for therapy today?" She looked at Joshua and then at Brad.

Suddenly, Michael needed relief in more ways than one. "Ah, speaking of facilities...would you guys excuse me? I could use a men's room."

"Down the hall, two doors on your right," Brad said. "Or you can follow this path back around to the main entrance, the way you came in. There's a men's room in the lobby."

Michael opted for the outside route.

* * *

Everything slowed down for Michael once he got away from the courtyard and into the restroom. He understood now why Scott had brought him there, but his emotions were getting away from him. He needed to take a deep breath and slow down. So much trauma. So much sadness. The kids were so young.

He finally gathered himself and slowly walked back outside. Scott was walking up the path toward him.

"They've started serving dinner, so I thought we'd go. Are you okay?"

"Yes…I'm fine. I think."

* * *

Scott seemed to be deep in thought as they walked wordlessly to the parking lot. Ten feet from the Caddy, she clicked the key fob and unlocked the doors, but instead of getting into the car, she walked past it to the guardrail and stood looking out at the ocean. Michael walked around the passenger's side of the car and stood beside her.

After a moment, Scott cleared her throat and said, "You see those sets forming out there on the sea? It's hard to imagine that those waves may have begun their journey from the other side of the ocean thousands of miles away, isn't it?"

Michael turned and looked out at the ocean swells that were bunching up, hurrying to end their lives on a beach in California. "Yep. All the way from Japan, maybe. Nothing to get in their way, I suppose."

Scott continued to gaze toward the horizon. A few quiet moments passed before she said, "You asked me if I thought parents were part of the problem with sports injuries to kids. Do they push them too hard? Do they get in the way? Well, I know for a fact in Joshua's case, the parents were definitely to blame. His father pushed him relentlessly to excel in sports. Called him a pussy if he didn't tough it out. Just like that cop friend of yours."

"He's not really my friend, he's just—"

"I don't care what he is." Scott's voice had an edge to it. Her eyes sparked. "He's endangering his son by playing him with an injury. Call him, Michael. Tell that prick whatever you have to, but get his boy to a doctor, now."

"Look, Laurie, I know why you brought me here, and I appreciate the fact that you did. I believe I can write something worthy of the situation, and if what I write prevents just one child from getting hurt—-"

"One child? Just one child, Michael? Can't you see? That's not enough."

"No, no. You know what I mean. I was—"

"We've got to do more." Scott's voice started to weaken. She turned to Michael, and a tear rolled down her cheek.

Seeing Scott so vulnerable was too much for Michael. He reached for her and took her in his arms. She buried her head into his chest and quietly sobbed. Slowly, wordlessly, they rocked together as the surf pounded below.

Several moments passed before Scott regained her composure. Still in his embrace, she looked up at Michael, and smiled. Tenderly, Michael kissed the tear residue from her eyelashes. Scott's chest swelled against Michael as she sucked in a deep breath.

When they finally separated, Scott dabbed her eyes and said, "I'm sorry. I…I didn't mean to get so emotional. Not very professional of me."

"Nothing to be sorry about, Laurie. You care very much about children. Nothing wrong with that. It's just that you just can't be responsible for every one of them. It'll drive you crazy."

Scott nodded. "I know, I shouldn't…"

"You mentioned you have a son. I think he's very lucky to have a mother like you."

Scott gazed back out at the ocean. "Yes, I have a son, Michael. You just met him."

Chapter 54

* * *

Michael didn't sleep well that night. He couldn't shake the image of the young girl named Becky, nor of Scott's son, Josh. He couldn't imagine how difficult it must be for Scott and how she must have felt the day her son was injured. And he couldn't dismiss the lingering feelings that remained from holding her in his arms.

The next morning wasn't much better. Michael sat at the kitchen table, coffee in hand, and stared outside into a gloomy fog that had settled in overnight.

Scooter lay at his feet, quiet as the fog.

The idea of writing about brain injuries and fractured lives depressed him even further. He tried in vain to think positive.

He missed his daughter. He missed his wife.

He wondered how his wife's Spanish was progressing.

He thought about Dr. Scott's eyes.

Finally, he put his coffee cup down and said in a voice loud enough to startle Scooter: "Come on, man. Get your shit together. I still gotta job to do here. Let's get to it."

* * *

Two hours later, he thought he might have enough new information on the NFL's pending agreement and related injuries, so he wrote it up and called his boss.

"Whaddya got?" Kimble asked.

"It's mostly legalese and stuff we've covered before, but I think there's a few nuggets you might find interesting. Kinda sad, though."

"I don't give a shit if it's sad as long as it's interesting. It is interesting, isn't it?"

"I suppose so," Michael said.

"Okay, send me what you got on that. Now, what about Scott? You get a chance to talk with her?"

"Yes, I did. I went to her facility. She was working with some people, but we found time to chat."

"Good. You take any more pictures? I'd like to have a couple more of her on file."

Michael laughed and said, "No, I didn't think about it. But I don't think she would have wanted me to anyway."

"Why not?"

"She was in her working clothes, or 'gym jammies.' as she called them."

"Hell, that woman would look hot modeling Eskimo wear."

Michael had a sudden image of Scott wearing nothing but a sealskin coat. "Yeah, I bet she would."

Kimble quickly burst that bubble when he asked, "She know anything about Winestein's brother-in-law?"

"No, she seemed genuinely shocked when I told her about the Florida thing."

"Hmmm...Okay, maybe there's nothing there. How 'bout the sports injuries in kids?"

Michael briefed Kimble about what he had learned so far but decided to leave out his trip with Scott to Moss Beach. He wanted to help Scott with more publicity but wasn't quite sure how to approach his boss with it yet. The image of Scott's son on a gurney and the girl named Becky lying in the hospital bed kept floating into focus.

"And I'm not sure if you want to use any of this," he said, "but for what it's worth, I found out that Pop Warner football was founded 1929 and is the largest youth football organization in the world. The NFL estimates that sixty to seventy percent of all of its players started in Pop Warner. I'm still putting that story together. We'll see where it goes."

"Okay, sounds good, Mike. Send me what you've got when you can."

"Will do. I—"

"Wait, what did she call them? Gym jammies?"

* * *

Twenty minutes after talking with Kimble, Michael's phone rang. It was Jesse's number, but it was Sadie on the phone.

"Hi, Daddy!"

"Hello, sweetheart. How are you?"

"Fine."

"Ah…is everything okay? Is your mother there?" Michael assumed that Annie or her father had placed the call, but this was the first time his daughter had initiated a phone conversation.

"Uh-uh. But she said I should ask you first."

"Ask me what, honey?"

"We-l-l-l, Daddy, I know what I want for Christmas!"

Michael's silent, parental alarm went off. Hell, he was already pressed for money to buy Christmas presents…then there was next month's rent. Cautiously, he asked, "Oh? What? What is it?"

"A pony! Can I have a pony, Daddy? Please, please?"

"A wha…Oh, now wait a minute, honey. Is your mother there?"

"I can ride a horse real good now, Daddy. Joaquin teached me."

"He *taught* you, honey, not teached."

"I can ride real good, really I can. Joaquin tole me I'm a…I'm a nature."

"A natural. You're a natural."

"I kno-o-o-w."

"Sadie, is your mother standing there? Let me talk to her."

"She's outside, with Joaquin. But she said I could talk with you about it. Can I, Daddy? Can I have a pony?"

Michael was silent for a moment, trying to steady himself. "Listen, sweetie, a horse is a big responsibility. They take a lot of care. You've gotta feed 'em all the time, and, you know, clean up after them, exercise them, do all kinda stuff. They're a lot harder to take care of than a dog or cat. Besides, how would you take care of one when you're back in the city?"

"But I wanna stay here, Daddy. If we stay with Grandpa Jesse, I could have a horse, couldn't I?"

"Look, honey, we'll talk about this later, when I come out to see you, okay?"

"But when will that be?"

There was a whine in Sadie's voice, but Michael was smart enough to know the reason for it. "Soon, sweetheart. But I...I've got a lot of work to do first. A lot of places I gotta go—"

"Why don't you work here, Daddy? With me and Mommy and Grandpa and Joaquin? We don't have to go anyplace. 'Cept to the market once in a while, but that doesn't count as work, 'cause that's fun."

"Well, I'm glad you're having fun, but...ah, be careful out there. I'll see you real soon, okay? I'll bring Scooter. Scooter's your dog too, you know. She really misses you."

"I miss her too. Is she all right?"

"She's fine, honey. We'll see you in a couple of days."

"Promise?"

"I promise. And *please* ask your mother to call me, okay?"

"Okay. Oh, wait. I'm s'posed to ask, what do you want for Christmas, Daddy?"

Michael smiled and thought about it for a second. "A story, honey."

"A story? What about?"

"Right now I'd settle for anything."

"Anything? Wha—"

"Don't worry about it, sweetie. I love you."

"Me too, Daddy. But I love you even more in person.""

Chapter 55

* * *

The Niners went on the road for the first two weeks in December, but couldn't make up any ground in their division. They managed to pull one out in Minnesota but then fell to St. Louis, putting their record at eight-six. Seattle was now at eleven-three and had already secured a spot in the playoffs. San Francisco was still mathematically alive for a wild card berth but would have to win their two remaining games and then hope for help from teams outside their division. The odds of that happening were very slim.

The writing was on the wall for Michael as well. Kimble had brought him in and basically told him that his services would no longer be required after the Forty-Niners' next home game. Brenda was recovering faster than anyone could have imagined and was being penciled in to help cover the last regular home game, on December 30. The paper would also rely on national media sources in case the season was extended.

None of this came as a surprise to Michael, of course, and he had already began his due diligence to find another job. He would honor the promise he had made to Annie. Hopefully, it wouldn't involve punching a time clock in a shipyard. The big question was, would it be enough to bring his wife and daughter home? The last time he had talked with Sadie, she'd told him not to worry about getting her a pony, because one of Joaquin's horses was going to have a baby. She was pretty sure Joaquin would give it to her.

Michael still had an obligation to write the final segment of his series documenting injuries to kids in football and hoped to complete it before the next game on Sunday. He had been saddened and shocked by some of the stats that he had come across detailing kid's injuries and even deaths associated with the game of football. In the previous year alone, eight high school boys from around the country had died as a result of hits they'd taken while playing a game they loved. There were even three deaths in three different states in one week. He couldn't imagine the grief that their parents had suffered. He sincerely hoped that the research he had done and the stories he had written so far would somehow benefit more people than just his boss.

* * *

On December 21, Michael sat at his kitchen table and finished his final story about injuries in youth football. It left him with an empty feeling. The rain that had been pounding the area for the last week did nothing for his mood either.

However, satisfied he'd done his best, he clicked "Save," followed by "Send," on his computer and then returned to his home page. A banner flashed "Navajo Indian Language," followed by the word "Dine" in parenthesis. Michael was slightly annoyed that the computer kept track of everything he'd ever Googled. It was as if it was saying, "If you liked the Navajo's way of saying hello, you'll really like this!"

He intended to call Dr. Scott and let her know that he would soon be let go from the *Chronicle* and that his writing days were over. He wanted to thank her for everything she had done for him and wish her luck with her work with the kids. He thought he might as well find out how to say "thank you" or "good-bye" in Navajo.

When he went to the site, he quickly learned that "Dine Bizaad" didn't mean to "eat naked," nor was it a native dish; it simply meant "Navajo language." He spent some time on the site and decided that Navajo was a language, unlike, maybe Spanish, that he would never need, use, or understand. He was about to click off the site when he noticed a link titled "Navajo Code Talkers."

Michael was vaguely aware of the role the Navajo Code Talkers had played in World War Two, and curiosity took him to the page. He wasn't surprised to read the definition of code talkers: "People who used obscure languages as means of secret communications during wartime."

Yeah, well, they got that part right about the Navajo language. What did surprise him was that the original code talkers, used by the military in World War One, were Cherokee and Choctaw.

The piece went on to say that the name "code talkers" was strongly associated with bilingual Navajo speakers specifically recruited by the Marines during World War Two to serve in the Pacific Theater. The Navajo code talkers were commended for their skill, speed, and accuracy demonstrated throughout the war. At Iwo Jima, six code talkers worked around the clock during the first two days of the battle. They sent and received over eight hundred messages, all without error. Major Howard Connor, 5th Marine Division signal officer, declared, "Were it not for the

Navajos and their code, the Marines would never had taken Iwo Jima."

Hmmm…all heady stuff. Maybe when he called Scott, he would mention what he had learned.

As Michael continued to peruse the code talkers' history and the system that they had worked out to send secret messages, something began floating around in his head, almost like a dream he'd had that, when he tried to remember what it had been about, *poof,* was gone, just out of reach.

He was just about to leave the page when it came to him. He quickly scanned the code again. Nope, not there. He went back again. None. He read the code a third time to make sure he wasn't overlooking them. Zero.

Maybe he did have a story after all.

Chapter 56

✳ ✳ ✳

Michael's first thought was to call Bo with his discovery. That would be the proper thing to do: after all, Kimble was still his boss. Chain of command sort of thinking, as it were. After a few agonizing moments of indecision, he picked up the phone and punched in the number that he now knew by heart.

Dr. Scott answered on the first ring. "Hello, Michael. How are you?"

"Yeah, well, ah…good. I suppose."

"You suppose? What's up? I haven't talked with you in a while. I've been worried."

"Been pretty busy. Christmas coming up and all, you know."

"Tell me about it. Been pretty busy myself."

"Well, one of the reasons I'm calling is to tell you that the game this weekend will be my last for the paper. Brenda, the gal that I stood in for, will be back on the job after that, and well, apparently I didn't impress anybody enough to stay on."

"I'm sorry to hear that, Michael. I think you did a wonderful job."

"Thanks, but—"

"And I'm hoping you're not calling to say good-bye."

"No, I…ah…I wanted to talk to you about something."

"Good. Are margaritas involved?"

"No, probably not."

"Michael, you sound a little mysterious. What's this about?"

"It's about your ancestors, the Navajo code talkers."

When Scott didn't say anything, Michael said, "You there? Did I lose you?"

"No. I'm here. What do you want to know about them? The code talkers."

"I'd rather talk to you in person. Can we meet somewhere?"

Scott took a deep breath, and then exhaled slowly. "I'm going to see my son tonight. Can we meet there?"

When Michael hesitated, Scott said, "You don't have to come into the building. I know it makes you sad. Just park down where we parked before, say, after visiting hours? Around nine-thirty?"

"Sure. I'll see you then."

After hanging up, Michael thought once more about calling Bo.

Naw, it can wait.

Chapter 57

At 8:45 p.m., Michael loaded Scooter into the Jeep and headed to his rendezvous with Scott. It was still raining, but he hoped it would let up enough to take Scooter for a walk, maybe find a way down to the beach.

Twenty-five minutes later, Michael turned off Highway 1 and followed his headlights through the rain until he reached the convalescence building. Two cars and a van were parked beneath the low sodium lights of the building's lampposts. Scott's Caddy was nowhere in sight.

Michael continued down to the empty cul-de-sac and parked where he had before with Scott. The rain had finally let up, but he stayed in the Jeep and waited.

As the minutes ticked by, Scooter pawed and nosed her blanket into a nest, plopped down, and sighed her contentment for the moment. Michael cracked his window and breathed in the wet night air. He pushed his seat back and reclined it as far as it would go. He could hear the surf crashing below the cliff.

It wasn't long before he began to doze. A couple of times, he twitched awake and took a look around. Still quiet and dark. He checked his watch again and decided to give it another ten minutes, and then he'd call Scott. As he settled back in the seat, Scooter emitted a low growl. Suddenly, a black-clad figure appeared at the passenger-side window. Scooter went into full barking mode.

"Holy shit!" Michael said as he grabbed the steering wheel. It took a second before he realized that the person looking in at him was Scott. She was dressed entirely in black: leather jacket, turtleneck sweater, skirt, and running shoes. She wore her hair up beneath a dark ball cap.

"Scooter! Shut up! It's okay! It's okay. Hush, now," Michael said. He reached over and opened the door, and Scott jumped in quickly.

"I'm sorry I'm late," she said without smiling. "I didn't mean to scare you."

Scooter settled back into low growling.

"No, that's okay. I...I didn't see you pull up." Michael took a quick look around. "Where's your car?"

"I parked up the road," Scott said in a subdued voice. "Not far."

Michael looked back at the building but didn't see her car. Scooter was still emitting a low grumble. Michael shook his finger at his dog. "Quit! That's enough."

Scooter finally quieted, and Michael turned to Scott. She was staring at the ocean with a distant look in her eyes. Slowly, she took off her cap and shook her hair free.

"Are you okay?" Michael asked.

A moment before she answered, "What? Oh. Yeah. I'm...I'm fine."

It was painfully obvious to Michael that she was not fine. He sat up and gave his seat a couple of tugs to adjust it, but it didn't budge. He made a couple more attempts, but finally left it alone. Scott continued to stare out into the night but didn't say anything more. A few silent moments passed before Michael noticed a tear flowing down her cheek.

"Is it Josh? Is he okay?" he asked.

Softly, she answered, "Okay? Oh, I suppose so. If you call being trapped in a useless body okay."

"I'm sorry. It's not fair—"

Scott stiffened and wiped the tear away. "Not to worry, Michael. Not your concern." She took a couple of breaths and composed herself.

An overwhelming feeling of compassion hit Michael, and he put his arm around her. "Laurie, if you want to talk—"

She turned to him, buried her head into his chest, and began sobbing. Her scent drifted over him.

Michael squirmed his hips around to a more comfortable position, put both arms around her, and let her cry. It took a minute or two, but Scott finally shuddered and looked up at him. "You're such a good man, Michael. You're sweet, gentle, and strong in all the right ways."

"Well, I don't know about that, but…"

Without taking her eyes off his face, Scott drew herself up and lifted a leg over his, her skirt riding up over her bare thighs.

"Laurie," Michael began.

Before he could say another word, Scott melted into him and softly kissed his mouth. The kiss only lasted a moment, but she didn't pull her face away from his. Neither one of them moved, their lips a half an inch apart.

"Laurie," he said again.

Scott leaned back slightly and slowly slipped off her jacket. She smiled and put her hand on his chest. Then she leaned in and kissed him again, light butterfly kisses on his lips and around his mouth, on the tip of his nose, his chin, his throat. Michael's breathing changed. Finally, her lips found his again, and they locked together. She heard him moan as she slid her tongue into his mouth and began an intimate dance with his.

After a few heated moments, they broke apart for air.

"Jesus, Laurie," Michael said. "I...I don't...I...we..."

Scott breathed hotly in his ear, "Oh, Michael..."

Their chests rose and fell in rhythm. Michael tried to gather himself, willing his pulse rate to go down. They stared at each other for a moment, and then she put her hand on his chest and moved back into him again. There were no soft kisses this time. They both responded immediately and began devouring each other. Scott took his left hand and guided it up under her sweater. She wasn't wearing a bra, and they both moaned as Michael's fingers found their mark. As he continued to caress her, Scott slowly moved her hand down to his crotch. She massaged him slowly a few times and then moved to his belt and unfastened it. She eased his zipper down and pulled his shirt up out of the way. Slowly, she worked her hand back down his belly and slid her fingers inside the waistband of his shorts. She lowered her head, her lips and tongue following her fingers.

"Oh, my God, Laurie...don't...."

Scott maneuvered Michael's shorts down, then suddenly lifted up away from him. She pulled her skirt up over her thighs and, in one swift motion, swung a leg over and straddled him. She wasn't wearing any panties either. She reached for him again.

Michael sucked in his breath and then quickly grabbed Scott's hand and stopped her from going any further. "No, don't...please. We can't," he panted. "Jesus. I...I can't. Jesus, I'm sorry. Please."

Scott wasn't interested in stopping now. She arched her hips and tried to guide him inside her. She threw her hair back and glared down at him. The fire was back in her eyes.

"I…I don't have any protection," Michael said lamely.

Scott held him fast. Her chest was heaving. "Goddamn you, I don't want any fucking protection! I want a child! A healthy one. I want yours!" She tried to mount him again. "Now!"

Michael's willpower was saved further torment when suddenly, the Jeep's seat snapped to its full and upright position. Scott tried to stay in the saddle but the horn she was holding slithered away. In a flash, the moment was lost.

Scott glared down at Michael for a second before she ungraciously dismounted and slumped back into her seat, stunned. She sat very still while she caught her breath, her skirt still up over her hips.

Meanwhile, Michael arched his back and worked his shorts up over a disappointed, confused penis. Silently he pulled his pants up, then zipped up and buckled up.

For several minutes, the only sound in the Jeep, other than heartbeats, came from Scooter lightly panting in the backseat. Finally, Michael broke the silence. "I'm sorry I'm such an asshole."

Scott lifted her hips and pulled her skirt down over her thighs. She pulled her jacket on and quickly tied her hair up in a bun.

Michael looked at her. "Well, I hope life treats you better soon. I hope you can find justice somewhere in this world."

"Justice?" Scott snorted. "Oh, don't worry about that, Michael. I *will* find justice. I'll find it the same way my forefathers found it. Without symbols and without numbers."

She slipped her shoes on and smiled at Michael's frozen countenance. "What? Did I say something?"

Michael finally blinked. "That's what I wanted to talk to you about. While I was researching some of the Navajo language, I stumbled on the code talkers from World War Two. I noticed they didn't use any numbers or symbols in their code."

"That's right, lover, they didn't. Have you shared this with anyone?"

"No, I wanted to talk with you first."

"Good. Then maybe you understand that the Navajo code talkers were all volunteers, and they weren't about to let some foreign nation bully their country into submission. Not your country, not my country, but *their* country. What they did helped humanity. And they found justice...for a while anyway."

She stared at Michael, daring him to say something. Finally, he did. "After Troy Polanksi died—you know, the hockey player? Well, after he died, the paper received an e-mail to the sports editor about how our society was the cause of his death. It was signed, 'No symbols, no numbers, no Polanksi, know justice.' The 'no' before justice was spelled k-n-o-w."

"Uh-huh."

"Yeah, like to *know* something..."

"I know."

The chill in her voice suddenly matched the one running up Michael's spine. He struggled to get the words out. "Do...do you know something about the letter to the editor that was published?"

"Of course I do. I sent it. I sent one after Lavorini died too. Maybe they didn't get that one."

"What? Why? Why did you send them?"

"Oh, don't be coy with me, Michael. You suspected that their deaths weren't accidents, didn't you?"

"Well, yes, but—"

"I would think you'd be happy to learn that you were right."

Chapter 58

✳ ✳ ✳

Michael's heart was taking a beating. His mind wasn't in the best of shape either.

"I know I shouldn't have sent those e-mails, but I couldn't resist," Scott said. "And I probably slipped when I mentioned Decker's ankle being bandaged. You seemed interested in that too."

"So, you know for a fact that the athletes were murdered?"

"Yes."

"And you know who killed them?"

"I do."

The silence was pounding. "Who?"

She smiled. "Me."

Michael shook his head. "Jesus Christ, Laurie! I don't believe that! For one thing, why would you tell me?"

Scott took something out of her jacket pocket, leaned over and adjusted the rear-view mirror toward herself. She slowly applied lipstick. When she finished, she ran the tip of her tongue over her lips and then looked at him. "I thought you wanted a story."

"Well, yeah, but not—"

Before he could say anything more, she quickly leaned in and kissed him on the mouth. It surprised him so much that he barely felt the slight sting in his thigh.

Trying to regain whatever composure he had left, he pulled his head away and wiped his lips. He took a moment to look at her. "Okay, if you killed them, why? Did you know them, or did you just pull their names out of a hat?"

She frowned and looked at her watch. "Don't be flippant, Michael. No, I didn't know them. But I'd seen them enough on television to know what they were."

"So you just decided to kill them? For sport?"

"Quit it, Michael. I'm not insane. You see, after Josh was paralyzed, about the only thing he could do was watch television. And when I would visit, I would watch with him. Not because I gave a damn about what was on, but because I was spending time with my son. Can you understand that, Michael?"

"Of course I can. I'm a parent too."

"Then try to understand how hard it would be to watch sports on television with your crippled son and see an overpaid, stupid, fucking bully take such pleasure in maiming other humans. What kind of a person does that? What kind of a message does that send to our kids? That they too, can make a fortune by pounding their opponents senseless? Great role models, huh?"

Michael shook his head. "I still don't believe you. You have helped so many people...so many kids."

"Thank you, Michael. Yes, I believe I *have* helped a lot of kids. And with Sam's help, I'll be able to continue to help a lot more in the future."

"But you don't help anyone by killing innocent people!"

"That's just it! Don't you get it? They *weren't* innocent! They were thugs! Thugs who were getting increasingly richer while demonizing and corrupting our society. Don't you see? Someone has to stop them. For the sake of humanity. For our kids' future!"

The realization that Scott might be telling the truth started to sink in with Michael. He was almost afraid to ask his next question. "So, tell me, how do you, a woman, weighing whatever, overpower three very strong professional athletes, kill them, and get away with it?"

She gave her answer with a smile. "Strength was not necessary, Michael. Just sweet seduction. Oh, I had to be careful, don't get me wrong, especially with security cameras everywhere these days, but for the most part, single men are so easy. Especially single men with big egos. They weren't like you, love. And I should tell you, I didn't start off intending to hurt anybody. I just happened to be watching the basketball game with Josh when that asshole punched that other player. It was horrific, sickening. I looked at Josh, and he had started crying. No player should be allowed to put his fist through another player's face and get away with it."

"But he didn't get away with it. He was fined and suspended!"

"Oh, please. He was probably proud of it." She looked at her fingernails for a second, and then said, "But you know, later, when I saw that hockey player doing the same thing…and, well, you know, the basketball player *was* pretty easy."

"Easy?"

"Oh, it took *some* planning and surveillance. I followed him around for a while, you know, watched his routine. One day I even took Josh with me in one of the vans I had borrowed from the institute. I was driving behind the guy when he pulled into a gas station, so I drove in next to him, got out, and acted like I couldn't figure out the gas pump. Didn't take long, you know: show him a little smile, a little cleavage. So the next day, we meet for coffee. I told him I had business in Truckee for a couple of days and wondered if he'd like to drive up and meet me for lunch. 'Sure, love to,' he said. What a fool."

"So you just push him in the river? Hope he drowns? A six-foot-six athlete? A sober six-foot-six athlete?"

Scott looked at her watch again. "My, my, what a cynic. But yes, you were right about that too—his not drinking, I mean. That surprised me, but...well...I worked around that."

"And I suppose you met Polanksi at a motel and politely asked him to lie down in the tub and OD on cocaine and steroids?"

She cocked her head to one side, as if she was trying to remember. "Something like that, yes."

"Okay, joke's over, Laurie. What—"

"The only hard part was finding a motel that didn't have an outside security camera on the corner of the building. But once I did, I told him what room to ask for. I also convinced him that for the sake of discretion, he should leave the patio slider unlocked. I think that part really turned him on."

"And I think you have a really active imagination. There's no way—"

"And to be honest, I kinda liked that part too."

"Oh, my God. Who are you? And what about Decker?" Michael asked.

"Ah, yes, Mr. Decker. What an egotistical fuck he was. He invited me down to his boat for afternoon cocktails, just the two of us. Said high heels and a short skirt would be appropriate attire. Can you imagine that, high heels on a boat? I think he wanted his fellow yachties to see me come aboard. Make 'em envious, or something."

"But you didn't, did you? Go aboard, I mean?"

"Oh, I went aboard, all right. At midnight, in a black wet suit."

Suddenly, Michael's head began to spin. A grainy, black-and-white, slow-motion video of Scott slipping over the rail of the *Deck Mate* ran through his mind. He rolled with the image for a moment before snapping back fully awake.

"Are you feeling okay, Michael?" she asked.

"Yeah, yeah. Just a…a little dizzy there for a second." He looked around at his immediate surroundings as if he didn't know where he was. His head started to spin again.

"It's okay, love. It's just the serum."

"Sea…rummm?" Michael drawled.

"Yes. An old Indian recipe. Made with the freshest ingredients. Burnt cactus skin, peyote, and other secret sauces. My ancestors used it to sedate horses and other animals if they needed to doctor them…or slaughter them. It made the animal quite docile and easy to manage. Plus, it didn't stay in their system long, as we learned later in a few necropsies."

"Oh…uh huh."

"Come on, sweet, we better step outside. Get some rain in your face."

"Yeah, Wayne face," Michael said. "Ha."

Scott got out, walked around to the driver's-side door, and opened it. Michael rolled out like a drunken sailor, and Scooter jumped out behind him. Scott took Michael by the arm and led him toward the guardrail. "That's it. You're doing good. Just keep walking."

As they neared the railing, a clap of thunder boomed. "No-o-o!" Michael cried, pulling his arm loose and pushing at Scott. When she slipped and fell, Michael staggered away toward the area that was marked off with yellow tape. Scott quickly got to her feet and hurried after him. She caught him by the back of his collar and tried to push him toward the edge of the cliff. He was wobbly and stumbled to his knees.

Scott was bent over, trying to get him to his feet, when Scooter suddenly attacked her, ripping at her sleeve and growling viciously. Scott stumbled backward, trying to fight off the dog. Scooter kept up the attack and forced Scott back through the yellow tape. Suddenly, the saturated ground gave way, and Scott screamed as she went over the cliff, taking Scooter with her.

Michael tried to get up but fell back down. Like a drunk pinned to the ground by gravity, he wrestled with the whirlies. He struggled on his back for a couple of minutes, trying desperately to stop the spinning, but finally, his mental gyroscope mercifully quit, and he passed out.

* * *

Two hours later, a teenage couple drove down the cul-de-sac looking for a place to park. When their headlights swept over Michael lying near his Jeep, the young driver initially spooked and took off. "We can't get involved, he's probably just drunk," he said to his wide-eyed girlfriend beside him.

But as he drove back toward Highway 1, the girl began to plead with him. "We should call someone. Maybe the guy's been shot or something. My parents won't have to know we were here. We'll just call 911, tell 'em about it and hang up." She rubbed his thigh. "Please?"

Chapter 59

* * *

The emergency response team found Michael lying on his side on the pavement. He was conscious, but when he tried to speak, his words were gibberish. One of the responders took a flashlight and gave him a once-over. The other attendant flashed a light in and around the Jeep. A few moments later, he walked to the guardrail looked down the cliff. After a couple of sweeps with his flashlight, he spotted Scott lying face down on a small ledge twenty feet below, her body twisted at a weird angle. Scooter was lying on Scott's neck. Within minutes, the two EMTs had a line attached to the emergency vehicle, and one of them had rappelled down the cliff. Scott was still alive, and so was Scooter.

* * *

Separate ambulances took Michael and Scott to the nearest hospital in Moss Beach, while an animal control officer took Scooter to a shelter. Michael's initial exam showed him to be physically fine other than a bump on the head. Mentally, he was still a mess, but showed signs of being able to put some words together. One of the medical staff guessed that Michael was asking about his dog and assured him that she was being taken care of. Meanwhile, the doctors decided to keep Michael in the hospital for further evaluation.

Scott wasn't so lucky. She had escaped head trauma but suffered spinal injuries. It would be a while before anyone knew if she would be able to speak at all.

Five hours after being admitted, Michael sat up in his hospital bed and tried to answer questions from the local police. The last thing he remembered was sitting in his Jeep, waiting for Scott. He had no idea how she had ended up going over the cliff. He remembered that he had called her earlier in the day to talk about something. After twenty minutes of questioning, Michael developed a nasty headache, and the attending nurse mercifully shooed the police away.

* * *

When Michael woke up later, Annie was sitting by his bed. He blinked a couple of times to bring her into focus.

"Wha's goin' on? Wha...where am I?" he asked groggily.

Annie moved her chair closer to her husband. "You're in a hospital. You've been in an accident. You're okay, nothing broken, nothing missing, but you are in a hospital."

Michael looked around at his immediate surroundings before looking back at Annie. "Why? Wha happen'?"

"That's a good question," Annie answered. Her voice had a cool edge to it. "We're hoping you can tell us. How do you feel?"

"I'm okay, I guess. Thirsy, maybe. Whersh Sadie? She okay?"

"Sadie's just fine." Annie went to the sink, filled a Dixie cup with water, came back, and handed it to Michael. She sat back down, folded her hands in her lap and waited.

Michael drank the water and then stared at the cup. The gears in his memory trying to mesh were almost audible. A few moments of silence passed before Annie sucked in a breath and said, "Your friend, Dr. Scott? She's in the hospital too, although I understand she wasn't as lucky as you. You want to tell me about her? You wanna tell me how she fell off a cliff last night? Some sort of lover's quarrel?"

Michael frowned and went back to studying the Dixie cup. He was coming out of his fog, but wasn't all the way out yet. What he said next was like a drunken mind speaking a sober tongue. "Wells, speakin' of lovers, how's Don Juan? Still takin' Spanish leshsons from mmm?

Annie looked stunned. "What are you talking about? Joaquin?"

"Yesh."

"Oh, God. Please. There was never anything between us, and you know it."

"Was?"

"Yes, was." Annie paused for a moment and looked down at her hands. "ICE came to the farm a couple of days ago. Joaquin had lied to Daddy. He didn't have papers like he had said. In fact, he has a wife and two kids in Mexico."

There was still a mist in Michael's brain. "You mean Joaquin got his walk-*keen* papers?"

"That's funny, Michael. Very funny. But you're changing the subject. What happened last night? How did your friend fall off the cliff?"

"Cliff? Wha…" Suddenly, he jerked his head. "Scooter. Where's Scooter?"

"She's at a shelter waiting for a vet to see her. They think her left front leg is broken, but she should be okay. What happened last night?"

Michael's eyes widened. His memory was coming into focus. He began nodding and sat up further in the bed. Finally, he said, "Holy shit."

"What? Holy shit what, Michael?"

"I...I think she tried to kill me!"

"Excuse me?"

"I think she tried to kill me!" Michael was nodding, as if to confirm to himself that that's what had really happened.

"What're you talking about? What the hell's goin' on here, Michael? Who tried to kill you? Doctor Scott? Why would she want to kill you?"

The question hung in the air like bug spray. Finally, Michael answered, "They *were* murdered! Decker and the others *were* murdered."

"Murdered? Others?" Annie shook her head.

"Yeah, Lavorini, Polanksi, and Decker. Remember? I wrote about them."

"The athletes?"

"Yeah."

"Okay, now you're scaring me. Damn it, Michael, please tell me what's goin' on here!" Annie sat back in her chair and folded her arms over her chest.

Michael took a deep breath and began describing the situation as best he could. He told Annie about the Navajo code talkers and why he agreed to meet with Scott in the first place. The more he rattled on, the clearer his memory became. He gingerly spoke of Scott's attempted seduction and wisely glazed over the minutiae. He told her what Scott had said about finding justice. He told Annie about the letter to the editor that the paper received that included "no symbols, no numbers." He remembered a sting in his thigh and Scooter barking. He remembered Scott pulling him toward the cliff. He thought he recalled Scott screaming as Scooter attacked her.

"Oh my God!" Annie said, and then fell in a stunned silence, trying to digest it all.

Michael respected her reverie for several seconds, and then he said, "There's something else I want to tell you. Something I need to say."

Annie stiffened, expecting more bad news.

"I want to tell you how much I love you."

Annie's expression turned to anguish. She shook her head as if she didn't know what to think or believe and then looked up at the ceiling, trying to keep her tears in place. When she looked back at her husband, she managed a weak smile but remained silent. When Michael began rubbing his temples, she took her cue.

"All right, Michael. I…I better let you get some rest." She stood up and said, "I'll check on Scooter on the way home. And I'll check with the hospital to see how long they want to keep you. I imagine you'll need a ride home too."

Michael looked at his wife. "Home? Where is that?"

Chapter 60

* * *

(FOUR MONTHS LATER)

The warm spring sunshine was enough to make Jesse and Michael sweat a little as they walked through the vineyard. Every few steps, they would stop and inspect some of the young grapes and their leaves.

"These look pretty good," Jesse said. "I don't think we'll have to spray for a while. Course, it depends on the weather. Damn drought makes it tough on everyone."

Michael picked a grape and rolled it in his fingers, feeling the firmness. "You said something about blowing out the sprinkler system; you wanna show me how to do that?"

"Oh, that's right. We'd better do that pretty soon. First, though, I gotta figure out what Joaquin did with the valves. Coulda took 'em back to Mexico, far as I know."

Michael diplomatically remained quiet. Months ago, Jesse had offered him and Annie equal working partnerships in Ireland's Acres. They were now in the process of tearing down the old cabin where Joaquin had stayed and building a, per Jesse, "whatever-the-hell-you-damn-want" ranch house for the Fletcher family.

Besides his new position with Ireland's Acres, Michael had found time for a part-time gig at a radio station in Santa Rosa. He served as a copywriter, and when a spot called for a young girl's voice, Sadie was a natural. He had also been contracted by the Healdsburg weekly newspaper to write a column critiquing local wines.

Jesse and Michael took a few more steps in the vineyard and stopped. They watched a young doe and her fawn saunter by at the end of the row. Michael said, "That reminds me, I promised Annie I'd pick up some fencing material today in town. Don't want the deer eating up her garden."

Jesse smiled and looked at Michael.

"You know, Mike, I gotta tell you. I'm so happy you guys are here with me now. Seeing little Sadie smilin' all the time, runnin' around playin' with Scooter…hell, the dog hardly limps anymore."

They took a few more steps and Jesse said, "Annie's happy too. I see it in her eyes. She's happy again. I've got you to thank for that."

"Forget it, Jesse. I know how lucky I am to be here. It's where I want to be."

Jesse kicked a dirt clod. "Life isn't always fair, as you know. I'm guessin' you're disappointed you never found a big story to write about for the paper, but sometimes it takes a tragedy to carve a different path for us. Like the accident you went through. Seein' your friend left paralyzed and unable to speak. That's gotta be tough. Tough for everybody."

Michael nodded.

"Good to see your man, Dorman, keepin' her office running though. I understand she's being cared for in the same place as her son now, huh?"

Michael nodded again.

Jesse took off his hat and wiped some sweat away. "Well, let's go see if we can find those irrigation valves, shall we?"

ABOUT THE AUTHOR

Radio talk show host and writer Terry P. Cubbins is a navy veteran, tugboat engineer, and carpenter. He lives in Washington State with his dog, Scooter, in a home that he built overlooking the Cascade Range.

Made in the USA
San Bernardino, CA
02 July 2016